February, 2014

To Ca

MW00438259

PRECINCTS
OF LIGHT

Thank you for thinking of me and setting this presentation

A NOVEL BY

HENRY ALLEY

up.

Best,
H. Alley

PORTLAND • OREGON
INKWATERPRESS.COM

Author Photo, Linda Smogor
Cover Photo, Warren K. Leffler, Library of Congress
Cover by Masha Shubin and Austin Gray
Interior design by Masha Shubin

This is a work of fiction. The character story lines described here, while based on historical events, are works of the author's imagination. The settings and characters are fictitious or used in a fictitious manner and do not represent specific living or dead people.

www.inkwaterpress.com

ISBN-13 978-1-59299-464-9
ISBN-10 1-59299-464-4

Publisher: Inkwater Press

Printed in the U.S.A.
All paper is acid free and meets all ANSI standards for archival quality paper.

1 3 5 7 9 10 8 6 4 2

This book was written over many years, and prospered through the help of numerous friends who read the various versions and drafts and attended my readings of my work as it was in progress. In particular, I would like to thank my mentor James McConkey for his unceasing help and my colleague Ben Brooks for his comments, both early and late, on the manuscript. Finally I would like to thank my mother, Johnnie Greer, and my brother and sister-in-law, Jack and Sharon Alley, for seeing me through a very difficult time in my life which this novel, as well as myself, survived. Austin Gray, my partner, has been a constant help and support as I decided to see this novel into print.

CONTENTS

Part One: Eleanor 1

Part Two: Harold 65

Part Three: Appleton 141

Part Four: Samuel 227

Part Five: Joanne 263

PART ONE

Eleanor

S HE HAD TO WAIT ONLY MINUTES AT FAMILY SERVICES before being shown into the caseworker's office.

"This isn't altogether easy," he began (he had introduced himself as Mr. Benton), "but you need to tell me a little about yourself." He held his pencil up—as if she might prove to be a very important person, based on what she said.

"My name is Eleanor Towning," she heard herself saying, "I own a collectibles business called 'Eleanor's Castle' up in Capitol City. I just got through seeing my sister in San Francisco. She was seriously ill. A stroke." But then she had to pause, at a loss, She could only think of the very thing which she couldn't mention. She felt restrained because of what her sister had revealed. "I have done many things in my life besides raise a family. I had my own television show back in the fifties, and later I became President of the Women's University Club."

"Very good, Mrs. Towning. That tells me what you do, but how do you feel?" Mr. Benton asked.

"How do I feel?" she asked.

"Yes."

"In general?"

The voice seemed to come out of a tunnel. "About

your son and the application he's making to adopt Derek. And let me say this—the reason we have to be so blunt is that Derek has taken a lot of battering. Especially at school. No doubt it will go on. He's one of those rare teenagers who not only admit they're gay but celebrate it. That means he's constantly paying the price. Especially now, with the way the climate is here in Oregon."

"Yes, Harold told me about that," she answered. And her sister had, too.

"So it stands to reason we need somebody absolutely secure in themselves as parents."

Something was borne out that she had felt since talking to Harold—everyone was speaking of Derek's mother and father as if they were one person, Harold.

"Well," she answered, not knowing where her answer came from. "I like Harold."

There it was, she remembered, that previous morning, walking across the park, and in recalling the stone Persephone standing there, modestly attired in the fountain, holding some chiseled flowers in her hands, amidst the bark dust, she realized that the reason she thought she hadn't liked Harold was because she had known all along there was a secret part of him. She had been resisting him, because things had not turned out as she had planned. But that could hardly be called dislike.

"You said 'like,' Mrs. Towning?" Mr. Benton asked.

"Of course it's more than that," Eleanor answered, "but you have to understand Harold has always

4

done most everything right. He's quite strong, in my opinion."

"Why do you think so?" Mr. Benton had begun to take notes, as they did on driver's tests. Why is that examiner writing? Nothing's happened yet.

"Harold's energy has always been very high. He finishes everything he begins. He keeps his temper most of the time. He's constantly serving others," she said.

"Anything else? Any special insights as his mother?"

Staring, she saw that the lines in Benton's face were like trench marks. Very suddenly. She had them also. In one glance, she thought—yes, he has grown children, too.

"Harold was always reliable," she said slowly. "From the very first. And he was always all-around. That's what his father insisted on, and I tried to help with that. His father never wanted him to be a total brain or a total athlete."

She saw him in their backyard with his View-master, years ago. Harold's secret life of fairy tales—and of being a woman, perhaps. Like being the bangled dancer in the *Arabian Nights*. She had caught him dressed as one, once.

"Balanced then?" Benton was asking.

"Yes, that's right."

"That's very helpful," Benton said. "That's a good word"—but he was agreeing with himself, not her.

"I mean," she said, now really gaining ground, "I could well imagine Harold helping him in everything—his algebra, his science projects, playing

5

basketball in the backyard. Doing in fact everything fathers do with their teenage sons but doing it better. He's accomplished that already as foster father."

Now Benton was picking up speed. The writing flew on the page. She felt herself saved—from her own past reservations.

"That's excellent," he said. "It reminds me of a saying my grandfather used to say which nobody around him could understand—so I don't mention it—but it's something I like to live by—*sana mens in sana corpore.* Surely *you* had Latin in those days."

"Yes," she answered, not very flattered. "Yes, that's right."

"Would you say that phrase is applicable here?"

"Very." But she considered she must have seemed dressed in much the old style. Meanwhile he went busily on, with his own creative writing, for she had only been his Muse. It reminded her of a story she had heard about an Italian oral exam given at Stanford, by a highly remonstrative native-born speaker. The student had not known a word of Italian, except for the phrase, "Oh, no, I don't believe it!" and had passed with flying colors. The examiner had done all the talking.

"Well," he said, in a virtual perspiration of rapid composing, "that's all she wrote. I mean, that really clinches things. I don't think I need to take up any more of your time. And we certainly do appreciate your willingness to come in on a Saturday."

Uncertain still, she stood up.

"One last thing, though," he said.

"Yes." She was just caught in rising.

"And I must say this in the strictest confidence. I think you ought to know that your son's wife has given her consent to the adoption but is what we would call a reluctant participant. If it weren't for the fact that Derek were such a hard case to place and the fact of your strong support—along with others'—there would, in fact, be no chance. So this makes us particularly grateful." She was about to reply, but he went on, "You have heard about the particular operations of the Oregon Protection Alliance? About what it's doing to 'protect' children from being placed with gay parents?"

"I have heard quite a lot, yes," she answered, thinking of San Francisco again.

"Well, Harold has never shown any signs of—of course you don't think—"

"That he's gay himself?" she asked. "How could you ask me that?"

"Wonderful," he concluded, checking a box. "Of course the OPA has no control in this office. But we simply can't have any extra stress for the boy, if you were to say Harold was—"

"Of course."

Nonplussed, she shook hands and left.

But outside, waiting for Harold to pick her up, she got more than she bargained for. For in front of her, without warning, there was a tide of a parade, and it pressed her near-lie upon her. Who have I spoken for, she wondered, as she stared into the procession, and saw that it was Arden's annual Rose Parade, of late summer. Myself or him?

Whenever possible, the idyllic town always had a celebration, with people travelling past, as though marching out of the city limits but actually only recirculating—all these t-shirted and costumed people were Arden's full citizens. Arden belonged not only to Renaissance celebrations but to the post-hippie world of organdy, spice, and multi-colored Volkswagens. Sometimes the place—a mediumish city—seemed like one large crafts fair, attended by sweet people who were all slightly out to lunch. How different from the perspective of California Street, down in San Francisco.

And she stood staring at the lovely Rose Queen, who passed, and a whole barrage of noble causes, which Arden was famous for. The Planet Earth was featured as a beautiful green globe, like the one held by Leonardo's *Salvatore Mundi* in Richard's, her brother-in-law's, den, while out of nowhere, there the *Salvatore Mundi* was once more, mounted high on a banner, the vision of the peaceable Christ, two fingers raised, followed by another banner for the Renaissance Fair Committee ("Look for us, October, 1992!"), and then headlined by Samuel himself, their Chairman—Samuel, professor, city planner, would-be congressman, Vietnam vet, her ex-son-in-law—riding in a bronzed Cadillac, a prologue to a rather severe-looking Queen Isabella, beautiful yet still ascetic, standing on the bed of roses of her float, which was as big as a battleship. She was just the way Eleanor had visualized her, from childhood on. In their *Litra Primers* of ancient grade school days, the Queen had been presented, in the engraving, as almost nun-like, with an oval face and perfected features—as Mary, Queen of the global Earth as well as of rotund Heaven would have looked. And all about her, in the parade, were carnival stars and flaps of orange, cut leaves and dahlias, boughs of sumac shaped into arches, and also with the Queen, a wonderfully well-built Columbus, with long hair in the old-fashioned sixties mode, but groomed, for the present day, and muscular legs that were shown off spectacularly well in dark purple tights. Also on their float—"Columbus Day is Coming! Renaissance Fair! 1492-1992! Look for us next year!"—as they rode through, circulated through, Arden's Columbus Square.

She could see Appleton, her new husband, in the face of this young Columbus, a face that looked as if it had slipped off Mount Rushmore and gained some life in falling, Appleton, the "new" man in her life of three years, with very grave hands, as though from a stonecutter, but highly living, vital ones, with veins like those visible in these Renaissance portraits, with the same vulnerability. And with that, a murmur was going up, for part of the crowd did not like who this was—the maligned Columbus—a "hero" no longer fashionable now, no longer grand. But wait a minute, she thought, this Columbus is also my Appleton. And as though in answer, the murmur gave way to a cheer, as the next entry arrived. The chant—"No on Hate! No on Eight! The Crime of Hate in our state!"—came as people passed, waving their banners and pink triangles, like stardust, some of it, like huge galaxies, too, with a huge sign marked "OPA," with a red slash mark through it. Next moment, she applauded and realized she was starting to cry, as Harold, emerging from a side street, pulled up in his car. The one thing she couldn't tell Mr. Benton was that she had a lesbian daughter, and, she was sure, a gay son.

"What's the verdict?" he asked, as she got in.

"Of course, Mr. Benton wouldn't say," she told him, wiping her eyes. "But it looks very good."

"Did he ask if I was—"

"Yes," she answered. "And I didn't say anything."

Without a word, he took her hand; she felt they were bound together, in a new alliance. "Bless you," he said. "I wouldn't have had a chance otherwise."

"But Harold," she went on, settling herself in, "please be careful. I saw Samuel just a minute ago in the parade. A man like him—who's said to be in the OPA—is terribly dangerous."

"I know," he answered. "He's keeping Sonya from Joanne."

⌒

Next morning, she woke up in Harold's spare room. She rested in bed, hearing the house fill up with time, the rooms radiant with sun and the sound of clocks. She heard another voice, ticking; it was Harold listening to himself on tape. She could make out the word "Alliance." She thought of the Axis Countries and the radio back in the 1940s—feeling descended upon by the "sheeted dead" of the Ku Klux Klan in the 1950s, and here her son's voice was, designing Sunday's sermon, trying to answer the Enemy, the Oregon Protection Alliance, the way any self-respecting clergyman in this state was. And so, feeling some pride, too, she got up, put on her robe, and went in to him and kissed him on the cheek.

"Is that your sermon for this Sunday?"

He nodded, shutting it off. "It isn't working yet. It doesn't hit, it doesn't move. There's that part about when I used to visit prisoners in Capitol City—I was trying to say how I felt but it only sounds like condescension."

"You'll find a way around that," she said, touching him.

He looked at her as if he had been browbeaten. "I really appreciate you being willing to stop over," he said at last.

"You don't have to thank me again."

He waited, a frightened, bearded Hercules. "I'm not sure how much Caroline is for this, and I think the caseworker senses it. We needed all the help we could get."

"I guess the main point is," she said, "does Derek sense it?"

"Yes."

In some ways—and just for a moment—he reminded her of Appleton, but she couldn't lay her finger on why. Going to the window, she looked out at the flaming dahlias, silver with rime. The crystalline garden seemed to form a miniature city, reminding her of San Francisco again.

"Your strength, Harold, has always been in planning things, you know that," she said.

"I'm not sure that's what I'm doing now, though," he answered.

"Then why are you going ahead with the adoption?"

"It has to do with Derek being gay. He's being harassed at school. He needs a full-fledged family behind him. There's no time to wait."

"That's all well and good, as far as he goes, but what about you? Does he have a full-fledged family behind him? Suppose," she said, "you do get Derek, what then?"

His eyes misted. "I don't quite follow," he said, taking off his glasses. "What do you mean—'what then'?"

"Will this be something you are ready for?" she asked.

Harold got up, rolling his cuffs, showing some veins in his arms. He took up so much space, the den seemed like an attic. "I've had time as his foster father. I love him. Besides—being gay is not something that has been very far from me in my life."

"That was what I was wondering," she said, frightened. "It came up when Mr. Benton started pressing me with his questions." And as she saw Harold again, as a young boy, out in the backyard with his stereoviewer, she could also hear catcalls coming from over the back fence, boys teasing him for his hobby.

"I wish I could say something more comforting,"

she said. "I don't understand very well, being old. I didn't even know what 'lesbian' or 'gay' meant until I was in my twenties. I was reading about women in prison."

"That's what most of us are," Harold said, "people in prison. That's the point of my sermon. And sometimes the only way out is to come out, I think. No matter how late in life it is."

"Is that what you're planning?" she asked. Had he just told her he was gay?

"Sure, maybe," he answered. "I don't know. There's my congregation to think about. And New Age people are hard to predict. Other than runes and Tarot cards."

"You might think, too, about Joanne," she went on. "All that she went through."

"I do think about her," Harold said. "A lot."

"You said yesterday Samuel's keeping Sonya from Joanne. I know for a fact that he's dead-set on doing just that." She had gotten up. "Well, I should get ready," she said at last, "and Caroline will be back from her trip any minute."

"One last thing, Mom," he said.

She caught herself in a mirror. "Yes, dear."

"Derek is the son of my friend Carey."

"Yes, I know that."

"Carey is gay. So adopting Derek is like adopting my own."

Restless, frightened, not exactly sure what he meant, she only nodded and then went up and kissed him again. Leaving the room, she changed out of her robe and took out her suit. It was beautifully tailored and auburn-colored. It had been her main outfit when she had sold clothes in Seattle. Day after day of working in the fancy dress shop, treating each item as if it were the last thing in the store. On that mall that was quickly becoming abandoned. Visiting her friend who owned the Mode O'Day Shop, and who shared her lunch hour with her. Together, although nearly broke, they had seemed to have the whole city at their feet. Going for a walk afterwards, through the square which had housed what her friend called "the magnetic statue."

For now, she put on her burnished stacked heels. How ready she was to leave and get back home! Harold would be driving her to the station. It had been a month since she had originally left for California, and everything, including her body, seemed stale with travel. She knew she smelled of lavender and sweat, and her clothes were all used up once again.

Packed, she was just about to the door, when Caroline walked in. The hug which came from her was cool.

"I'm so glad I haven't missed you," Caroline said in a rush of enthusiasm that was a strange variation of Harold's. "I have so much to tell you about my trip."

"I would love to hear about it," she answered. "But we have to leave in a few minutes. I'm going to take the noon train back. That will put me in at a much better time."

"You're not spending another night?"

But she heard the question mark fall over on its side.

14

"That's very thoughtful of you, honey, but I can't. I've been away from Capitol City for too long as it is," Eleanor answered.

But Caroline looked slightly ponderous. "And did your interview with the caseworker go all right?"

"Yes. And," she added, "I hope that it's best for you."

"Yes," she said. "I think it is. I love Derek in my own way, too."

Eleanor looked at her, wondering if she could fathom whether she knew about Derek's father and Harold, but she didn't need to plummet every family secret. Having just been to see her sister, she had enough of them as it was.

At that moment, Derek and Harold came in together—football and sweat—and Caroline's attention beat a hasty retreat. "When you get back up to Capitol City, you should go to the Willamette Art Museum. There's going to be a beautiful art show there. Women painters. We were talking about them at my women's retreat."

"I wonder if my niece Gloria's work is there."

"I don't know. But the women painters are part of the antiphallogocentrism we've all been fighting against—"

"Antiphallogo—what?" Derek asked.

"Anti-roosterism," Harold answered. "You know— no cocks in the hen house. Or at least the art house."

All four of them just stood there frozen in their tracks—Derek and Harold dripping on the hardwood floor, Caroline holding her beautiful blonde hair back,

15

and she, tired old lady, wanting to move her luggage at least one more inch toward the door. How long had it been since she had seen Harold and Caroline touch?

◇

Weeks back, when she had gotten into San Francisco, she couldn't bear to go to her sister's hospital right away. She took the airporter into the downtown, and, arthritis notwithstanding, managed all the way up Sutter to California Street. Her heart nearly broke as she looked at the old woman being helped past the iron gate into the Cathedral Apartments, the chauffeur of the round-town limousine seeming always to be at salute, condescending and wiry, with the sun hurrying on past the towers of the west hills, ready for a plummet into the Ocean.

Here it was all around her, these wonderful curved and squared stone buildings, as though pastry decorated, with the sashes always up, fire escapes and curtains lacing the windows, while she travelled back on down the hill, southward. And there she saw one apartment room empty, all white inside with a cut-glass mirror and doorknobs.

And she crossed down toward Market, into the vulnerable hour of seven, it not being dark enough to have her purse snatched immediately, and in moving into the flow of the avenue, she crossed over into Harold's mind, and she could feel him straining, although he was miles away, where things were going mad across the state. She knew now why she was taking this walk northward up Post, all the way back into time, her childhood, girlhood. It was the myth that many of the sojourning city dwellers felt—that if you just climbed up to the top of the hill like that, you could triumph over the sunset and all the shadows that were forming and happening lower in the city— you could walk straight up from seven o'clock right back into six, outpacing the light. As if the chime from St. Mary's would lose a toll just because you kept moving upward.

All these shadows, all these reflections within the precincts of light, because she hadn't wanted to think about Harold or her sister, Olivia. But no sojourn could change that. It was like having an aerial view as they had lifted off out of Arden towards California—of the lakes and countrysides (now they were climbing), of being aware of what you could not change, of what was inexorable. And she knew that something was wrong.

She had always been a kind of angel of mercy, really—a title which, when sometimes given by her closest friends, embarrassed her. Nevertheless here she was, here she was. Her sister had had a stroke, had undergone a quick rally, and then called for her. As though something—and not her condition—had come up that simply must be aired, discussed. And not just with anyone.

She could see herself, just as she had seen herself in that room in the building opposite, just a moment ago—the cameo of a woman framed on the wall, carefully cut from the dye, struggling to fulfill her intended purpose, against an onyx background, not perfect exactly, but dedicated at least to a larger idea.

She walked back to the airporter station and called Richard, her brother-in-law, who picked her up in his maroon Cadillac. In the glass of the car, she saw, still, that she did look distinguished, dressed in her auburn suit—slender, with her hair not looking anymore than full of light, in its silver-gray rinse. She was aquiline, a bit equestrian, as her Appleton would say. Aquiline. Perhaps borrowing a bit from Eleanor of Aquitaine. Imperious like her, but subdued, now, after all these years.

"What's our future going to be?" Richard asked at last. For they had hardly spoken anything but pleasantries until they had reached the hospital. "Years and years ahead of watching Olivia like this? Confined to her bed."

"A stroke doesn't end everything," she told him. By then they were alone on the elevator. "There are remedies. There's rehabilitation. You and Olivia know that better than I. We went through all of that with Mother. Mother came back with a vengeance. She had all of Horizon Haven hanging upside down by the time she was finished."

"It'll be different with Olivia," Richard answered. "She's too elegant for a rest home. You know that."

From the seventh floor of the hospital, there were views of the city, of even the house where they used to live. 252 Balboa, with her mother holding imperious reign over the entire family, until their father got back, whenever that would be, from wherever that would be. She could remember, for some reason, an evening of travelling south on the bus to St. Augustine's bookstore, and a coffee-colored cloud forming in huge magnitudes and lovely, softened magnolia shapes, above the traffic, above the oak and eucalyptus; winds had flown in like witches on broomsticks. Now as if a filter had been added, all the stucco turned rose. Patches of fog began to trail, as if a huge fire, from a hundred miles off, had been started.

They went into her sister's room. "Tell me how you are," she said to Olivia, who had been lain back on pillows.

"Well, I'm better, amazingly better now," Olivia said. "But not so good when this all happened. I was starting a letter to you when it dropped on me. I began to put my fountain pen to the page and everything went blank. I was trying to focus on you, and even you started to fade."

"I understand," Eleanor answered. But she was taken aback by her sister looking so white and tarnished.

"There's something I've got to say," Olivia said. "When I was writing you that letter where I lost my mind or at least part of it for a few minutes, I was going to tell you something that's been eating at me ever since your Joanne went through that terrible dark night of the soul she went through."

"Joanne?" she asked. And she was still surprised to see how much she didn't like speaking of her daughter, especially to her own sister.

"When Samuel divorced her and took Sonya away

because Joanne was lesbian, I knew a secret. And I vowed if I ever got my voice back, I'd tell you."

"Tell me?"

"That my Gloria was married to Samuel before he married your Joanne. For six months or so. Back East. Years ago. It didn't last, of course, and then after that, she died. And then he married your Joanne. But I simply had to tell you."

"I know that," Eleanor answered. "Joanne knew that. She in fact met Samuel at Gloria's memorial."

"Memorial?" Olivia asked. And looked agitated in way that was frightening. "Gloria didn't have a memorial."

"I mean at the memorial dinner for her," Eleanor said. "In Seattle. At the Athletic Club. Joanne after she married him couldn't bring up the previous marriage to Gloria to you. It was out of delicacy."

"Just the same," Olivia went on. "I'm at fault. I knew all about him then, fresh from Cornell. I knew about his ambition. But then when he came around to marrying Joanne, I kept my mouth shut—as advised by Richard here. And now Joanne's been through this terrible ordeal in her coming out process—" She stopped talking and reached for Eleanor's hand.

"She's fatigued," Richard said. "We'd better go." Also, he was embarrassed.

"But Richard knows something else," Olivia told her. "He knows Samuel is devoted to protecting Sonya from Joanne. Will not allow much visitation"—the word was hard for her to articulate. "Because he sees Sonya as fearing her mother's lifestyle."

Eleanor pressed Olivia's hand, kissed her. "We'll see about that. For now, you just lie back. That's enough. We'll be back tomorrow."

Her sister nodded and closed her eyes.

"What is this?" Eleanor asked, following Richard out. "Samuel keeping Sonya from Joanne? Joanne's suffered enough."

"He has good intentions," Richard said. "He wants Sonya to feel safe."

"Safe from her own mother, who loves her?"

They sat down in the waiting room and he held his head. "I've been getting ready for this for ten years," he told her. It took her a moment to realize he was speaking of the stroke. "But now that it's come, there's no getting over it. Certainly that must have been true for you when you lost Frank No matter how hard you try, you always think of it as the life going out of somebody else, not out of you, because you're married to them."

"The life didn't go out of me when Frank died," she answered. "Especially now that I've got Appleton. And it's not going to go out of you."

They waited. Richard raised himself.

"Listen, Richard, I'm getting a headache. From the trip. From this information. I need something to eat."

He complied—at least to the point of getting up. He went down the hall to a pay phone and ordered dinner to be delivered to his and Olivia's home from the Townhouse Restaurant. He took her back to the car, still refusing to talk about Samuel and Sonya, helped her nevertheless with her luggage when they arrived at the impressive stucco, lit a thermoflame log in the fireplace. The fire burnt green, then blue, then the pure cordial red you rarely see, except in old-time fireworks. Her headache subsided, after dinner came. The variegated flame was so much like him, the decorator of restaurants.

"You haven't been in this room since your mother had that stroke herself," he said.

Richard's *objets d'art* were crowding in and distracting her from the fire. Certainly a scene like this could never happen in Oregon—never, because the entire room, although luxurious, seemed to be narrowed within the circumference of light coming from the lampshade and the flames. The crowded homes outside (tight upon the hills, protected behind bars and sashes of stucco) caused everything inside to seem locked in. Oregon, however, continually knocked out walls, knocked on your door, knocked about its hills, welcoming the groundskeeper and the grounds in and causing a blend with the landscape.

"But I've been here so many times since," she answered.

"But not recently. Not this room. I had this closed off. I had it worked on for almost five months."

"It's beautiful," she said, not really looking.

"I was thinking back on that time when your mother used to crochet here—and I was thinking you're someone just like her—someone we scarcely appreciate. (And listen to me, I had to wait until I'm seventy to say it.) You're always here when we need you."

"Thank you."

"It was all very strange," he began. "Going back to that time." He was standing in front of the fire, the colors changing on his suit, a rich, perfect brown. "You know how Olivia was with your mother. Always harried, always guilty. And so when your mother came to stay for a couple of weeks we just had to get out every now and then. And one night, just before we were to see the premiere of something, she asked me to go downstairs and bring up from the basement something I didn't even know was there."

"The memorabilia that pushed her off her trolley," she answered. "Memorabilia does that. To all of us. Do you know where it is now?"

He smiled, reflecting. "That cigar box? I suspect it's back down there. Do you want it?"

"Not now, not now."

And she thought of Richard's treasure trove in the basement, like something in the second illustration in a fairy tale—the first showing you the boulder in front of the cave, the second opening up into over-whelming brightness. Richard was probably worth millions in that basement; stamps with inverted airplanes, the one-cent Magenta, perhaps, a golden cup—questionably pure but still golden—found in a lagoon off the Florida Keys; perhaps some stream of loose coins from the Devil's Triangle had found its way through an underground channel into his cave. Those *objets d'art* around her upstairs were nothing more than the tip of the pyramid. Push the secret panel and you're plummeted into the underground chamber of the million-dollar mummy, where the loot really is. It was down in that basement that he had found a fragment of what they were now calling the Shakespeare *Passion*. From an old box he had brought over from England. Supposedly the literary discovery of the century. And the academic community was going wild with it. Especially Oregon. New lines—a whole mystery play segment, by Shakespeare, and Richard had found it, enterprised it, industrialized it, going ultimately into cahoots with Samuel, who had given him this information about how he was going to "protect" her granddaughter.

"Now, Richard, tell me about Samuel."

He didn't have to ask what she meant. " I had no idea," he said, "he would prove to be the man to be so hard on Joanne when she wanted joint custody of Sonya. And now that he's won, he sees that the state of things in Oregon is creating a danger for anyone associated with gays and lesbians. He's heard about a child being hounded out of school because his peers knew he had a lesbian mother. I think he may, in fact, have joined the Oregon Protection Alliance for just this reason."

"Are you still connected with Samuel?" she asked.

"Yes."

"How connected?" she asked.

"The 1492-1992 Festival," he answered. "In Arden. We've been planning it for years."

"So," she said, "you're still seeing him. After all he did to Joanne. Is still doing."

"It's good business," he answered. "This is the year we announce what we do in '92. That's when we announce the play, announce the unveiling of the manuscript. We'll be bringing a major showcasing to Oregon for the quincentenary. That is, Samuel and I. All for next year. We'll both be in the Rose Festival Parade then."

"My headache has come back," she said, and left the room.

◇

How would she describe her daughter's ex-husband? This mysterious son-in-law. Samuel. He's a man you think you know. She had in her possession still some books he had given her. And at the time she had been surprised by his arrow-like perception in knowing just what she would want. Proust in the original. A biography of Dostoevsky. Record albums—Schumann— with no coaching from Joanne.

Smooth-faced, Kennedysque, Samuel still had to him a certain nutcracker-like sweetness; it was as if by x-ray you could see the jagged features underneath. There was an air of sugariness about his grace, too. At a party, at a Christmas gathering, his most witty ironies caused everyone to laugh, and the most solemn moments were broken up—in every sense. Rising out of the Peace Corps and Cornell graduate school and miscellaneous forms of social science, he was quickly heading for enormous political power both at Arden

University and in the state at large, and whenever her friends would ask her about Joanne, she had scarcely time to answer before they more comfortably switched to Samuel.

"How is he managing that long commute?"

"It's wonderful the way he's living in Capitol City, so Joanne can teach there. Wonderful."

And it was true. He was willing to make the sacrifice.

And he took time out for his daughter, even more so after the divorce arrived. He drove her to school, to her ballet lessons. Was often the parent who did the teacher conferences. He had in mind the best for his daughter.

But, as they say in the Bible (she could remember sitting in the pew in the old church in San Francisco, becoming listless, embroidering in her child's mind every quote from the King James Bible she heard), "And there was with the angel—"

There was with this angel something she couldn't define, not even after many years. What was more— he reminded her of her daughter-in-law, Caroline. It was as if her children had gravitated toward two beings so entirely alike she wondered whether they were brother and sister. Caroline's pauses on the phone were exactly like Samuel's long pauses in seeing her. At first she thought no two people could be more different. But there was, however, a slant in Caroline's letters just like the one in Samuel's suppressed but handsome face: a slant of overagreement that bordered on coolness. Caroline (1960s) dressed up in flamboyant prints was Caroline (1970s) dressed up in bib overalls was Samuel (1960s) dressed up as bermudaed Youth Corps worker was Samuel (1970s) dressed up—coat and tie—as post-liberal. There was the faint flickering of the houselights—and the sound of the bell in the theater lobby, before all went into darkness.

At her own birthday celebration, Eleanor had watched Caroline give the first toast, her face quite exquisite close to the crystal: "I toast Eleanor, because she taught her children the great values of feeling— even though one of them was a man."

And when the wave of embarrassment and laughter had gone through the party, Samuel, as if on cue, had said—"Amen." And then raising his glass: "She's taught her men how to feel so that she can always keep them in line."

Uproarious laughter.

But there was "with" both of them, as with that angel, a multitude of the heavenly host. She had to say she always faintly disliked them, Caroline and Samuel, because they gave off a scent of flamboyantly recycled paper, fashionable health food, and down-hill skiing. But their power was remarkable, because while it seemed to be staunch and American and indi-vidual, it actually came from the Invisible Choir and was always only one step ahead of the next change in the wind and humid herd mentality.

Later, certain political developments in Oregon confirmed her suspicions. The Governor had sent out a referendum protecting all government employees from discrimination on the basis of sexual orientation.

But Samuel, she learned later, had actively and secretly pressed the Governor to change his mind, using his academic influence and their friendship as crowbars. When the Governor, persuaded by another, older friend (Appleton!), had gone ahead and issued the Referendum anyway, the Oregon Protection Alliance had arisen in the backfields like a slow and gigantic toadstool, appearing in loathsome manifestation in the Balboa Inn complex just south of Portland, to start creating a vanguard against the Referendum in the form of Measure Eight. It was then she had had a sneaking suspicion that Samuel, for all his parading academics, had a great deal to do with that toad-stool, on the rise, just as she had known for sure that Appleton had been the old friend of the Governor who had taken the train all the way down from his beloved Seattle (he was in a rest home then) just to speak to his longtime pupil and persuade him in the opposite direction. Sometimes, you'd never believe Appleton had been the one, because he was such a tough old bird anyway, and his Pendleton facade made you think more of a Marlboro man aged thirty years (without the tobacco) beyond his prime rather than what he really was, a liberal ex-law professor who specialized in writing ironic recollections and could move quickly as an activist.

At present all the state was in an uproar over that Measure Eight which the Oregon Protection Alliance had succeeded in getting on the ballot. "Let's Strike the Governor's Protection of Gays and Lesbians

Down." On both sides, everyone was starting to go into high gear.

As now Capitol City neared, it hovered there, as she sat on the train, under its own lights, just the way it had two years ago, when the devastation had come to Joanne. The town, the city, had stood there in momentary Saturn rings of fog, the state capital at Halloween, with random lanterns on porches, and the sheeted children, sentineled by grown-ups, running back and forth across the streets.

◇

Arriving back at the Capitol City train station, Eleanor found herself exhausted. As she pulled her luggage off the cart, and phoned Appleton to meet her, she had to admit that Samuel had been looming over her. On the ride up from Arden, Samuel had seemed to be in every "Yes on Eight" sign that went past.

Appleton drove up in his collector's DeSoto. The one with the profile of the explorer on the crest.

"You look like you've been through it," he said, after they had kissed—and pretty passionately, considering all their rattling bones.

"This has been a week of revelations," she said. "I'll break them to you one at a time."

"I guess I should say thanks. I take it Olivia's health is not the great revelation—that she's O.K."

Almost immediately, they were under the shadow of the great Dome of the Capitol. A workman all of gold stood on top.

"Yes, she is O.K. Olivia is not the great revelation,

29

but she provided it. It has to do with our none-too-favorite, Samuel."

Appleton assumed his lawyer's squint, as they drove into the late-summer sun. He put on his sunglasses. At the end of the long parkway, there would be her beloved "Eleanor's Castle: Collectibles and Antiques."

"Well," he said, "what is it?"

"It turns out," she said, "that Samuel plans to keep Sonya away from Joanne as much as possible."

"How would Olivia know that?"

"Richard is close to Samuel because of this 1492-1992 project that is in the offing. He told Richard Sonya fears a lesbian lifestyle."

Appleton drew in a moment. "If Sonya genuinely feels that, it will be hard to get more visiting time for Joanne."

"Unless," Eleanor said, aware of quests all around her, "unless we can find out something devastating about Samuel."

"Something that we could use for leverage," Appleton said smilingly. "I've never been beneath skullduggery."

"My dear," Eleanor heard herself saying, "you follow my thoughts exactly."

She had them detour past an old DeSoto emblem on the side of a dilapidated building. It was early evening. And as if commanded, a curtain of light was thrown across.

"Well, that wasn't necessary," she said to the light. "But I thank you for it."

Underneath the layers of paint was the explorer in profile and then below, the ship in a circle—Plymouth. A beautiful white and-now-almost rose brick wall.

The clouded sun was setting, looking like one of the Columbian silver pieces she had seen in a coin store once. "Look," her Sunday school teacher used to say. "Look at the full moon tonight and see if you can't make out the picture of Jesus holding hands with all the children 'round the world." How much better, however, to try to see the profile of Columbus—silver—in the sun.

A sense of explorer's excitement was coming up inside her. "And do you remember, Appleton?" she asked. "Do you remember Isabella on that dual portrait stamp you bought? That's the way she was in the engraving in my reader going back to my second grade. I saw her in the Arden parade yesterday."

"Yes, yes, not at all like that schoolmarm in the parade a year ago." Across the street was a little park and a strange proscenium, with a baroque plaque with cherubs and arrows that all the trees and Scotch Broom had overtaken.

"I used to have, too," Appleton said, following her thoughts, "a Columbian Expo silver dollar, with Columbus in profile on one side. My father brought it back after visiting Chicago in '92, along with a clock that chimed, and a full-tinted portfolio book, stereoviewer cards, and enough stamps to make anybody independently wealthy at this very moment."

"I just feel like we're on to something now," she

said. "Like them. Columbus and Isabella." Her own Eleanor's Castle was coming up, a dark three-story 1920s house with a collectibles sign out front. "We can knock Samuel from his pedestal, win custody for Joanne, and win a No on Measure Eight."

He had pulled up in front. They leaned over and kissed again.

◇

Next morning, she left the Castle in the care of Appleton, and went down to the No on Eight Headquarters to talk to Joanne. Eleanor found her alone in the office. She knew that down in Arden, the very same headquarters would be a beehive of activity by now, but up here in Capitol City, you couldn't expect much, even though it was the capital, because this was a resistant county. It was as though Joanne and her friends were blazing a trail.

Her daughter held out her hand when she saw her coming, warm but uncertain.

They hugged at last.

"Will Harold get Derek?" Joanne asked. "And was your trip all right?"

The place had once been a fifties restaurant. They were standing before a full-glassed front.

"I think Harold will get Derek," Eleanor said. "The social worker seemed to like me, I think."

"Harold has been on a tightrope all this time," Joanne said, looking as though she were on one herself. "He told me."

Eleanor wasn't sure how to answer.

"I mean a tightrope," Joanne went on, "in that it's been so important to him to be a father. I know how he feels. They still won't let me see Sonya."

Eleanor had wanted to go all morning without hearing that.

"I don't see how Samuel can keep you from her," she answered.

"It's not as though he does—directly," Joanne said. "But I think he's influencing Sonya. Somehow he encourages her to say, 'I don't want to see you,' and then I can't force her. And when I watch Derek and Harold together, I think—Derek wants to be with him. If Harold only understood how I want that from Sonya."

"It will come, dear. It will come. And if Family Services will let Harold adopt Derek, they'll finally approve you at last down there, too."

"I don't know about that. It depends on if Harold—" And she stopped.

In that moment, Eleanor felt her complicity in the near-lie she had told just a few days ago. Beyond her, in the reality of the windows of the headquarters, she could see the Capitol's late-summer rose garden even from here, and was reminded of every sad-looking flower she had seen from the speeding train. Along with little delicate-shaped pieces of ancient pottery with faces. There was some of that in the abandoned lunch counter of this cafe, once called "The Hub." All of discarded Oregon seemed to have made a stopover here and then come to rest. And then she wondered,

What would it mean to topple Samuel? What would it take?

"And Aunt Olivia?" Joanne asked. "How is she?"

"Recovering," Eleanor said. "I think she may even come up here when she's better."

"That's the main thing," Joanne said. "That Olivia's better."

Eleanor, contemplating and embracing the enormous capitol symbol in front of her, also thought again of De Soto, Columbus, Isabella. Perhaps she had been hoping Joanne would be distant, cold (which she wasn't), so that there would be a reason not to broach the past, ever.

"I have something else to tell you," she said at last. "Olivia told me Samuel has every intention of keeping you from Sonya."

Joanne retreated—she was close to the lunch counter now. She seemed near to getting behind it.

"At first," Eleanor went on, "Olivia was burdened with what she thought was a secret about Gloria— that she was married to Samuel before he married you. And then she told this other thing."

"Samuel?" Joanne asked, her full eyes wide.

"Yes. I honestly believe," Eleanor said, "that it helped her recover from her stroke to tell me about it."

Joanne's face had become the same as Harold's.

"There's no understanding Samuel," Joanne began slowly. "He worked so hard for so many things, including our marriage. He's a devoted father. But there's no room in him for a variation on the family. After a few years with him, I realized I could be

34

Gloria's stand-in. He just wanted a wife, a house, a conventional life, and that was it."

Eleanor had often reflected that there was something of the Art Nouveau goddess about her daughter, but she seemed also tough now, and in a political frame. High cheek-bones and a radiance of dark hair. She remembered this radiance following in her wake, the moment she had finally emerged, smiling at last, from her depression. "So what do we do now?" she asked. "That's my question."

Joanne answered, "I'm not sure."

"I had something in mind," Eleanor said at last. "Something more directly torpedo-like for this ex-husband. Something like blackmail to help you and the campaign."

At "blackmail" Joanne raised her brows. "I need to be strong right now," Joanne said. "Is that being strong?"

"I don't mean crude blackmail. I mean subtle."

"Subtle or not," Joanne said, "when I said strong, I meant imaginative."

"Then what do you have in mind?" Eleanor asked.

Joanne, getting tea from a tinny pot for hot water, said, "I'm imagining meeting with Family Services and getting this all out on the table—I need time with Sonya. I'm also imagining a small coming out session at our rally, one to match Samuel and Richard's heraldry of the Renaissance Fair. I can read my poetry, and we'll have others speak. And we can do it in Isabella Circle down in Arden. That circle, you know, is sort of blessed by Gloria. She used to live there."

To Eleanor this seemed very light-handed indeed, especially now that her own anger was going up to its highest pitch. Also she wasn't so sure she wanted to think for long about Gloria. Nevertheless, she nodded. "Well, it's an idea."

"Good. Let me know what you finally think. And as for Samuel himself," Joanne went on, "we have no tangible proof yet that he's a member of the OPA. But what we're doing now"—she was at the locked office cabinet—"is keeping a file."

And Eleanor, walking up and finding the folder, saw a photograph of him, with the Dome behind, with a caption saying he saw himself as the next state senator. It had become clear, as Joanne had spoken, that the Measure Eight they were presently fighting was only the beginning—that there was something coming round the bend next year when Renaissance Fair 1992 really hit, and that was Measure Nine—a machine gun proposal to eliminate gays and lesbians in all Oregon schools, and on all levels. Silence children, silence teachers. After that, who knew? In some ways, it wasn't so much the issue of being gay or lesbian that the OPA was interested in; it wasn't so much the matter of education; what it was, really, was the effort to control the family, define what was natural, and this would be the beginning of an ultimate rise to power. And control. And the end of all differentness.

But clearly Joanne was still thinking about the threat to her visitation rights. What would she, Eleanor, have done, if she had found out such news?

"Wait we will, I guess," Eleanor said, putting the

clippings away. "And if the poetry reading and coming out session will fortify you, so be it."

"Fortification is the name of the game." Joanne smiled. "Coming out publicly on Columbus Day will be a big step for me, so I'll need all the support I can get."

"You coming out?" Eleanor heard herself ask. "I was thinking you meant other people."

"That's what everybody thinks," Joanne said, still smiling. "It's always a good idea for somebody else."

"But you?" Eleanor asked. "In front of everybody?"

"Yes, me. In front of everybody."

For a moment, Eleanor felt crestfallen.

"Maybe," Joanne concluded, "when you're thinking of it, you can tell me a few recollections about Gloria—and Grandmother Lucinda. I can't find that journal I kept when I was sick. So your writing might help me go into a few poems. Stories about relatives frequently do. And Gloria's always been an inspiration."

"Yes, I could do that," Eleanor said. "But give me time first to catch my breath."

Joanne came up and embraced her. "Absolutely."

◇

When Eleanor and Appleton had first visited Capitol City as a common law couple, they had been called there on emergency. Joanne had been distraught. Answering the cry, Eleanor had seen Capitol City as a place for witches, so enormously different from Harold's Arden, even though the two towns were only seventy miles apart. The hills of Capitol City got you lost—altogether unlike Harold's Eden-like and user-friendly Arden. Too many ups and downs in Capitol City, too many sheer cliffs—too many extremes, from the exclusive Ash Grove to the penitentiary. Completely unlike Arden, with all its bike paths, and walks, and running trails. On that night, two years back, when they had driven up and through the Capitol Park area, through the pornography district, they had passed a house in the dark, whose gingerbread yawned open: in the living room was one of those old merry-go-round horses, restored—with the monstrous jaws ready to snap at you.

After first knocking and receiving no answer, she and Appleton had entered Joanne's home, going into her living room, one that seemed to possess floating rings of light, with Joanne missing but with her papers and her poetry scattered all over—a shock; for even as a child, Joanne had always kept her writing neatly filed and frequently hidden. Appleton had taken her arm, instinctively.

"Looks like there's been an upheaval," he had said.

"No kidding."

"Well, let me finish. But it looks normal—usual. Everybody throws things in arguments."

"Not Samuel and not Joanne," she answered. "And certainly not her manuscripts. And where's Sonya? She's always doing her homework at this hour."

In saying this, on that night, Eleanor found herself edging against a sense of panic; there was something calculated, considered, in all of this. It was at perhaps this moment that she had known this would be the night Joanne would be coming out to her.

Then the sound of a car—and Joanne and a strange woman at the door—the woman, introduced as Alice, was stout and wore a broad-brimmed hat. The dress seemed elephantine.

"I ran off to my woman's group," Joanne said. "I couldn't wait any longer." She started picking up the papers. "I was trying to find the right poem and I just left everything scattered. Fortunately I forgot to lock the door."

Eleanor found herself introducing Appleton, who was leaning against a table. Perhaps to steady himself.

Then she had to take Alice's hand, as an introduction. A suspicious handshake between two suspicious women. She felt strange being one of them. Holding Alice's hand, she felt observed from along a slant, especially when she turned and hugged Joanne. And in that moment, Eleanor saw her daughter as thinner, felt her as thinner, more porous, and her eyes were more on the verge of spilling. Not because she was about to cry, but because she seemed to need to sleep but couldn't. She was dressed in the kind of clothes she wore when she worked in the yard or cleaned house.

Finally her daughter sat down, away from her, in one of the pools of light. Alice disappeared to make a phone call.

"Where's Sonya?" Eleanor asked.

"She left with Samuel."

"For where?"

"Arden."

"Why in heavens' name? At this hour?" Eleanor asked.

"He's taken her and gone. They're going to the apartment he keeps down there. Tomorrow they look for a house to rent."

"What's the matter with him?" Eleanor asked. "What's happened?"

"I've been seeing a woman," Joanne said.

"You mean he's been seeing a woman."

"No—I've been seeing a woman. A woman named Clare. I told Sonya about it three weeks ago and at first it was all right. Then she started shutting herself away in rooms with her father. Talking and talking. I think," she said, crying suddenly, "I almost didn't survive the talk. At last, they left. This morning, Sonya said she never wanted to see me again."

Eleanor was furious. "And it's this Alice, isn't it? This Alice who roped you into this cock-and-bull woman's group, and they encouraged you to have this—connection."

"She told me about the group, yes. But that's just because she worked at the college."

"But it's this woman's group, isn't it, where you met Clare?"

"Yes, but you don't understand," Joanne said.

"Apparently not."

For long afterward, Eleanor would remember the flatness of her retort. She found it hard forgiving herself for it. And the way Joanne looked at her at that moment said that she was absolutely alone.

"I'll stay here with you," Eleanor went on. "Even

though I don't understand. You have to realize, honey, that these ideas came late to me. I always thought of lesbians and gays as people who were thrown into prison."

"Of course, prisons," she said, echoing Harold later. "That's the only way lesbians have been seen up until now, and Sonya—"

A lance-like movement crossed her body, and all Eleanor could remember was when Joanne had had rheumatic fever and she had nearly fainted from her daughter's pain. Appleton stood up, but Eleanor was at her side again before he could come over.

"You must stop suffering," Eleanor said, holding her once more and yet having no idea what she was saying. "Whatever it is, I know it's not your fault. You've been duped, misled, and once Sonya learns that, she'll come back to you."

"No," she answered—and gently pushed her away. "What's been done can't be changed. I've been this way for years. What she's realizing about me is the truth. And Samuel brought a counselor up here one night, and the counselor told Sonya how lesbian and dangerous my poetry is."

Eleanor could not fathom it. Not then, not even now. All that she did know in that moment was that she was glad to have been pushed away.

"But you must do everything you can to get her back," she said. "She's your daughter."

"On what grounds?" Joanne asked, defeatist then.

"I don't know. We'll get an attorney, and find out."

"Sonya," Joanne said, "is twelve years old. With her the way she is, there is nothing in heaven or earth that would change her way of thinking."

The thought of her bowing out like this angered her. In memory, she saw her own hands bathing Joanne and later Sonya. To think of her two children divided when she loved them both.

"The only thing to do," Eleanor said, "is to take the situation in hand. I'll simply stay here until Sonya's come back."

"You can if you like," she answered. "But I'd also understand if you never wanted to see me again."

"Stop feeling sorry for yourself. And don't talk nonsense. I'm probably as shaken up as Sonya is, but you don't walk out on your children."

Joanne obviously felt so much relief, she started to cry again. Mindlessly, Eleanor began to pick up Joanne's poetry, the scraps of her journal. "Who's that man with you?" Joanne asked finally. For Appleton, too, had disappeared for the moment.

"That's too long a story for now. His name's Appleton, and he's about a million years old."

"Will you be using the same bedroom?"

"Yes, as a matter of fact."

"Then I'll get it ready for you."

◇

The rally Joanne had spoken of at the No on Eight Headquarters came on Columbus Day, and with a rapidity that nearly caused Eleanor to catch her breath. All the excitement was heightened, for her, by the arrival of Olivia and Richard, on an extended visit. They had been in the Castle hardly ten minutes, when immediately her sister and brother-in-law had a falling out over what they would do on the renegade holiday—go to the rally or Samuel's Great Unveiling of Shakespeare—with Richard storming off, still in support of Samuel, and Olivia calling after him, "Good riddance. If you can't be there for Joanne, how can you be there for anybody?"

Within a matter of moments, these two Californians had become what Eleanor now privately called "Oregonized"—at odds, divided, at each other's throats. This Great Divide, general all over the state, was just on the upswing. On the eve of the rally (Columbus Eve? Eleanor wondered), she and Olivia drove down to stay over at Harold's, with Appleton (seeing to things again in the Castle) and Joanne due the next morning. They descended into that magical valley just about sunset, with the smoke from the field burning wrapping the road and the fields in a pink haze. Small one-seater planes darted through, like horseflies—or "darning needles," as they used to say in Texas, as though mending the fabric of light ahead of them. But hardly had she and Olivia stepped through Harold's doorway, when there was trouble afoot. Oregonization again.

The living room was covered with leaflets for the rally. "Don't forget C-Day! Come out! Show Up!" they all said. Derek, higher than a kite, was stacking them into a news carrier's sack like wildfire, ready for another dive into the neighborhood. Caroline looked on disapprovingly and seemed to shoot objections all over the room.

"Please let us take your things," Caroline said to them. "And I'm afraid you'll have to share the same bedroom. There's been a last-minute rearrangement. And Derek, you need to come back for your home-work," she went on. "Remember what we agreed. Not too long after dark. No one's safe after that time."

"Let him go," Harold said. "He knows how to take care of himself."

"Of course that's what you'd say—"

And she wheeled away from him, out of the room.

"Caroline," Harold explained, "is not showing up for Joanne tomorrow, either. She's going to hear Sam-uel's project."

Eleanor exchanged a glance with Olivia. "Well, then, she and Richard can stand together," Olivia said. "They'll make a charming couple. Odd, but charming. Defectors from the family."

Eleanor couldn't fathom it. Why she'd not show up for her own sister-in-law—who was even a client of hers at one time—just so she could hear that horse's ass. And yet somehow it did make sense, since, as she'd often noted, the two of them seemed so much alike.

"Do you mind if we take these to our room?" she asked, suddenly feeling the weight of her luggage.

With Olivia, she crowded herself into their new quarters, narrow but cozy. The windows presented a few spangles of light in the evergreens. In the street, not far from the center of town, she could hear a constant hubbub, reminding her of that October night, two years ago, when Joanne had come out to her.

"Are they getting revved up already?" she asked Harold, who was still attending them.

"Yes," he said, pulling out linens, "by some strange coincidence, there's also going to be a March for Christ tomorrow. People from all over the world are pouring in."

"That means there's not going to be a square inch of room left in Arden, once you also add in the Shakespeare people."

She was aware, once again, that Arden felt like an enormous archaic party, to which everyone was invited. Mad hatters, March hares. Which was usually the case. Like the parade she's seen.

She settled into the room completely, as Harold said good night. And she had to admit she was absolutely thrilled with the politics of it all. The idea of "showing up" tomorrow sent a current through her nerves such as she had never felt before. She had not realized until then that Joanne's depression had been such a freight upon her shoulders, ever since that October night. And now both she and her daughter were letting go of it—with her sister there beside her! Joanne speaking tomorrow!

"What do you think?" Olivia asked, turning down her bed. "Here's my tulip needlepoint on a pillowcase."

"It certainly brightens up your side of the room." She turned, caught by the discarded bric-a-brac of their quarters, the spot she had stayed in just a month ago. "You know, Olivia, this reminds me of when we shared that garret just before you and Richard were married. And all the funny things that happened."

"Yes, talking like this, planning like this, up to all hours, describing the places we would visit, like Egypt, because we had seen DeMille's *Ten Command-ments* or Claudette Colbert's *Cleopatra* or *Antony and Cleopatra* on stage—"

"—remember when that sphinx, that was speared on the top of that pyramid, and how it slid off and landed, like a sled, straight into the lap of Enobarbus, who was in the midst of some speech over poor Cleopatra? (I believe he was panting.) We couldn't stop laughing, all the way through the last act?"

"Or the times, when we were married, when we'd go out horseback riding in Golden Gate, or speak fancy French in front of Richard and Frank at the L'Auberage, and how provoked they'd get—"

"Or when you and I stole on to that train to Seattle to go looking for Father!"

"My oh my," Eleanor said, "we've come such a long way together, haven't we?"

And so her dreams that night were first of Olivia, and then of the old water tower in Volunteer Park in Seattle, with two little girls in early century dress playing in front of it, and then of an old souvenir book called *Seattle Story*, with the city presenting itself in all its angles, in its bays, its totem poles, and its ivy. She was about to set herself upon the grassy bank of the 1948 campus of the University of Washington,

and hear, perhaps, some chimes (taking her to the
top of a San Franciscan hill, and the sounds from the
tower, again, of Grace Cathedral), but she woke up in
the middle of the night, in the middle of a memory
of visiting Joanne at Woodland House, when her
daughter was at the very center of her depression, not
long after what she and Appleton had witnessed at
Joanne's home. Like the eye of the storm. She could
remember approaching the old, done-over twelve-
bedroom Woodland House and Convalescent Center
as it rested in a beautifully mixed hub of sunlight and
shade, its lawn crossed with daisies, yellow violets
and strange, unidentifiable flowers in the shape of
spades—just as pointed as those in a deck of cards. As
she and Appleton mounted the steps, it seemed as if
a whole, one-suited bridge game had been brilliantly
strewn over the lawn—reminding her of a meadow
she had seen once in the Cascades that had flashed
out in the same way, the flowers the same shape and
dyed gold as well.

And there they had found Joanne, defeated in her
bed.

And in Harold's house now, Eleanor felt she was
falling asleep again. The spell of Arden arose once
more in her dreams, dispelling the depression. Like
a sunrise.

◇

In the morning, she put on her robe and went out
into the dawn of this promising Columbus Day. The
hoarfrost had touched everything just so, to give the

things in Harold's wild garden a sense of fruition. Finding some scissors, she cut some heroic October roses and put them in a vase before the front hall mirror. Turning, she caught herself in it.

She still looked good—not old, really, with hands still crisp with veins. Her eyes were blue and sharp, and she was still proud of her figure—clearly drawn, supple, responsive. Even if she did forget or postpone things like memoirs requested by her daughter (at last she had supplied some), she felt so in love with herself at that moment, before that vase of flowers, that she could dream and recollect even while awake. Standing there thinking, I will soon be off to a rally, she also considered all the names of people she had known and perhaps was about to know. It was thrilling to think of them sometimes—how strange and altogether entirely unique they were. The names. James, Ivy, Nick, Carlotta, Jacob—like a great clustering flower, opening up, further and further.

But soon after that moment—of what she could only call exultation—she heard Caroline's quick step in the kitchen, and felt she must get dressed in order to be that name she most certainly was that moment: Eleanor. For her own protection.

Sounds continued to echo through the house, of a family, getting up, rising for the day. Harold's thunderous cough. The low complaining of Derek, who sounded as if he didn't know where he was. Olivia's motions, precise always, in the toilet. Richard's unzipping of his shaving kit.

But once they were buttoned and strapped, and

fed—once they had acknowledged and kissed each other goodbye—strange to say they were a divided family again, as though on their way to opposite sides of a war.

Standing there later at the center of the city in Isabella Circle, waiting for Joanne and Appleton to arrive, with Derek on one side of her and Harold on the other, she felt those edges again, felt so strangely divisive and vulnerable. For as they stood in their narrow throng, she could see Samuel's Grand Procession beginning to form around Columbus Square, not with pomp and circumstance, but with bombast and profusion, with Leonardo's *Salvatore Mundi* flying high above them all, on a banner that looked more like a kite. The preview, once again of next year's 1492-1992 Renaissance Fair, with a magnificent podium and bunting and regalia, while her, Eleanor's, No on Eight group only had a little skeleton of a microphone and a few pink triangles.

And music was coming in—the music of autumn.

Here Joanne was at last—looking quite beautiful in a sun-colored dress, and sitting down in a line of chairs up near the microphone at the top of the steps of City Hall. And Appleton was coming in close and taking her hand. Now they were a quorum, yes. A Saturday quorum. The steps were filling with slow lines of the motliest group ever. Banners were being raised, slowly but everywhere. "Hate is not a Family Value!"

A series of dignitaries proceeded in and, in the case of a few, came out publicly—on that poor little skeleton of a podium, wowing the state nevertheless. A senator, a clergyman, a nurse, a doctor. And then Joanne. A college writing teacher and poet. They were an hour long into the rally when it finally came.

Joanne was now standing to read her poem. A poem, she announced, dedicated to her cousin. And so, as the lines came, the woman, Gloria clearly, became a mermaid, in a sojourn of light. She was also in a wheelchair, this cousin, with a Hades-like man pushing her and then she was on the top of a diving tower, vanishing as though she were nothing but an orange lily, tossed toward the audience. And there was a rainbow above a sea wave, then a little pavilion park with girls chasing hoops, their cap ribbons flying, and then gold strokes upon a painter's canvas—Gloria's, too, perhaps: images which moved and affected her, Eleanor, strangely, as though she were a wind chime, or as though she were all the people, the names, she had contemplated this morning. She could remember drawing Gloria close at one moment—and the beautiful line of her shoulder and the sweet scent from the nape of her neck. At dinner, when she would visit, she would be a candle flame.

Just then, at just her ear, Harold was saying, "My God! What a poem! What a speech! I wish it was me." And as soon as he was saying it, the whole throng was bursting into thunderous applause.

Oh, that's my daughter, she wanted to say, ashamed of her moment of doubt. My daughter, people!

◇

They won the battle but lost the war. Measure Eight carried. She could hardly believe it. Oregon-wide, state employers could now hold open season on gays and lesbians in the work place. They had a license to hunt, as their No on Eight campaign said they would. Discrimination, generally, was underwritten.

Eleanor was devastated. It had not been just her children, after all. She had had a stake in it, for herself. And the rest of the world. And just as she had felt all the enthrallment of that rally, so she felt all the disastrous letdown, when they had gone to the fairgrounds and watched the election returns come in.

And more than that, it was an impossible winter that followed, one that turned cold with the most extraordinary viciousness. No one in the state could believe it. Rains would sweep in from the sea and then a lowering Arctic ceiling would freeze everything over into a lethal glaze. People would pick or shovel or salt themselves out, and then they would have another blizzard. One time she could remember travelling on the Amtrak down to see Harold and looking out at the frozen rivers and the veins of still-white branches—at the sheep huddling together beyond the farmhouses that would disappear because of the white-outs—and she would think that the train was the last vestige of the nerves of the state, the last way of getting from one place to another. With the Interstate closed, telephone lines down, sidewalks roped or sawhorsed off,

51

this one means was still in operation—perhaps three or four or five hours late but still in operation.

It was then she began to fear that Joanne might go into another depression, because Sonya moved more and more into her father's grip. That was the particular pain of Christmas. She, Eleanor, could not see where any healing would be coming from.

She slowly discovered that Joanne had thought that Coming Out would mean that Sonya would withdraw, of course, at first, and then things would start getting better: there would be a return of her daughter, inch by inch, on the horizon, no matter how distant.

But it had not turned out that way. In her history with Joanne, Sonya would sometimes draw in closely, by writing letters, only to back off. Eleanor found that she herself was still in a state of shock or disbelief or resistance, because all of this went completely against what Eleanor had known of Sonya before—directness, concern, and courtesy (and not phony, overblown, or party-like). Even beyond that, all of this went against the previous bond between daughter and grand-daughter—open, laughing, close. Now it was simply wiped out. Sometimes Eleanor imagined that Sonya had her own fears concerning Joanne's lifestyle, just as Samuel had been reported as saying—and then her actions made sense—sometimes but not always. For herself, Eleanor was passing through a state of secret withdrawal from Joanne which was still quickly flowering into a tenderness which almost frightened her.

"Don't think you're so special," Eleanor would tell

her. "I remember when you started retreating from me when you were fourteen. You'd go into your room and slam the door until well past midnight."

"Yes, yes, but I was still under the same roof."

Christmas Eve was, she supposed, a turning point. Olivia had come up again for a visit, leaving Richard behind. They were still quarreling over his connection with Samuel. Joanne and Olivia once again spent hours talking about what they might do to stop Samuel.

For a family gathering that night, she had invited Harold and Joanne and Derek and Caroline up for presents and eggnog, but Harold had said over the phone he would be the only one coming.

She was sitting with Olivia and Joanne by their narrow tree of angel hair and old-fashioned light bulbs, the pink glow on the walls reminding her of a neon sign she had seen somewhere, when Joanne said, distractedly, "Did you know that Sonya's in town tonight—I made a Christmas call this morning, and Samuel said she's up here with her old candy-striper group. They're out caroling this minute."

"Well, good for her."

"I'm hoping against hope they'll come by here," Joanne said.

"Well, don't plan on it," Eleanor answered, trying to model coolness. "It's better that way."

Still and all, Eleanor felt as though they were being set up. The hearth log burned iridescent; the gold cupids turned and chimed above the candle flames. And through the windows, the entire neighborhood was winking and flashing at them. She could see that merry-go-round horse once more; it was as if it had crashed its way through the window and was now galloping into the living room.

In a moment, all of them—Olivia, Joanne, Appleton, and herself—did hear caroling. Joanne rushed to the window. "It's a group of girls and one of them's brunette."

But as the sound approached, Joanne's face fell. It disappeared. It wasn't Sonya at all.

They sat in silence.

Someone was at the door. Harold.

Taking off his coat and seeming to breathe steam into the house, he was all energy and muscularity. "This certainly is a subdued group," he said.

"Why isn't Derek with you?" Eleanor asked.

"What with the Election," Harold answered. "Derek's turned to drugs."

"Oh, my heavens," Olivia said, "really?"

"Yes. We've got him in an out-patient program now. The addiction may have gone back to even before the Election." Harold's glasses were misted. He wiped them.

"Would it help if I talked with him?" Joanne asked.

"Nice thought—but why you?" he said.

"Well"—she hesitated—"I am out."

She could see the emphasis hit Harold hard. "Yes, yes, that's true. And Derek was extremely moved, by the way, by your speech at the rally. Knocked out by it, in fact. But then we all got so elated, we thought

we were going to win. The disappointment was too
much."

"Exactly," Joanne said, "and so I know how Derek
feels."

"And you think I don't?" Harold's face was almost
in alarm.

"I didn't say that."

Harold wiped his glasses again. He had been
crying. "You know Caroline's moved out—"

"Moved out?" Eleanor heard herself asking.

"Of course she would move out," Olivia said.

"Anyway," Harold went on, "since Caroline moved
out and the Election Disaster struck, Derek's been
dead set against me coming out, because he's afraid
he'll lose me."

"You coming out?" Olivia asked.

"Lose you?" Eleanor asked.

"Yes—his real father was gay and abandoned him,
too. He wants to be open himself but have his parents
stable, as he calls it. For him, that means straight."

"Does that mean that Caroline might be the one
to grab him?" Joanne asked.

"Very possibly," Harold said. "She's got this notion
that if he ever stays clean, he'll go straight, too."

Eleanor knew they were, all five, on the edge of
a precipice—just like Persephone in the story. The
Christmas tree was the fatal bush—winking flowers
of every hue. The underground yawned underneath,
and she knew this was as true for Harold as it was
for Joanne, for there was something fatal about him
tonight, in his being here utterly alone.

◇

The confirmation and confrontation at last, near Easter. The eve of going to Family Services, in Arden again, this time in behalf of Joanne, who was going to defend her right to see Sonya. With all this on the horizon, Eleanor had taken a nap and had slept on through to evening. There was a red light through the window. She had dreamt she had been asleep in the catacombs of a castle, and there had been a gossiping among the sepulchres, a general whispering of wings along the eaves. What was that red light? An airplane beacon. She remembered, now, the Columbian Exhibition as her mother had reported it, with a statue rising high above the waterways, of the botanical gardens and the rhododendrons, pink and purple, with bottle-green leaves, in the stereoviewer which he handed round. She dreamed, too, back to when she had been living in that garden of waters named Seattle, cooled by backdrops of mountains, rockeries of heather, and vermilion dahlias, caught in the expensive Kodacolor of those days: the district called Magnolia, misnamed and yet so appropriately named. Where she and Appleton had met, and she had lured him out of the rest home.

Later the next morning and within hours of her dream, she, along with Olivia (visiting again—she and Richard had now separated) was being ushered into a small county room by the same Mr. Benton, with everybody there except Caroline and Joanne—Sonya, Samuel, Appleton, and Harold, along with the two attorneys, were sitting waiting. Her heart misgave her—where was Joanne?

"I'm here to try to dissuade you," Benton began. "You're all bound by blood and or by marriage, and I'm here to try to dissuade you, for the sake of Sonya, to forego going to court."

"In other words," Scripps, Samuel's antique attorney, said, "we're in agreement with our consulting psychologist, who will be coming in shortly."

"We're not here for just the sake of my granddaughter," Eleanor said. "We have my daughter to think about, too. If things are allowed to go on as they are, she will go on being shut out from Sonya's company. That will only make her suffering worse."

"I'm a licensed counselor," Mr. Benton said, as though he were directing traffic. "And I have to take issue with you. Sonya is better off setting her own timetable for returning to her mother. We have to even congratulate Sonya on this point. Most children would have refused to see their mothers ever again, if they had been given the same information. Sonya has not said that. She's just made an indefinite postponement."

"What is this, the Middle Ages?" Appleton asked. "When is it that a child has to be congratulated for not being bigoted?"

Elsa, their attorney, pulled out another file. And as she did, Joanne arrived. She seemed distracted and angry.

"Why in the world did you start without me?" Joanne asked.

No one answered.

"I would like to point out," Elsa said, directing Joanne to a chair, "that the divorce agreement stipulates visitation such as is 'reasonable and mutually agreeable.'"

"That means," Benton said, "that whichever of our judges you would defer to—and I might remind you that one is a man and one is a woman—they would still rule in favor of honoring the child's wishes, especially at her age, and especially with this new initiative, Measure Nine, coming on the ballot."

"I am in favor of honoring Sonya's wishes," Joanne said. "But I am not afraid anymore of any ballot measures, and I am only asking that I see her enough so that she knows who she's choosing. And I wish these proceedings had not begun without me. She's been kept away from me so much, she's forgetting, I'm sure, who I am."

Eleanor felt that this exactly was the point.

"Could I be blunt?" Scripps asked.

Benton nodded.

"We're saying that we're doing you a favor by not going to court. For if you do, we'll have to say that we doubt whether you're mentally competent enough to be a mother."

"All right," Samuel said, breaking in, waving his hands. "What's more to the point is—you've got to let things be and let Sonya grow. You have to remember that at any moment her classmates could hear about you, and she could be ostracized—when right now her peers mean everything to her."

"More than me?" Joanne asked. She held out her hands. Eleanor wanted to take one of them.

"You see, you're superimposing guilt upon her by saying that," Benton insisted.

"Let me add something else," Samuel said. "Who's going to take care of her if you do get the full visitation rights—'full' as you see it? Certainly not you."

"Why not me?" Joanne insisted.

"Because at any time you could take up with another woman. And what sort of competent arrangement is that going to be? I used to deal with cases like that when I was doing social work in San Francisco."

Benton nodded.

"We're talking," Samuel went on, "about women coming in who don't shave their chins. Women who are here one day and gone the next—because they've waltzed off into religion or New Age or God knows what and then turn around and do the opposite. Joanne, I've seen you bring some of them home. They scare Sonya and they scare me. Women who haven't the least idea of family life beyond some kind of commune in the woods where they form circles and dance around campfires every night until they're dizzy as witches. Is that what you want for Sonya? Who's going to see to it that she has the money necessary to go to college or join the honor society or meet the right boy down the street and be sure he's safe for her to be with? Who's going to see to it that she has a presentable parent show up to meet her teachers when there's an Open House at school? Joanne, you exist in a talented and visionary world of music and poetry—you have supreme sensitivity and under-standing—but you've never had good sense. You're like my father."

"She put you through graduate school," Eleanor found herself saying. "Isn't that sense enough?" But although she was ready to jump up and defend her daughter, his sweep of talk had caught her up. Again.

"If only you would understand," he answered, pressing forward. "When Joanne started wanting women so badly in our marriage, she went completely off track—on all of us. Don't you remember when you just left Sonya in the park during that Gay Pride march and she was crying, and someone got it on video tape."

"It was just for five minutes," Joanne said. "The crowd had pushed us apart."

"Maybe," Harold said suddenly, looking at Samuel, "maybe you, Samuel, weren't enough to keep her interested."

This was so much against his better judgment, Eleanor wanted to stop him. At least with a signifi-cant glance. There was, however, a slowly burning fuse in the room. What's happening? she wondered. And then she saw it was coming from Harold, and he looked funny. Queer.

Just then, Caroline entered. "Sorry I'm late," she said.

"Yes, we had to go ahead without you," Benton told her.

"It seems to me this alone would decide things," Scripps went on, pulling out some pages. "Regardless of what we think, if fear is what Sonya feels, we have to go along with it."

"But, Sonya," Eleanor said, "you love your mother."

"Of course I do," Sonya answered, speaking for herself at last. Frightened by the commotion around her. "I'll always love her." Eleanor saw the beautiful child there. The one she used to bathe. The one who would take her aside and tell her secrets on the porch.

"Wait a minute, wait a minute," Benton replied, "that's laying way too much on the child. Mrs. Towning, you must simply start thinking about others and not just yourself."

Appleton folded his arms. "The insights in these chambers are wondrous indeed."

"May I say something?" Caroline asked. "I come from a similar position of being a mother of an adopted child—who, in this case, is the one who is gay—I think that if he were afraid of me, I would want him to go with the safer parent."

Suddenly it dawned on her, then and there, that Caroline saw herself as a kind of consulting psychologist in this case, that Harold hadn't been told either, and that his wife had just advanced the burning fuse.

"He is afraid of you," Harold said, getting ready to blow.

"Could you explain further?" Benton asked.

"Yes, of course," Caroline said. "Of course I'm outside the situation. But I am Sonya's aunt, and I can't help but say as a practicing psychologist myself, that Sonya clearly belongs with her father."

"You treacherous bitch!" Harold said. "Your own sister-in-law!" And with that he came up and gripped her by the shoulders. Gave her a hard shaking.

Instantly Eleanor saw that every man in the room was on him, and Benton was shouting for the security guards down the hall of this very civil building.

In the next moment, they—all except Appleton—had Harold pinned in a corner. Someone at the door had whipped out a walkie-talkie and was talking into it. But Harold, breaking free, went back to the table and hurled a chair against the wall. It went into pieces.

Eleanor looked around the room and saw Samuel sitting there beside a terrified Sonya with a protective and ironic expression on his face, so smug it almost lit up the already exploding room. But the expression was there only a moment, for Olivia had gotten up suddenly and, walking across, was slapping him so hard, he toppled off his chair.

"You killed Gloria and you're trying to kill Joanne. But you have me to deal with—and you'll regret that the rest of your life."

Appleton was starting to laugh.

Caroline, recovering herself, was immediately coming in between. "Aunt Olivia, please—you'll have another stroke—"

"Get away from her," Joanne said, giving her a shove, "you cheap psychological extortionist—you ought to be horsewhipped!"

In the room, the "professionals" were flying around like startled geese. Or confetti. It was a sort of hospital panic. "I've only begun to fight," Harold yelled from underneath the dog pile of men.

Appleton was still laughing. "That's it, son, give it to them both barrels!"

But in moments, Harold was being hauled off, and Sonya was being confiscated by Samuel.

Joanne, coming up, put her arm through Eleanor's. But she was speaking to every one. "Harold's right," she said. "We've only begun to fight."

And Eleanor, recalling Joanne standing at the rally, thought my daughter's back! my daughter's back! returning to the time Joanne had first emerged from her own mental prison.

PART TWO

Harold

ALSO CLOSE TO EASTER, DEREK'S HIGH SCHOOL WAS having "Turnabout Day," a spring fling when the men dressed as women and the women as men. The Theatre Department put on an assembly, which was usually pretty uproarious, and that was supposed to be the end of it. But this time Measure Nine was approaching. Harold had to remember that—Measure Nine was approaching. It had created an atmosphere. That was the OPA's great power—he was admitting that more and more—it could create a new world, and disclaim all responsibilities for it.

This spring, the drama club put on *The Wizard of Oz* with Derek as Scarecrow. The idea was, this time, to showcase Dorothy's arrival in Munchkin Land for the assembly, with some special "turns" in honor of the turnabout. One was—to have the hunkiest of the football players come out and do an added ballet number. As Harold was to hear it later, everything was going well, until Glenda called in sick for dress rehearsal, and Derek volunteered as stand-in.

Even the director knew this might be going too far, and told him so, but still was argued into giving in.

And it all seemed to come off at first. There was, very much to everyone's surprise, a hilarious moment when the Wicked Witch of the West appeared in a burst of "flame" before the frightened cowering Munchkins and shouted, "Who killed my sister? Who killed my sister?" and some wiseass at the back of the auditorium yelled, "I did!" and the whole assembly roared with laughter. This led into the "Rite of Spring" number from the football ballerinas, which was well received during "Ding Dong—the Wicked Witch Is Dead!"

But something happened, just when Derek-Glenda was speaking her parting words to Dorothy. Harold had listened closely. Ms. Curtius the director said later she could see it in the wings as she stood there with her woman "friend" of two decades. They both agreed. Somehow the football drag number had made things bad for Derek. Perhaps it was also the fact that he spoke quite tenderly and non-uproariously about Dorothy's ruby slippers. It was just then, at that moment, that Ms. Curtius said she felt something flicker in places in the auditorium—as inexorable as the laughter just minutes before. She had gone into an actual sweat.

Derek had not noticed, and in fact, was all hepped up, because the entire scene had brought a standing ovation anyway, and besides, he had just given his boyfriend (who was as out as he was in school) an erotic greeting card of an Easter "bunny" who was all beard and chest. Out of bravado, he'd worn Glenda's necklace of costume amethysts through the rest of school and right on into the late afternoon, which took him to his part-time job at the nursery just outside of Arden.

Somewhere around closing time, two young men came in. No one knew for sure whether they had been at the assembly or not. They spotted the necklace and drew their conclusions, and waited in a parked car just down the road. By this time, Derek had completely fogged himself in with marijuana in the bathroom, and, getting on to his bike, was feeling quite well pleased and hilarious with himself. He was to meet Kelly, his boyfriend, at the shopping center, just before the eight o'clock curfew Harold had given him.

According to what Harold learned later, as Derek rode out, the car slowly followed him, and then roared past with the usual yells. Derek flipped them off, and then pedaled into overdrive, turning on to a back road, before the car could make a u-turn and come back. The bright neon oasis of the shopping mall was just on the horizon, and soon he would be off the road and on to the bike path.

Nevertheless, the car's headlights were engulfing him now, just on the edge of the path; he tried to race past a barricade, when suddenly a club came to the side of his head, toppling him off his bike. Derek, cornered, pulled off the chain and lock and started swinging it. The two men dodged. Then there was another set of headlights. Some motorist had seen. Derek, terrified it was yet another basher, somehow got back on his bike, and pulled away. The blow had not been heavy.

Slowly the lights of the mall focused for him. Somehow it meant everything in the world that no one know he had been bashed. Not even Kelly.

Besides, they had planned to have some Pepsi and valium together and look in all the florist shops, bright with Easter, and later try on women's clothes. It was to be so cool.

But that's not the way it turned out. Meeting and having their own little private kiss-in—scandalizing all the people by the fountain and at the ice cream tables, too—they ran, head-on, into the two men once more, standing right there in front of the Emporium.

Derek told Kelly to run and run they did—around the displays of Levis, Fruit of the Loom underwear, the racks topped with dismembered stockinged legs. At last they ducked into two dressing rooms, standing on the seats so their feet could not be seen. They could hear the men outside, saying "faggot, faggot, faggot," over and over again—and Derek had still not taken off the necklace.

The men passed by at last. And Derek, extremely scared and now feeling dizzy, had to go to the Men's. Slowly, cautiously, they sidled their way across the mall, and stepped inside the bathroom. There the men were, as if planned. A fist went into Derek's stomach, and his face was pushed into the toilet. Kelly was thrown to the ground and rolled into a corner. Derek lost consciousness.

When he awoke, the two men were gone—so was Kelly—and he was in such pain, he took two of his favorite blue pills—the ones whose names he'd never learned. The texture of the mall changed for him. Outside, he wasn't even sure anything had really happened.

He got back on his bike. Fog was slanting across the highway, and now on the mountain road, he saw the Silverdale Nursery below again, surrounded by cedar. He could smell the branches, with their newly shellacked lace, could smell the fertilizer and insecticides, and he could see himself watering the flowering trees out by the statuary the next morning, with Mary, Joseph, and an angel opening their hands above the birdbaths.

Harold knew he must have planned then to sneak inside the house without his stepmother seeing— his shadow must slip down the window shade. He would not tell her what had happened. He must get in somehow without that firm, proprietary voice arresting him and calling him back on the carpet— "Derek!" as though saying, "front and center"—with the patio windows behind her, the candelabra of the dining room reflected back a dozenfold. She would arrange her own political (but decidedly non-gay) stuff in front of her and then say, "From now on, I want you to check in by nine."

Now, Harold imagined, the fog was descending upon Arden in sail-shaped waves, reminding Derek of a moment he had spent in a foster home when he had been locked in and the imprints on the blankets had been anchors and helms. He had plummeted down into sleep then, safe from the voices in the next room that were busy determining what to do with him next. Yes, the fog lifted for an instant and he could see, suddenly, the acres and acres of water in the field with the hawks—wings reflected—flying over. For somehow the sun was rising, now. The dots of color in the nursery became visible and then were subsumed, answered by the bluebells and winter roses in this mountain glade, this fen. Derek remembered his stepmother's threat again—"We will be moving to Capitol City, where I can put you in Treatment"—and a sheet of sun shone out like an ensign, and he wondered what he could do to salvage himself, salvage this green garden of mist and waters. In two months' time, all of this would be flowering into irises and daffodils, crowned with rain, and Derek, Harold knew, wanted to be there, working among the plants, without his shirt, the sun warming his body.

Tonight, whatever night it was, Derek must take the money, flee the house and go to the concert. There the mix of music and lights would be just right—as if you could feel and see the earth rotate beneath you, and the singer would come out with the song—with the chink of metal, as if it were a command.

The bicycling had stopped. There was nothing definite, nothing demarcated within him, except this one need to settle on one particular point of land, under this rotating canopy of mist, enfolding this fen and meadow, this forested mountain above the town. The music echoed across the floods, as he stood there on the mountain road, and he thought of the journey he had taken long ago to find his natural father. And when he had met his goal, Carey, his father, had said, "Why yes, if I had a lifestyle which could tolerate children, I'd take you in."

All vanished now in the shadows of a tunnel; he

had only one direction now, and riding out of the glade, he seemed to tumble over rocks, stumps, clefts of water to the highway. Ahead, the sun was sending out its spokes, moving its bright-ribbed fans through the fog; it rose toward him, out of the thicket of blossoming cherry trees, like a promise, or a mirage worked up by a spell. He abandoned his bicycle and hitched and walked, hitched and walked. At Eleanor's Castle, he found his grandmother sitting in front of a computer screen, the green shining on her as though from the forest of ferns outside.

She started when she saw him. "Derek! You almost gave me a heart attack. What happened? Where have you been?" She stood up and steadied herself against the table.

"Where's Harold?" he asked. "I have to talk to him."

"Harold's in jail," she told him.

That's all he heard. He didn't stay for anything else. To his mind, that meant he was gone forever—the way his first father had been. Harold would put that gloss on it later, too.

Outside, running, Derek could feel the whole neighborhood shake to its foundations. Basketball! I could be playing basketball with my stepfather just now! Outside, he could feel a blindness overtake him, as if the fog now were obscuring all and his hands were running along the surfaces of the street, trying the globes of the lamp posts, and the theater along the mill race. But there was the park—and, as if a tent had been torn, the fog opened up to tables and roses and pines and a phone booth under the brightening sun. He called Kelly's house.

"Kelly?" his mother asked. "Why, Kelly's at school," she said. "And why aren't you?"

◇

Derek was missing for four days. Harold had not known that Caroline had secretly retrieved him after two. He would find that out later. She had simply hunted him down through her own channels and found him in Capitol City, and then moved up there herself, a place where chances were better he might turn out straight.

When Harold got out of his forty-eight hours in jail, he simply did not connect Derek's disappearance with Caroline's. She had always kept her distance from Derek, and he simply concluded he had vanished because she had neglected him. Perhaps— and this was very hard to admit—it had been wishful thinking on his part. He had found himself in a blame game, like pin-the-tail on the donkey. If Caroline had been the reason Derek had headed for parts unknown, then he didn't have to think about what had landed him in jail.

He was up shit creek in so many ways—maybe it was real therapy for him not to think about himself too much and undergo a desperate search, leaving no stone unturned in Arden and finally calling the police. He kept trying to reach Caroline at her new number but there was no answer. Trying to piece the story together about Derek, he never thought of Capitol

City until Eleanor had called him, saying Derek had "dropped in," and that it was the perfect place for Caroline to put Derek, since, of course, Capitol City was the capital of straightness compared to Arden.

Meanwhile, Harold groped his way all over Arden, and then all over Capitol City, supported by Eleanor, Appleton, and Joanne. Then, suddenly, a full twenty-four hours later, the phone rang. It was Eleanor. "Harold, you need to come at once. Caroline's just put Derek in the drug treatment ward of the hospital up here. He wants out."

"Drug treatment? As we speak?"

"He's addicted to some pill which takes away his sight. He only got to the telephone by stumbling."

"I'll be right there," Harold told her.

Dressing and flinging himself into the car, Harold felt the panic come over him again—it was as if Caroline had slammed the doors of a prison. The time was Easter morning, and the light in mist above the highway lit up a cross, right above the hospital, as he arrived from the south.

At the front desk, there were two nurses. "I'm sorry," one said, "Derek Rourke is in detox right now. No non-family are allowed."

"I'm his father. I was called here because he's in trouble."

"You're Harold Towning?" She looked up. "We have explicit instructions not to admit you."

"I'll give you ten minutes," Harold said. "After that, I'm going in."

He turned. There stood Eleanor and Joanne.

"We've just seen Derek," Eleanor said. "He's starting to withdraw from his drug. He'll have to stay here at least two days before we can see about a transfer."

"Well, they've got me blocked," Harold told her. "Caroline must have some kind of restraining order through Family Services."

One of the nurses put down the phone. "That was Eileen Till, Derek's counselor. She'll be down to talk with you in a moment."

And at just that instant, she came out of the elevators. She was a floating graceful drapery, with a large set of keys on her belt.

"You'll need to fill out these forms," she said. "Derek's withdrawing from a very severe drug and we want everyone screened before visitation."

"But I'm his father—" Harold began.

"You may think you have a right," she said, heading him off, "but think better of it." She put her hands together. She made Harold consider an iron on an ironing board—and consider Caroline, too. "We have several legal papers in his file, including your transitional status, Mr. Towning. We could never let you see him, in view of his condition and status as a minor, until we receive additional papers and have a clearance from his stepmother."

"She'll never agree," Harold said. "And this is the weekend and Family Services doesn't open until Monday morning. Even then it will take me three hours and three dozen forms to get an audience. My son needs me now."

Harold could hear that he had raised his voice,

and in raising it, he noticed that Eileen Till had lifted her brows towards a security guard, as fresh and wound up as if he had dropped off a flying saucer. Not that again. In fact, the whole lobby of the midnight hospital seemed to be just that—a space ship—flying within the magnetic pull of Venus, which was to snatch him off and hold him under restraint.

"We'll see to it," Joanne said, "that Derek is out of here in two days."

"You'll do no such thing," Eileen Till said. "Not until we have his stepmother's signature."

"You have an unlocked unit," Joanne said. "No one has to stay against their will."

"In the instances of a minor," Eileen Till said, "we have the right to detain him. And if he keeps on isolating the way he has, we're going to have to bring in a psychiatrist, because we suspect psychosis."

"You don't know what you're saying," Joanne said.

Eileen Till got up and, without another word, disappeared among the space apparatus.

"Come away, come away," Eleanor said. "There's nothing more we can do until morning."

"And even then, what then?" Harold asked. "Sunday—Easter Sunday—everything will be dead. I can't let him stay in there another hour."

"We'll ask Appleton," Eleanor said. "He's down in the all-night gift shop trying to pick out a card, of all things."

He followed her down two flights, and they found him surrounded by porcelain and paper flowers. He listened to their story and gave his legal take on it.

"Wait," he said, "wait until we've had a chance to talk to Family Services again."

So very soon Harold found that they were heading toward Eleanor's Castle once more, the specter of Eileen Till following at close range, perching itself on wires. The whole night avenue rushed at him like a locomotive.

"It seems to me," Appleton said in the car, "we could use the Proteus Precedent in this case. What goes back to the experience of a Dr. Wren. The case was decided—where a minority plaintiff is concerned, the burden of proof is on the majority. We could argue that the hospital is coming between you and Derek because of his orientation—that his mother wants him to be straight."

In the Castle, Eleanor got a room ready for him. In the morning, he would have to decide what he was to do about his Easter sermon. Letting the blankets receive him, Harold felt as though under a turret which was turning slowly. In sleep, he saw some wrought iron curtains separating. He found he was in memory up in the attic, watching fireworks with Joanne. The starshells burst apricot and sapphire above the lake. All about—and through the house—there was the haze of summer; the red roses were wound tight upon the lattice just below the window, and he thought, I can imagine myself moving through the Seattle of my childhood with a Roman candle in my hand, just like the boy pictured in my old *Golden Almanac*, the soft sparks creating a trail like petals wherever I walked. Somewhere framed in the window,

I can see my sister's face, can see her holding her doll for dear life, in cut-out silhouette, the filigree of her night dress like something on a nineteenth century nursery screen.

"Joanne, why don't you ever let loose of her?" he remembered asking.

But she didn't answer, only became a shadow when the fireworks had flashed their last.

Something was crossing into the dark, as Harold dreamt on. He remembered folding down into the bed and feeling the outlines of something. A curve upward—a chest—and downward, thighs—and he could remember seeing a framed picture somewhere—a man in uniform—but now the jacket was off, and he could feel the firm planes of his back and neck. Carey, Derek's father, just as he had remembered him—naked. We had entwined ourselves against the sheet, Harold thought; we had been nothing more than a flowering vine—a clematis—hovering in mid-summer under eaves of sunlight. It was as though we had given birth to an idea—of my adopting Derek.

Then there had been what had happened when Harold had been in jail. Two men in the next cell over had been trying to get it on. No, no—it shouldn't be that way, he had wanted to tell them. It hadn't been that way between Carey and himself. It had been ennobling. And yet here, in the jail, he could hear it, just the way the OPA said it was. And there was no escape.

"Quick before someone comes," one of the cell-mates said.

"You know how I like it," the other had answered.

And he could hear all the noise, pornographic, that goes with hurry, danger, lust, secrecy.

And the debased feeling of being turned on while he listened, knowing this was the way all those OPA politickers in the state saw it! In jail, doing it, shame-faced, under the table, up against a cold wall, beside the toilet. Never proud, never open. Isn't that the way the military wanted it too? Under the cot? Behind the latrine?

Just a few days prior, when Joanne had come to bail him out, she had asked, "What is it? Did you let them convince you you were wrong for being gay?"

"Maybe," he had answered, "But not now. Not now that you're here to see me home."

But at Joanne's house, he could not reach Caroline. And sometimes Derek answered the phone, but he wasn't answering now. Joanne took out some more pamphlets against the new Measure Nine, while she lit the gas flame and got dinner going. He looked over and thought how much he liked her, suddenly. All that envy gone. Through the window, he could see the rain forming the halos of an Art Nouveau print. Liked her, yes, yes, he liked her. But then there had been the terrible sick feeling when he had learned that Derek had visited Eleanor and vanished with blood on his clothes.

"Joanne," he said, "will you get to see Sonya? Did my throwing the chair ruin everything?"

"No," she answered. "I've talked with Sonya since. She still won't live with me. But she's starting to talk more. She may even visit. The fear is lifting."

"Thank God it's starting to work out for you."

But now he was awakening here in the Castle again, and as he did, he thought of nurse Vy Coburg and Woodland House. A possible way out. He opened the curtains, to a high cylinder of clouds breaking gold upon the morning. Easter. What was in my dream that could go into my sermon? (For he had decided he would go back down to Arden and give his sermon anyway. Not a Coming Out sermon, not yet. But still a resurrection one, the Coming Out of Spring.) What could be dug out and transformed for these people who specialized in Tarot cards, New Age, and healing crystals? Even now, he knew that his parishioner Mrs. Agnes was arranging her Easter and tiger lilies on the altar, tying things with a huge white sash, she herself as fresh and full blown as a morning glory, heavenly blue and opening.

He ducked into Woodland House before driving to his church. Perhaps Woodland House could take Derek.

Woodland House was now a crown of sunrise, the light dispelling itself in the random dandelions on the lawn.

"You couldn't bring him here," Nurse Vy Coburg told him as he came in, "because we have no one else here right now, and for withdrawal, you need other people to get you out of yourself."

"But do you understand why I can't go on having him stay at Capitol General?" he asked.

"Yes. Capitol General is the right place for him to detox in, but probably not the place to stay forever.

Yes, you're right. It's a cold network. I don't know how you're going to work all the legal particulars, but if you can do it, send him to Mead House right down there in Arden. It's an unlocked unit, and there's a spirit of humanness everywhere."

Harold thanked her.

Now he could arrange his sermon in his head as if it were a bouquet of lilies, one opened and three closed, as the next move.

But at his church—when he touched down for a moment—he found that someone had called the Board President and given out the news—and therefore eventually everyone else—that he had been in jail.

"Which means," the President said, "you're going to have to visit each member of the congregation personally and explain what happened."

"Yes," Harold answered. "That's a worthy goal— and a worthy penance."

And so his sermon was that bouquet of lilies, one opened and three closed; one was for the casting out of St. Paul and his booming, condemning bell, tolling from a tower, but another was for the long-suffering and weariless Mary as she waited for her son at the foot of the Cross, or waited for him to return home from his temptations in the heavily pined wilderness, her robe a rich blue; the third was a purging of the nails from the hands and feet of Jesus, a cleansing of self-negation; the fourth was a blooming into the light of the Easter star, the highlight of the heavens on Easter eve, the reminder that suffering for suffering's sake has been conquered; the stone has been rolled away and the ensign torn; and now Christ's narrow ankles can be seen among the clouds, his hair laurelled with lily because the soul no longer needs to be in anger at itself. He ended by quoting a line from the exquisitely beautiful Chester Shakespeare *Passion*, which Uncle Richard had discovered.

—*Lo, the eastern star calls the shepherd home.*

Afterwards, he thanked Mrs. Agnes, his star parishioner, for her flowers, because they had given his sermon a direction, a center; he kissed a baby, holding his soft terry jumper against his cheek— almost losing himself when he handed him back— and then, leaving the sanctuary, turned toward Mead House. There was a cherry tree waiting for him in the courtyard; its blossoms spread above a stone fountain—gnomes holding loose fish. This was indeed different from Capitol General and served as a welcome.

"We could take your son on transfer," Nurse Alice, the nursing director said, "provided he's out of detox. To interrupt him now would be dangerous. It doesn't matter how bad it is. You're going to have to sit it out, but we could take him in a few days."

All about, things were quiet but not hushed in the hallways. Here and there, outside on benches, people in gowns or street clothes sat, smoked, talked. Different, different—yes, yes, it was different! Downstairs, the coin telephones were rattling with change. In the cafeteria (which she had shown him), a sign said, "Still hungry? Ask the cook."

"So do you wish to make the arrangements? Shall I call?" Nurse Alice asked.

"Please," Harold said, almost losing it this time for sure, perhaps from the strain of the sermon, perhaps from the long dreams of the night before, or the strain of the lobby scene before that. "Please do."

Now everything must be set on springing Derek as soon as possible. And as he thought of this, outside in the courtyard, the blossoms snowed slantwise upon him, and he stopped for a moment, hesitating among scents and colors, feeling Vy's imminent, recommending influence in the winds that touched this place, inside and out.

Now back up the freeway again—to Capitol General, where Eleanor met him once more, but looking frightened.

"Derek is going through intolerable pain withdrawing," she said.

"Is anybody there with him?" Harold asked.

"His father."

An ice storm in his chest. His father!

"I haven't seen Carey in so long," Eleanor said.

"You may as well go home," Caroline told him, emerging from the ward. "I have a restraining order to keep you out."

"Well, we'll see about that," Harold told her. "For now I just want to know why you put Derek in here in the first place."

She turned to him in hard angles of light, as if she had been in a museum—darkened—with the door just opening. "I'll tell you why," she answered. "While you were in jail, Derek was gaybashed."

"No," Eleanor said. "We weren't told!"

"He was gaybashed—struck on the head with a club and punched in the stomach. And all because you encouraged him to be all that he could be"—her stare still taking him in as he felt himself sinking. For all in the lobby to view.

"Why didn't you tell me?" Harold asked, fending her off. "Why did you let me look for him, search for him, desperate all that time—"

"Because I needed to protect him from you, Harold."

But Harold saw Caroline couldn't silence the menacing looks Eleanor, Olivia, and Joanne were now giving her. For perhaps the second time in her life, Caroline must have felt unpopular. She went to the desk and told them she'd be seeing Derek again.

But just as she was about to go in, Carey emerged and had to brush past her. Harold was terrified to see their exchange of glances, and in the mirror the perfect configurations matched each other; a curtain was parted, revealing a mirror—yes—flesh, skin, and bones answered the analogy in the glass. He had been in bed with both of them. Man and woman—husband and wife to him in such different ways—were much the same.

As they passed, Caroline held a paper up in Carey's face. "And I see your attempt here"—looking at him—"to take Derek with you. You want to explain this?"

Harold tried to rise.

"Just look at you," she went on, still staring at his former lover. "Just standing there like you'd know what to do if you did have custody."

"Tomorrow I go to the authorities," Carey said. "You're finished. I am his father."

"That's an interesting statement," she answered. "Where have you been all these years, then? So you've surfaced yet again. And let me ask Harold here a question as long as we've got him—would you sign custody over to this man?" Now he was being watched. "Probably not—am I right? And do you think even together the two of you are capable of bringing him up? What kind of life is he going to have? Can your plan get him sober? Keep him safe? Can you do as well as I can?"

But fortunately she left before Harold could answer. Carey seemed to feel the pain of his hesitation. Because Harold knew she had a point. Just as Samuel had had. But as if to stop his thoughts, suddenly Carey embraced him, spoke into his ear. "I'll see you tomorrow. Family Services. We can take it from there."

But Harold didn't know if he wanted Carey back.

◇

For weeks following, Harold's life seemed tracked by Derek's recovery. Derek did not last long in Mead House, either, even though Harold considered it a real coup to get him transferred there. Caroline had lifted the restraining order. Derek refused, periodically, to take his medicine, and, several times, he shut himself in his room, foregoing meals. The papers he turned in for his written assignments were something out of Dick and Jane. Harold considered that his son was back to being seven once more. And Derek's dreams, by his own report, were splintered and scattered; he talked of being chased by mutant children, then later his Easter bashers, and this cycle of insomnia was said by the experts to have been started when Harold had taken him out of school for the No on Eight campaign. Thanks, Dad. Harold added that as another heavy item to his list of sins.

Nevertheless, Derek began to recover there, at the new place, at last; his dream of the children and the thugs and a luminous clock dial began to change. Mead House was built on a meadow on the idyllic edge of Arden, and not far from it, there was a lake which itself had been a meadow until some beavers had built their dams and decided otherwise. From the shoreline to the glass of the House were wildflowers— as variegated as the isolated gems in a piece of English alliterative verse. Daily, Harold knew, Derek would look out and see the dandelions rising, opening in the mist, the bachelor's-buttons as blue as Joanne's eyes. The paintbrush formed even lines of fire, and whenever he rested, he saw the lake glowing with it, a coverlet for sleep, sealing out the nightmares. The scene was like an assemblage of all the hues of meditation, rising to a perfect crown, which transcended color, which was a beholding of the incarnate Christ—the *Salvatore Mundi* by the apocryphal Leonardo, perhaps, above the lake, near the sun, descending with a green globe in hand. Derek told Harold he recalled it from the parade. In Mead House, they called it a

Higher Power. Derek felt strange, he said, borrowing
Christ, when Christ seemed to belong to the OPA.

"If I believed that," Harold said. "I couldn't do
my job."

Derek had more to say. "I prayed and prayed and
prayed that God would make me straight. I prayed
that for a long time, after I saw you and my real
father together. I'll never forget when I saw you take
his hand one time—I prayed that it wasn't what I
thought—it was like I had put my spell on you, that
I had made both of you into me, and that was why
you and Caroline were splitting so fast. I so wanted
you straight."

"But why, Derek?" Harold asked.

"So I could lean on you, believe in you. Have you
show up when you said you would."

"But I will show up when I say I will."

"I don't believe you." Derek began to sob, bitterly.
"Not with Dad the way he's been. Wasn't he supposed to come and get me? Take custody?"

Harold hesitated, felt all the pain. "Yes."

"Well, where is he?"

Harold had to be honest. "You're right, he's disappeared again." Carey had not shown up at Family
Services.

Suddenly Derek clasped himself across his
stomach and rolled over on the bed for a moment.
"I'm sorry—it's just this damned drug pulling at me."

Harold drew up and patted his shoulder, hoped he
might sleep.

As he looked up, evening was coming in through

the window. In shadow, the needles from the field were rising on the wall. The scene seemed almost a black-and-white photograph, where all the outlines are hazy. Staring at this meadow, Harold said, "I don't care what I have to do to help you get well—Carey's gone, but I'm not—"

Derek tried to rise again. He moved his legs back and forth. The pain, obviously, was intolerable. "I'm at the end of my taper—they're tapering me off of valium—and the rest is just white knuckle. And I'm having trouble making it, having trouble talking. Sometimes I get toward the end of what I have to say and my lungs shut down before I get out the last word. But let me have a last word—although I'm disappointed that it turned out this way, I wouldn't change you."

Harold took his hand, looked at the clinical band on his stepson's wrist. All the information on it. It reminded him of Brenda's. He had hoped at one time that his daughter might have lived long enough for him to say something like this to her. "I'll be there for you."

In the days to come, Derek got even wilder as they removed the drugs. His entire system went into revolt, as it got better. He would run from class or group therapy and grab the phone and shake with crying the entire time. "Either I'm crazy or this house is." He felt sure that his room was bugged, and that the patients were really nothing but actors in disguise, hired on by a psychological institute to conduct some experiment called "Derek." His craving for his drug caused him to bungle through meals, and sitting there for a moment trying to swallow milk, he became convinced that the blouse of the woman sitting in front of him was a set-up—the bills of the ducks printed on the cloth seemed to be pointed at each other's rear ends. He was sure that by afternoon she would change into another blouse, subtly different, to see if he had been watching—and also, subtly, to drive him mad like Ingrid Bergman in *Gaslight*.

All avalanched one evening when, during music therapy, and according to report, Derek screamed that they were trying to destroy his intelligence by playing nothing but dipshit folk songs. He tore up his copy of the lyrics and bolted from the room declaring he must hear some real rock and roll or he'd go crazy. By then, that's what everyone thought had happened anyway. The staff was up in arms and insisted he be thrown out. Harold thought Caroline would seize the opportunity and order him up to the psychiatric ward in Adamsville, but she surprised him. She mentioned Mead's sister house in Hamilton—Star of the Sea Recovery by the Sea.

And so the two of them decided, in accord for the first time, that Derek be transferred to the Coast.

By the sea, Harold knew Derek started to sleep; his vision began clearing. For the rest of the world, his face came more into focus. Nights, he told Harold, he would look at the globes of the promenade and would feature them as floating upon an infinite coverlet of sleep, becoming stars, infrared, ultraviolet. He saw the blue icon of The Lady in the distant cove, shepherding the boats with raised hands; the dream dipped and he went under, finding a deep somnolence; without his drug, he was allowed to touch the bottom of exhaustion, and then come back up as if touching the bottom of a pool. Mornings, he would sit in the courtyard underneath the flowering cherry and gaze out over the ocean like one who has escaped drowning. Afternoons he would go to N.A. meetings. The horror of the rage was over. He accepted his medicine dutifully. Harold said to himself, that like Joanne, Derek had smashed through the mirror and come out on the other side. The specters of the supervisors were past, and he had a new treatment counselor, along with a new psychiatrist, Dr. Long, who was sufficiently eclectic to acknowledge his recovery and yet ask, also, about his life, his psyche at the same time. His nervous system was on the mend, and as it was mending, the strategies for his recovery came at last into accord. Caroline had veered very close to sending him to Adamsville, but had swung back and had come up with this magical Star of the Sea (in an emblematic card deck, wouldn't it have been symbolized by a robed secularized Great Lady in blue?) What she had done was no more explainable than why she had not pressed charges against him for what had happened in Family Services. He owed her an amends. The curtain had been pulled, revealing an old-style refuge, where Derek lived protected, one with Salvation Army bed fixtures—but still with a courtyard.

Here Derek sat, or so Harold imagined, in shade

as closely woven as that of the webbing of willows. Ahead of him would be the first of the Ektachrome roses, which, within his vision, would not be quite yet in focus, but soon would be. As if in answer to the blue waves, which broke into a white toil on the shore, the house would spread its slow green shadow. Spangles of sunlight would fly on the page Derek would be working on. A dragonfly would hover down and point itself on the hat of a stone gnome, its wings still moving, glittering with iridescence. And Harold, imagining all of this, would himself drift off at last, allowing himself to sleep finally, because Derek was on the mend.

It was in this courtyard state that Harold found him one afternoon. Very full of life.

Beyond them, the waves were really hard at it. The wind was so brisk, it nearly blew the notebook off Derek's lap, and a pencil went into the violets. Somewhere, Harold knew, his dead cousin Gloria had drawn Natura, in pen and ink. "But why Natura?" his cousin had written in an article somewhere. "Why not Naturus?" And the emblem that had emerged was Mr. Nature holding up the world with wondrous shoulders.

That emblem seemed to be rising among the columns of water. The spray dashed up and fell against the stone like finest white sand. To Harold's mind, the image of Natura was also that of a woman, in graceful limestone and marble drapery, windswept, creased, gathered. Perhaps she was in a chariot or perhaps was about to drop an olive branch or lightning bolt. And then, as he was taken back to the scene, everything shifted; a bee headed in on an iris; a butterfly flopped down, almost colliding with the first of a hollyhock; its wings were gigantic in profile, like a bird's—scissoring the air. That salt smell! And over by the entrance were the beginnings—like starts—of a wisteria arbor.

"You look," Harold said, "happier to see me this time."

"I am," Derek answered. "And I'm ready to go. When's the next rally?"

"My dear," Harold answered, "you can't jump from hitting bottom to activism in two split seconds. Take your time. Get better, get recovered—"

"You don't ever fully recover, remember," Derek answered.

"Excuse me," Harold corrected himself. "I mean— get yourself to feeling better, and then you can jump on the bandwagon. For now leave the politics to me."

"But I can tell there's something going on," Derek answered. "Tell me. What is it? What's our next move? They won't let us read newspapers here."

"Our next move is for me to go on television," Harold reluctantly told him. "Against Measure Nine."

"Television! Fabulous!"

"But for now," Harold concluded, leaning back and taking in the scene—another vision of Natura, Naturus, if at least for a moment—"you let me have the limelight."

◇

For while Derek was spending his months recovering by the sea, the Oregon Protection Alliance had gotten enough signatures to get Measure Nine on the ballot. It had capitalized on the atmosphere it had created. Harold's design, then, for another Columbus Day rally had to go into full gear and many months early.

The measure, which would amend the state Constitution and ban all funds from anything even remotely gay or lesbian, also outlawed any positive presentation of "that lifestyle" in the public schools and colleges. In fact, the institutions, by mandate, "shall assist in setting a standard for Oregon's youth that recognizes homosexuality, pedophilia, sadism and masochism as abnormal, wrong, unnatural, and perverse and that these behaviors are to be discouraged and avoided."

The liberal of the state gasped in disbelief. Harold himself had to hold on to his desk while reading it. What had been implied in the previous campaign of Measure Eight had now come with vicious boldness to the fore. For all his past struggles over Derek, Harold had a hard time believing that anything so outrageous would be allowed out in public.

Even in late summer, his Ministry and Laity Involved group started mustering a counter-attack. A No on Nine office popped up on the Arden downtown mall. And Harold was enlisted to do everything he had done before, particularly now that he had visited all the members of his congregation and had found them willing, most of them, to forgive him, even though he had been a brief jailbird, and had been ratted on to his congregation, presumably by some spy in it.

Nevertheless, as Harold sat on committees planning all the next political moves, as he felt the state split straight down the middle in another full-scale embittered dispute, as he searched every corner of Arden for those thugs who had beaten Derek up, he slowly decided that being merely a concerned minister was not going to cut it. Not this time, not this time. He had hidden behind his mother's "no comment" to Mr. Benton and people like him too long. Suppose it jeopardized the adoption of Derek? The way it had jeopardized Joanne with Sonya? But of what value was he to Derek this other way?

He wondered sometimes if anyone understood what it was like to always be on the outside looking in in these profoundly inside situations. That is, the one who, during midnight vigils, holds the umbrella and observes while the gays and lesbians have their camraderie, while he only has camraderie with his wedding ring, which flashes like a torchlight in the candle flames. If you can't be it, organize it, workshop it, facilitate it, rally it, sermonize it. But never be it. Yet how many men at rallies, at vigils, had he wished to be intimate with—and how many had he recognized as his former dream men when he had seen them later *incognito* at the bar?

Until he had been in Benton's office on Joanne's behalf, he had never openly admitted to himself (although with Eleanor he had come close) that he was gay, even though he and Carey—prior to his disappearance—had been intimate several times, always on fishing trips or "fun runs" away from home. It's quite extraordinary how the mind can perform those magical tricks, he decided. I'm not gay. He is. Particularly when the man in question has that muscular beauty like Carey's which some would call Come-Fuck-me-Gorgeous.

However.

However, because of what had happened, that was no longer good enough for him. He was getting ready to come out. Derek already knew. Joanne already knew. Eleanor, Appleton, Olivia. But there was that whole world out there, still demanding he stay in that straight clerical closet. Yet sometimes when he took his collar off, along with his tunic, in a hot car, he could feel his sweaty body almost burgeoning out, like the Incredible Hulk's. Coming out. Maybe the Hulk was gay, too. Really, he was certainly hunky enough. Beautiful forearms (observing himself in the mirror), a back well constructed and fanned with muscle, and a chiselling of strength along the jaw line. He belonged more in a knit polo shirt.

There was, though, that overpowering sense of inferiority—from having watched Joanne emerge from her chrysalis into the extraordinary sister he had admired in his childhood. Overpowering because, as she had come out, he had felt himself remaining the same, like an insect trapped in amber, rather than wrapped in tissue, and so all of Arden had brooded over him, had caught him up in its web, dictating a

very precise protected life which was always frightening, because he always expected to be found out.
Christmases he felt it the worst—mere decorative
window dressing for the straight flocks (Where did
he belong, anyway?), reminding him of a tableau he
had seen in a neighborhood front yard one time—
of Santa coming down the chimney, toward kneeling
and perhaps praying windowed children below, pious
in their pajamas.

So, it being summer now, it was time to take the
first step, just before Derek was to be released from
Star of the Sea. And after Carey had disappeared again.

He was down at the Court House, demanding
that some further action be taken on tracking down
Derek's two bashers—had met with another run-
around, when he was tapped on the shoulder by one
of the most infamous of the OPA. One who had a particularly personal vendetta against him, because the
attempt to get him thrown out of his own church had
fizzled. He knew that unfortunately this man was no
dummy, and that once more he was being set up. Be
the straight man (right!), the paper tiger.

Nevertheless, as he stood there in the District
Attorney's office, waiting for someone to say there
was at least an initial investigation, the Major Repre-
sentative nudged up against him and challenged him
to a debate. On TV. Very unlikely and yet Harold was
surprised to find that he always considered himself TV
material. Why not? His mother before him had captivated all of 1950s Seattle (those antennas! reminding

him of *Them!* the new science fiction sensation) with all of her magic deportment. So why shouldn't he?

He was so angry, being in that office, he said— "You're on!" without thinking, knowing full well a second later that this man, this so-called minister, Reverend Hanshaw, meant to libel him on the air, north, east, west, south. This time they would not fail. This time it would extend to more than just the church, it would be the entire planet.

"So where do we meet?" Harold asked.

(It could just as well have been, "Pistols at noon?")

"Everything will be arranged," he answered, speaking with that characteristically smooth diction Harold had come to know all too well. "At the KILT studios at four. It's to be done live on 'Northwest Message.'"

He was gone before he could say more. At just that moment, Harold's turn in the waiting room came up again, and word arrived that the bashers were in custody and had already been put through a plea bargaining. On the loose again before Harold could speak a word. Sentencing was to be in two months. Two months! Harold stood there, and felt as if the whole world had been invaded. They were already out in the world at large.

Leaving the Court House—the District Attorney was not available—Harold felt his anger rise, boil, and begin to pitch him toward a "public coming out," the very thing the Oregon Protection Alliance wanted. But he also began to kick himself for having waited for so long—if I had come out sooner, I could have helped people sooner, I could have nipped the OPA in the bud. But I did not come out sooner, so I'm fucked, and if I'm fucked, I may as well stay in the closet, where I might get fucked the way I want. But that was a voice he didn't listen to anymore.

<>

With the TV debate on the horizon, Harold drove out to get Derek at the Floral Hill Nursery. He saw small doubtful things that had grown under strikes of rain. Caroline was now allowing Derek to stay with Harold whole weekends at a time, and now that summer was here—weeks at a stretch. In Capitol City, Eleanor was having a family dinner to celebrate Derek's three-month N.A. birthday.

Harold waited by the sundial and watched its shadow advance through the roses, the hydrangeas, and the shy vines of the clematis. The statues—St. Francis, Mary, a gnome—seemed to pass through matins, vespers, as the racing light caused alternating night and day, in miniature, as if in a hurry to enter into autumn. Inside, in the hothouses, Harold knew there was the green floral smell—misted—so intense still it seemed almost bottled. That's where Derek was now, watering the begonias.

As he waited, he saw a figure moving among the plants, weaving, changing color. Proteus, as a woman. She was gathering autumn bulbs the way one might gather eggs—Mrs. Inge, another parishioner of his, first looking at him from this perspective, now that. With her magic touch, she had enough in that basket to set all those hills behind her home on fire with flowering reds and yellows of the spring. It was as if she were carrying those color crystals which grew, miraculously, in a fishbowl of waterglass—save here the medium was light, soil, and water. Harold could remember watching them rise in a Mason jar down in the basement, where he kept his chemistry set as a boy. The smell of that basement! But now Mrs. Inge was pausing; she wasn't looking at him but at the vats of the water lilies—gold, red, orange. For a moment, a cat came up and drank, leaning its paws on the wooden lip, its shadow draped across the pads.

And just then Derek appeared.

"Well," Mrs. Inge said, more brightly, looking at him, "still the fully recovered young man? You see, I've bought some of your wares. And we're all looking forward to the time we get you back into the choir. I still need someone to sing off key with!"

"I don't know when I'll be back, Mrs. Inge," Derek said gravely, shading his eyes, trying to look at her.

A few minutes later, they were walking toward the car. "How was the home study today?" Harold asked. "How did Geometry go?"

"It's still like the way it was in Star of the Sea. When I tried to play checkers. My whole brain is washed out. Back then, I couldn't remember how to jump over the different pieces. And today I just stared at the different triangles. I couldn't jump over the different places there, either. Sometimes I wonder what I'll forget how to do next."

"You put in an afternoon's work," Harold said.

"I can't imagine how you could do any better than that."

A gauzy veil of cosmos lined both sides of the parking lot. Harold had never seen it as high as that. They had to part it with their hands as they got into the car. The lavender composite blooms were just beginning to deepen in color, looking like autumnal flowers pinned to a screen. All of this, as they pulled out of the lot.

"You grew those, didn't you?" Harold asked, nodding toward the flowers. "Going all the way back to last January. What did you grow them in? Some miracle elixir?"

"Bat guano and turkey manure," he said, smiling.

A few minutes of silence.

Beside the freeway, Oregon sunshine—bright yellow wildflowers—were sashaying. In one field, there was a "Yes on Nine" sign. In another a "No." "So has Carey moved in?" Derek asked at last.

"Yes," Harold answered. "Effective this morning."

He didn't answer. Harold knew he was angry, because he hadn't been consulted. And himself? He didn't have a word to speak in his own defense. He had been so afraid Derek would say "no," he had gone ahead and acted unilaterally. "Don't you want him in the house?" Harold asked.

"He's only made me suffer all my life," he answered. "What do you think?"

"Try to see it from his point of view—" Harold began.

"I've been doing that ever since I stole his address

from the orphanage. I wrote to him. Would he like to see me? Sure he'd love to see me. So I hitched on down to the Courtland address on the envelope. Know where that was? The fucking jail. Just like you. And that's where you're going to end up permanently if you let him stay with us."

"Don't knock jail," Harold said, surprised at himself. "It's free room and board."

"You really are a shit sometimes, Harold," he said. "You don't care how I feel."

"No, I don't care how you feel," Harold answered. "I've only been looking after you, night and day, for the past three months. And going to those goddamn parent support meetings."

Derek was now slammed into silence. What a wonderful achievement! Harold sat there, fuming, disgusted with himself. He had worked so hard to get past Caroline's restraining order and won. But now he was sabotaging what he had with Derek. He knew that it was the thought of Carey's body which had driven him to this. The birds flying over the fields that were now a steady amber reminded him of how he had felt when they had been together—pinioned back, crucified by the weight of him. It wasn't possible for him to act in the best interests of the family and especially Derek when he thought of this; he only wanted the heat to return.

"What would you like me to do?" Harold asked. "I'll send him away tomorrow if that's what you want."

"Send my own father away," Derek said. "Thanks,

Harold, for that job. Have you ever noticed? You put everybody else in the world first except yourself, so that I always get fucked over. I bear the brunt. Make the decision on your own."

"You're right," Harold said at last. "I have put it on you, but the question is—what do we do now?"

"Fucking faggot behavior," Derek went on. "Never being able to make up your mind. Wanting everything both ways."

Now he was slammed into silence. Maybe he ought to send Derek back to Caroline before they hurt each other any further. But that would be to protect himself, not him. The silence, as they say, you could cut with a knife, and if it was bread they were slicing, they had enough to feed an army. At the appropriate juncture on the freeway, the fields gave way, miraculously, to beautifully shaded arbors that meandered, slowly, toward the river. Suddenly the incandescent maple was spreading its leaves into the open spaces, then over small brooks of gold, and then at last they were getting out beneath a spangled Rose of Sharon at the Castle. He could imagine Eleanor and company all waiting for them on the third floor veranda. But the Rose of Sharon was fading—tinged, perhaps, with their anger.

As they climbed, Eleanor's "finds" became larger and larger. Felix the Cat posters. The 1950s Reagan Camel ad. A picture of Gena Rowlands. In the second story window, there were giant hollyhocks, the blooms reminding Harold of faded rose lampshades. Impossible. Yet, nonetheless, Eleanor had gotten them to grow that high. Maybe they had been fertilized with old ground-up Agnew buttons, Harold reflected. No shit better than that.

"Well, you sleepwalkers," Eleanor said, "sit down and have some lemonade. That should wake you up. Or maybe you need tea. Here's the man of the hour," she added, kissing Derek. On the patio, they were invited to sit at tables with umbrella stands.

Over to one side sat Sonya and Joanne, shyly looking on. After all that heartache and fight, at last Sonya had come back on her own. She was staying with Joanne on weekends, too. And here was Richard, sitting beside Olivia.

"We've been talking about some problems," Joanne said. "Our Columbus Day Rally is completely blocked, after we've advertised it all over the state."

"How?" Harold asked. "Why?"

"Samuel's torpedoed Columbus Square for us again. He's hung us up by scaring the Permits Board."

"How'd he do that?"

"He said there might be a riot," Olivia said. "And what with the display, there, for his precious Renaissance Days, of the priceless da Vinci, guarded by the Feds, security, according to him, is going to have to be tighter than the bark on a tree. Even the Arts Council is backing him up on that one."

"Oh yes?" Harold answered. "Tight enough to lose us the Election, he means."

"Well, we can't just continue to sit on our apathies like this," Eleanor said, "and let Samuel steamroller us into oblivion. We've learned the hard way with him. I propose a two-pronged attack."

Harold stared into the sky, exhausted with strategies. Since the firebombing of his church, he hadn't been able to sleep. He kept seeing those marauders defacing his walls, even with swastikas, throwing fire, even though he hadn't been there. He could smell the smoky broken glass, could imagine the flames striking at the portraits of what few saints they had left. All his congregation knew now why it had happened. Word had gotten out. Now he was just another vulnerable not venerable gay, unprotected by closet or wedding ring.

It was a 3-D afternoon, as Harold tried to pray into it. There were arches and little footbridges of cloud above the evergreens, torn veils of cumulus revealing deep, underseas caves of blue. Just let me cross those little footbridges. Perhaps I have never seen blue like that except for one time before—in the Hope Diamond. Or Caroline's eyes.

Suddenly he was aware of Eleanor taking him in. "You're staring off again, Harold. Pay attention. I propose we do some investigative research on Samuel, proving once and for all that he is linked with the OPA. If we do that, his campaign for state senator is down the drain. He will lose his credibility with the intelligentsia. When he's gone on record as supporting 'all things intellectual and disinterested.' They'll see him as loony as Hanshaw. He'll lose his behind-the-scenes-control."

"My father is not a member of the OPA," Sonya

said, breaking into tears. "You all say he is bad. He's not!"

She left the patio. Joanne followed her.

"Way to go, Ellie," Appleton said.

"I didn't mean to insult her father," Eleanor answered. "But when I even think about him, I get livid. I see him again in that room in Family Services."

Harold was looking at Olivia. "I need to get something clarified. You mentioned, Aunt Olivia, something about"—he couldn't say the word "kill"—"Samuel and Gloria. That he did her in."

"It was back in the Cornell Days," Richard said.

"I was there in the Cornell Days," Harold answered.

"Not that far back."

"She was ill," Olivia went on. "He took care of her, but in a cold way. She went back to her work as a champion swimmer to escape him. She died from the diving tower."

"Does Joanne know this?"

"Yes," Eleanor said. "But that's nothing as far as having the goods on him is concerned. Who knows why he protects people the way he does?"

Appleton seemed sort of folded down into himself and was smiling across a distance.

"Well, what do you have to say, oh cat who just ate the canary?" Eleanor asked

"I was just going to say," Appleton replied suavely, "that we can still get the goods on him."

"He seems unstoppable," Harold said.

Harold found himself going back to his 3-D visions. "Lo, yon Eastern star calls the shepherd home." He pulled the umbrella of his patio table around, so that the sun was more squarely out. He could see the group better, now. Eleanor was dressed in red (pants suit) and Joanne was coming back in blue. Sonya, returning also, was staring at him, frightened. She had bib cords on. That moment caused all their faces to collide in his mind, like cards slanting off a table. He was reminded of a *Hamlet* bridge deck, with Ophelia as the Queen of Hearts, calling up a memory, and when he had finally sorted everything out, he realized that Richard had exited and returned, first carrying a martini and then trying to hurry away again. He wanted to tell him something, but Eleanor virtually had him by the throat, with everyone else crowding around and bumping into one another. But something else was up.

"What the hell do you want to do—spoil Derek's recovery? We can't have alcohol around," Eleanor said.

"Listen to me," Derek said. "Listen."

"I'll take it right now," Olivia said. "There's a sink about two steps from here."

"I'm sorry, I'm sorry!"—Richard tried speaking above the hubbub—"I just wasn't thinking."

"Everybody just sit down," Derek shouted, and Harold found himself sitting down, along with the rest. "I can speak for myself."

"I'd like to know—" Harold started to say.

Richard began slinking off to the kitchen, as instructed, very dainty and guilty in his maroon cardigan.

Then he noticed that Derek was staring at him

from behind the gates of his eyes. Were they locked or open? They were luminescent, pale green, like the wings of a luna moth, sailing their way through the forest-scape of evergreens, with spiders weaving cautiously between the branches.

Below stairs, there were manikins in the windows of the courtyard of the Castle. They were wearing Mardi gras masks in different colors. One girl figure, costumed in pink as a butterfly, had gilt scrolling around her eyes. She seemed to press her face to the glass.

Eleanor brought in a cake, lit with three sparklers. "Happy Birthday, Derek!" she said.

Derek came up and took Harold's hand. "I'm all right," he said.

◇

There was still anger inside of him, with the advent of Measure Nine, with Samuel even blocking their efforts at a rally. If the man Harold was to debate with was a member of the OPA, then he most likely was Samuel's henchman.

Harold sat on his fury, steamed on it, for the next twenty-four hours, but ultimately found himself too clever and cagey by next morning to walk right into Hanshaw's clutches. He called KILT, the television studio, and told them that this man, Hanshaw, was notorious for his interruptions on camera (which he was), and had recently turned a whole national talk show into a public shouting match on the same subject. Before he would go on, he wanted a statement, signed by both him and the studio, that Hanshaw would be publicly escorted off the set, if he engaged, more than once, in what the moderator saw as an unfair attempt to silence him. They agreed, and said they would call Hanshaw and have him sign. Of course Harold would have to do the same.

Going into his study, he pulled out all the OPA material he had collected from his files. It was like running through all the gay misnomers of the past 2000 years. A Dantesque descent into anatomical fixation, that OPA material, particularly with the more private sectors of our guts, Harold thought. How is it possible, he wondered, that this so-called religious group is more obsessed with our assholes than we gay men are? For the material was filled with diagrams, quotes, photographs which supposedly documented the way gay men, in particular, confused their sexual and excretory functions in late Roman Empire orgies. And for a moment he was held in check by their arguments—perhaps they have a point, he thought. Men, when they make love, do make a difficult fit. But what, after all, he asked, is fit? A woman's resource of love, Harold considered, has other functions besides that of welcoming a man, hosting him inside her. It is meant, also, to bear children. Just so, a man's rectum and mouth may have many functions. The OPA was insisting, over and over, that a penis' only proper place was in the womb.

Harold came to see at last that all these arguments about natural place and position were merely a front for a fear that would never be admitted, but in order to deploy it, the OPA was willing to blow up the entire state, cause the whole nation to crash and burn if necessary. Male lovemaking. To lesbians it was really indifferent, although their liberation it would take on, as a package deal. But ultimately, what emerged from all this reading and from their obstreperousness and hysteria and scheming and global networking and fundraising and boldfaced lying from pole to pole was the stark raving terror that men might legally and openly and lovingly be prone to one another. As he continued to read and their own private hell sunk its pit deeper and deeper into an enormous sewer, he could see that this was the point, the issue, the goal—to keep men disconnected physically, for otherwise all power such as they understood it would be lost. To save themselves from connection, they would even go so far as to bring in AIDS, their divinely appointed curse on this foul wrong-way down a "do not enter" alley.

And as he thought it through—well into the next morning and afternoon—as he prepared his notes and went to the studio, he came to the conclusion that yes, they're right, sex between men is awkward, unsightly, but so then is all sex. Tear away the veil of privacy, and everything goes into toilet stall graffiti. If I were to talk, Harold decided, in this soapbox manner about the anatomical specifics of Caroline and me together in bed, it would also come down to the same nasty newsprint, which they have been dropping on every doorstep in every precinct in this town. That indeed is sin. The *reductio ad absurdum* of sex to the obscene.

He refuted them in his mind this way—in an

elaborate conceit, in a sermon on sex which he would never give—that the OPA said intercourse must always take place in the nursery of the woman's womb but never in the bathroom of the man's anus. But they had it all wrong. Sex, far from being a nursery or a privy, was much more like a master bedroom, if you will, in the sleep center of the brain, where everything was amorphous, transsexual, androgynous, anamorphous, always changing—with the bath and nursery adjoining but still separate. And as one embraced his or her beloved in the act of love, one was much like Menelaus the King, as he embraced Proteus, who changed into serpent, fire, bird, man, woman, lion—or into Helen, Calypso, and even Odysseus himself. Or one was Sappho as she embraced all the elusive forms of her love, in those wonderful shifting monodic meters—Helen again, Aphrodite, Hermes, the Lady of Cyprus, and Persephone herself in the dark center of sleep, where those strange healing elegiac rhythms were. Was it not true for him that sometimes in his master bedroom, the person he beheld was Caroline, but then again it was Carey? And also, in even more unguarded moments, the man was a masked bandit, who fucked him with a rubber; or a human lion, whose tawny paws gripped his muscular back as he beat against his gate, his soft flanks touching his as the animal long-dicked him in one long roar of ecstasy. They say One in Every Ten. But in the master bedroom, try One in Five, One in Two, One in One! One on One!

Wasn't anything possible there? And didn't

everybody belong? And, yes, we do have to get up to pee and to tend to our children, but then again, when we come back from the bathroom or nursery, do we not resume our lovemaking without the least hesitation? Were we ashamed after we had tucked our children back in, after they had fallen asleep or out of bed or needed a drink of water?

So why do the OPAs view themselves as moral, he asked? What's so moral about insisting that everything go on in the nursery, that children or their potential must be present in the chamber in order to make lovemaking all right? Isn't that perversity itself?

For his part, he thought up a story, which he named Desire. It was set in the future, where people go to Incarnation, Inc., a bureau where they can find the mate of their dreams; in fact, that's the guarantee; the mate has been in the client's dreams for a stipulated amount of time. And so the hero goes to the building of the future, made of chromium and steel, but lined with art deco neon, and he or she sits before a screen to hear the spirit speak. A changing shape appears, a bearded face, then a thin flat one, then wide and stodgy, handsome and lean. Perhaps it is a woman's. Quite angular. "I have loved you," it says, "in darkened sun-cornered parks. I have loved you on the street when I have been nothing more than a passing mist in the crowd. I have loved you down alleyways and on thoroughfares, when I had only glimpsed you once through the windshield. I have followed you in family reunions and in the sheer loneliness"—here a bearded face changes to a star—"of the back row of a movie theater where only the singles sit. I have loved you as a guard in a museum and loved you through the eyes of the roped-off portrait itself. All in the shifting, gold and silver of the river-lined afternoon, I have loved you."

The client gets up and goes to the main desk and tells the attendant he does not want this spirit to enter a body; let all remain just as it is, in his master bedroom of sleep.

◇

KILT studios. In the dressing room, Harold found himself sitting before a mirror behind the set, now lit, and putting on make-up—just as Eleanor, by telephone, had directed, remembering her old days on television. Indeed, in more ways than one, Harold was "KILT's Lady" of the nineties. The day was warm, as was the studio, and since Harold was prone to sweat, the pancake make-up was to help keep everything in place. All his family, all his congregation would be watching. And instead of having them cheer him on down at the bar, they were doing it down at the local No on Nine office, with all the Xerox machines politely and reverentially on pause. You've come a long way, he told himself in the mirror, giving himself a nice, hail-fellow-well-met pat, you've come a long way since losing it in the Conference Room of Family Services. (Yet he still owed Caroline an amends.) He picked up his copy—also—of an OPA newspaper which he had brought.

As he came out on the set, there it was—the studio

audience. And as he sat down, he fixed, for some reason, on all the lip gloss their M.C. was wearing. Why that? Envy, maybe—she had something better than pancake make-up to hide behind. And a beautiful Japanese face.

Hanshaw started in with his "special rights" argument—that is, if you protect gays and lesbians as a minority under the law, you are giving them protection over and beyond what is given normal citizens. Before he could reply, however, he then launched into a personal attack—on the way Harold "hired out" his church during the regular days of the week, making it the center of gay and lesbian activity, which had nothing to do with Christian outreach.

"Last I heard," Harold answered, "hospitality was a fine Christian virtue. In my book, serving the particularly oppressed is not only a goal for the wayfaring Christian, it's required."

"Have you read Leviticus?" Hanshaw asked.

"Yes, I have read Leviticus," Harold answered. "But even assuming, for a moment, that Leviticus is right or even that the way you interpret it is right, the Bible never says we ought to neglect what is adjudged as wrong. Otherwise, our very soup kitchens would have to hand out moral questionnaires before they could actually lift the ladle."

Laughter. Hanshaw was openly annoyed. "I still can't understand," he said, "how you can do God's work, given the level of political activity you and your church are involved in."

"That political activity, as you call it," Harold

answered, "is mainly in response to the divisive Measure which your so-called Christian agency is presently circulating and trying to sign into law. If you people had not tried to tamper with our Constitution, perhaps the political activity would have been different, or not political at all. However, I would also have to say that even if you didn't exist, it would still be our business to attend to hate crimes—as foisted upon Jews, black people, the homeless, as well as the gays and lesbians. We must always be a bastion against such groups as the skinheads, the Nazis, and others."

"Are you equating the OPA with those groups?" the M.C. asked.

"That's exactly what he's doing," Hanshaw interrupted. "He's drawing a direct link between us and the hate crimes, which I deeply resent."

"Hate crimes have gone up dramatically," Ms. Kuromara put in, "since the arrival of the Measure. That I will have to say."

Harold felt he must put in something, make the connection, as distant, as elusive as it was. "I have no evidence to draw a direct link, but I will say this— when you create a statewide political pressure cooker such as your OPA has, the hate crimes are bound to happen. They are what are in the pot."

"You're steering awfully close to libel," Hanshaw said.

"Let's turn to a major issue," Ms. Kuromara said, responding to a danger—but speaking as if they hadn't been on the major issue already, and adjusting her dress just so, she seemed to suggest they were in a richly furnished restaurant, and just about to get down to polite business. "The Oregon Protection Alliance constantly insists that gays and lesbians are trying to corrupt the young. Recently, it scored a victory by getting a children's book on gay parents and gay family life banned from the Capitol City Public Library. I would like to know what the OPA's fears actually are."

"It's quite simple," Hanshaw answered. "It's covered in our most recent handout. It tells the story about how a young boy in an Oregon mill town is convinced it's all right to have sex with another boy, because his teacher says the lifestyle is O.K. Teachers have an enormous impact on our children and what they read to them. As do those books that we have tried to remove."

"So what you're saying," Harold replied, hiding behind his good Socratic fashion, "is—if I teach about gay lifestyle, the way the book does, I'm actually teaching them how to do it and that it's O.K."

"Exactly."

"Well, under the same logic, then, if I teach *Macbeth* in high school, all the parents ought to worry about being murdered in their beds."

Uproarious laughter. Hanshaw snatched something from the floor. "I would like to show our jovial studio audience here another little book they probably haven't seen. It's called the *Spartacus* manual. It's a guide that you can buy on almost any newsstand which tells gay men where they can find public sex in almost any part of the country. Especially the parks and the restrooms." He made ample display of the two naked men on the cover. "The way you're talking, this could also become a supplementary text in the public schools."

Harold had his trump all ready, however. From where had it come? He could not say exactly. Had it been from his thinking about Greek elegiac verse? A breath somewhere from Lesbos, like the exalted smell of spice from off the coast of Zanzibar? No, it was more from Plato himself. Hanshaw had no idea what he was in for. Going through the files had paid off. But he hadn't even thought of this until now.

"You seem, then, Dr. Hanshaw—" Harold began.

"And I want to show them something else"—also pulling out other material.

"Excuse me," Ms. Kuromara said to him, "Dr. Towning has the floor—"

"I insist," he said.

"No, you can't insist. Dr. Towning, do continue."

"It seems to me you're very concerned about what reaches the eyes and ears of young people, am I correct?" Harold asked.

"Yes."

"Then I"—and Harold pulled out the OPA newspaper from his file—"am going to show Ms. Kuromara something which you and the Oregon Protection Alliance dropped on every doorstep in Oregon last week. I'm going to ask if according to present TV codes, it's fit to be read over the air"—Harold passed across the handout and pointed to the passage which was so anatomically specific. "And if by some chance I do get her approval, I will have to ask every parent who is watching to take their children from the room."

Ms. Kuromara put down the newspaper, which she had clearly already seen. She was extremely nettled, whether with him or them, Harold couldn't be sure. "No, Dr. Towning, obviously you can't read this on the air."

"You listen here—" Hanshaw said.

"No, you listen here," Harold said, "you and the OPA put that on every porch in the state last Saturday, where any six-year-old could pick it up and read it, and yet you talk about gays and lesbians corrupting the young—"

"It's just the filthy acts you're trying to legalize and push our children into—"

"Dr. Hanshaw," Ms. Kuromara said, "this is my last warning—"

"This man here," he went on, outraged with the trap, "is what we call a homophile of the cloth. I wouldn't be surprised if—"

But Hanshaw was yelling and interrupting so much this time, he was escorted from the set. "I wouldn't be surprised if he was gay!" came from him in the wings at last.

"Which I am," Harold said, staying seated and surprising himself with a forced smile.

There was an awkward TV pause. Completely unfilled. How much do those pauses cost, Harold wondered? A million dollars? We should be plugging Easy Off.

"Fortunately, Dr. Towning," she laughed at last,

"we're out of time. We want to thank you so very much
for coming—"

"—out," Harold answered, "and thank you"—and
suddenly the studio audience stood up and cheered.

But that night, Harold's church was firebombed
again and covered with graffiti.

◇

He waited for Carey at the edge of the Filbert Festival.
Dusk. He idled in a heavily patroled unloading zone
for the fair. Through the cyclone fence, the midway
seemed to grow—its neon like the flame of a lighter,
when on a patio, someone suddenly lights a cigarette, and the walls of dark fall back. From across the
street, the beautiful butane blue of the spook house
was coming through the twilight, whose yellows and
oranges seemed to stand like potted roses in all the
October gardens.

Harold sat and made notes for his coming-out
sermon and didn't get very far. Somehow he didn't
expect that Carey would ever find the "No on Nine"
booth, would ever deliver the buttons and bumper
stickers and still find his way back. It was a simple
matter of going from point A to point B, but everything was conspiring to waylay Carey in the interim.
He would run into one of his old flames. He would
inadvertently lay the materials aside while buying a
hot dog. He'd get a sudden urge to test his strength
at the Sledgehammer Palace. Spiritless, anonymous,
energetic, he's the man every man dreams about,
cropping up at crossroads, in alleyways, at bus stops,

a male Hecate. His body was the coverlet of darkness, a sheath of Shakespeare's metered lines, read without understanding, which, as an actor, was frequently his way. And now surely Carey was passing through the needle's eye while winding his way through the brightening carnival, with amphibious footfalls, through this early-autumn fair, and, as far as keeping his original goal was concerned, all bets were off.

But Carey surprised him. He came back wearing a "No on Nine" cap and holding a blue balloon.

"No problems with the button handoff?"

"No problems." But Carey seemed uncomfortable once the door was slammed. Harold's small car could scarcely hold the full six and a half feet of him. The balloon bumped the roof the car.

"How is the booth doing?"

"Just fine, just fine—except that every closet queen in the state seems to have turned out for this election. Men I've known in the Park. They're safe with their 'No on Nine' buttons—it's their one chance to express themselves and still stay safe. Big deal."

"Well, their votes are all the same in the polling booth," Harold said.

"You know perfectly well what I mean—and then on my way out, some pervert handed me this."

A lavender sheet from the Oregon Protection Alliance: "What do gays and lesbians, pedophiles, adulterers, fornicators and rapists have in common? Answer: Homosexuals indulge themselves and others in unhealthy, unnatural sexual perversions."

Harold tore it up.

"You know who's behind this?" Carey asked.

He didn't have time to answer.

"Your former brother-in-law," Carey answered himself.

"Unfortunately, that's just a rumor. Appleton's out to prove it's true as we speak."

"But it's a pretty damn good rumor."

The carnival seemed to glow now from within a goldfish bowl, a lit underseas city. There the darkness was festooned round like seaweed. The house beside them had lost all its majesty; the lamp above the porch was on and that was it.

"If you believe the rumor—and I believe it, too," Harold said, "why are you going to take part in Samuel's Renaissance Fair? Especially when it upstages our rally?"

"It's just my job. What does Shakespeare have to do with politics?" Carey asked.

"Everything when it's a mastermind operation going back to Samuel."

"Well, I don't see it that way," Carey answered. "Anyway, I'm getting out of all this. I'm not political and never will be. I'm sick of trying to satisfy you and Derek, hoping you'll accept me. I'm odd man out and there's no two ways about it."

"You don't have to be odd man out," Harold said.

For once Carey looked directly at him. "I don't? I try to seduce you for years and then when you finally decide to be a come-lately, suddenly you've got the world's story to tell. Now that there are supports and running groups and men's choruses. You don't have a clue what it's like to be gay all your life and be as old as I am. I don't fit into this."

"How old are you, Carey?"

"Fifty."

"I thought so—that's good to know, too, after all these years."

"Do you get my drift, Harold? Do you have any idea what it's like to be seduced at ten and begin the bar scene at sixteen?" Carey asked.

"I don't want to hear about it," Harold said. And unconsciously he found he had raised his hand to fend things off. Instantly, Carey pushed it back and slapped him hard.

"You will listen to me. We're not doing nuances back at Sylvester's Bar. For years I laid low in the parks and was fucked in the bushes every Sunday afternoon. For years in Hawaii, we had group sex on the beach. You see, to me, being gay is just slime. It's as simple as that. Some got lucky and were born straight; the rest of us queers were relegated to fuck in the bushes. Your campaign is ridiculous because in the end everything the opposition says about us is right."

Harold had to catch his breath, stop the blood on his lip with a handkerchief. "What are you saying? That you want to move out?"

"Yes."

"Well, I'm not holding you. You never were forced in the first place," Harold said.

Carey had another handkerchief out. A bandana. "Here let me—"

"No. Keep back." Harold put the key in the ignition.

"Where's it going to be, Carey? The bus station? A freight car? What's going to take you to the end of the world this time? And is this going to be the time you drop clear off?"

"Maybe." He had started to cry.

But Harold felt himself becoming like an iron gate. Nights when Carey came home to bed at all hours, he could feel him upset the whole rhythm of the house, as if the pendulum of the grandfather clock had been nudged, and the smiling moon had gone down under the waves always a few hours too late. He was bringing the bar back with him, into the household, keeping them from dreaming their deeper dreams.

"I never wanted Derek to be like me," Carey went on. "I was afraid he'd have the same kind of life. That's why you were my only hope."

"That I can understand," Harold said, wiping more blood away. "What I don't understand is—why you don't want to make things better for somebody else? And here's your perfect opportunity."

Carey sat there crying while his balloon continued to bump against the ceiling; he seemed like a shunned six-and-a-half foot boy at a birthday party. On some level, Carey was still trying to seduce him.

Harold started the car. He was getting signals from the fair monitors to move on. "Let me make it easy for you. Your job at the bar is affecting Derek's recovery. Either you quit or pack up and go. Is that clear?"

"Perfectly." His tears had stopped. "And thanks for making it so easy."

As they turned down the next street, all the porch lamps shone, touching them with their spokes of light.

◇

But when Carey left, he felt a void.

And in trying to write a sermon for Columbus Day, it seemed to him, ever since he could remember, it was important to be, always, on the morally enlightened side—the one preaching from the sanctified pulpit, the one leafleting the neighborhood with the correct pamphlets. He admitted it—he wanted to remain picture-perfect. First for Eleanor, then Caroline.

When had the crack come? And he didn't mean in the perfection. Which had never existed. But in the desire for it?

He supposed it was when he had seen Carey for the first time. With his shirt open. Men were rarely that massive and thin at the same time. He was a good worker, a good actor, and a strong member, eventually, of Harold's congregation. The Shakespeare Theatre of Courtland could always rely on him. And so, after so much imperfection had entered Harold's life, Harold gave up that goal for himself.

But then he had plummeted down, too. When the dip in his marriage to Caroline caused him to try to remake Carey over, then he began to slide. He tried to usher him into Caroline's position—for even the shape of her face was the same as his—and he sent him on his journey downward (across country, really), with himself closely following.

Should he confess more? Their daughter Brenda

had died of crib death. And when that was over, and he and Caroline were finished, but didn't know it; he wanted to reshape all into another family life. He would put Carey and Derek in the photograph rather than Caroline and Brenda. There were times when he found himself following Carey to the ends of the earth, and, yes, he had been seeking the shape of him—the man with the beautiful mustache who knew how to give him a massage with those multi-colored oils—the man who could sing and act with such sound delivery on the stage—but there had also been some idea (to compensate for the loss of perfection) which he had been seeking. The idea of the male family. Harold was ruthless for it, and in his ruthlessness, he lost so much of his sense of being the loving husband.

And so he had lost it with Caroline in the Committee Room. And therefore he lost Derek, for a while, in the legal system.

What had it been like to be cut off from Derek? It was only now he had the luxury of asking himself that. I can remember, Harold thought, being out on a run along the river and seeing a figure much like Derek's at the far end of the path, just by the rose garden. Was the figure for real or was it just a trick of the shade in the foggy February light? The rose vines were arbored on the trellis; the next day, at sunset, the trellis was in the sky, flaming rose, as I drove past Caroline's house, hoping to get a glimpse—but all was shut out—nailed closed; there was no use—and all the trees seemed to be those dark cut-outs reflected in water, a brook.

The male had turned; it was not Derek. Then unimaginable pain. Could there have been anything more important or wonderful than sitting by the afternoon living room window with the book of "Euclidian" geometry open and talking about a theorem for supplementary angles and Derek's Puckish face becoming one "aha" at the right moment? Later they would go out and play catch among maples that wore garments of leaves like smoke—reddish, rose, brown.

He could remember, now, the first time Derek had come up from behind and hugged him—without stopping. What had been the reason? His decision to let him take the car out on his own? Or maybe he had decided to let him out of mowing the lawn so that he could spend the Saturday racing his bike up and down the lilacked hills. He could see him now, furiously speeding away with the sun glinting on the metal, the yards seemingly covered by a vast purple wisteria, as fine as sifted gray rain. Perhaps he had had no reason—for that would have been like him—no reason, no reason at all—but Harold did remember where they had been—in a park, much like the yard which his landlady kept for him. There was surrounding laurel and hanging golden chain. The wild roses were there in their sketchy pink. It had been when they, the three of them, Caroline, himself, and Derek were still all together.

"A few more sit-ups, Dad," Derek had said, hugging him tighter around the waist. "We're getting a little soft."

He pulled him forward and tousled his hair.

"We're? You need more meat on your bones and I need less. Deal?"

"Sure."

"All right, all right. Break it up you two," Caroline said, smiling. All about, the clover was radiant.

"Mother," Derek said. "Let's go get Mother."

"Better not," Harold said, "or she'll sic her women's group on you."

With that remark, the carnations vanished from her face. How could he have said such a thing? Always wrong with her lately, as much as he had always been wrong with Carey. How could he have sent such a shadow through the park? It continued, that shadow; it was at one with the impending evening. Silent, Caroline flipped the picnic basket closed, picked it up in one long hoist, furious.

"I didn't realize we were leaving," Derek said.

"Not we," Harold answered. "She."

Harold followed her at close range to the car. She was behind glass by now. Had locked herself in.

"Would you roll down the window?" he asked outside the car.

Silence.

"May I talk to you?"

Silence.

How could anyone look that beautiful while brooding straight ahead? A crystalline blue to her eyes, aquiline nose. She could have been the radiant replacement of Catherine Deneuve—now the symbol of Liberty for France. In her eyes, a maze.

"Caroline, roll down that goddamn window or

127

I'll break it. You know I can take anything but silent treatments."

The window came down. "Why is it, Harold?" she asked, "why is it you have to hit on the very thing that matters to me most?"

Well, he had not thought it through very clearly.

"Can't you see," she said. "You have Carey as your friend. I need something for me."

"You have your counseling," Harold said. "It's a whole profession."

"But I mean something private. And every time I look at Derek, I see Carey. It's like he's always taking you away from me."

The sun laced its fingers through the park. Alone, Derek threw the football up high, catching it in meandering circles. He let out a whistle every time it fell.

"I just can't take it seriously," Harold answered, "some kind of women's psychological Rockettes routine."

Why hadn't he understood her feelings? Why?

"Of course you can't," she said, retreating still, "because you're not in that group. But you've got to understand it's all I've got left."

"Got left? What about me?"

He looked at her, wanted to touch her rose skin, but the least gesture from him brought her to withdraw. "There's nothing of you left," she said at last. "It all started when Carey showed up from out of hiding. Sometimes I would swear you love him, not me."

Harold could hear the river nearby and imagined all that he had imagined about Carey. Some green was thrown on the canvas of landscape; there was the brown of a masculine shoulder. He remembered all the seed dahlias, fiery jewels beneath his bedroom window. He remembered, once, under the green transparencies of a green house, Carey had come up and held his chest against him as he had clutched the basket of color spots. That was adultery; that was infidelity. Standing there and breathing in the scent of earth from this sun-darkened man.

"Harold, when am I going to start getting your attention?" she asked.

"I'm right here," he answered. "Steady on. Just let me in the car."

"No, I mean in bed. I feel myself shrinking. Don't you remember the time we went to Portland and saw *Gone with the Wind* and made love for two hours afterwards? Don't you remember? It was way before Derek was sent for. It was almost like you were dashing— dashing me off my feet."

"Me in old rusty knight's armor," Harold said. "That's hard to imagine."

Caroline did not look at him. The moon would soon be out, circled with violet. He kept crushing her sense of romance. It was embarrassing, thinking about Portland. He had been *gallant* then, opening car doors for her and walking with her on the insides of curbs. Nevertheless, what she had said was true. His attention had become scattered; it had become like the display of lights down at Sylvester's—that bar. He could not rivet on his wife. And he was pretending, in the pulpit, to be something he wasn't.

Derek came up. He had found a white cat. Sometimes Harold wanted to call Derek Ulysses. There was nothing he couldn't search out and rescue. He had even tracked down his own father through a series of leaps of detection—letters, rifling the orphanage post office. For now he was presenting Caroline with this Foreign/ Oriental White through the car window. She kissed the cat. It had blue eyes, like Derek's. Driving on the highways, along the back roads, Caroline could burst into tears when she saw lost or dead animals. In the bedroom, the oval of her mirror was brightly scrolled with the woodwork of squirrels, meadowlarks, loons, all embraced by foliage. Her father's creation, through woodwork. So she was never vain when she looked at her reflection, for there was always a reminder of the things which needed sanctuary, and she made sure it was provided for in the gold, green, and maroon petitions which she circulated. She carried petitions for an initiative to preserve river front parks and wet meadows and everything else. I remember, Harold thought, we had run through one once; we had been out on a hikeathon to protect wild flowers. Ahead of me I had seen her stoop suddenly. How much she had looked like Judy Collins then—on the front of that album which everyone has. Wildflowers. A beautiful escapee from the 1960s, too exquisite for anything except the slightest make-up. Oh, lo and behold it's that cat again. For one had approached her then, too.

"It's a male," she said, way back in that sanctuary. "Please, Harold, can I keep him? Some campers must have left him behind."

"Who am I to give you orders? You're the boss."

She was standing in a lake of camas lily. The wind blew in fresh, clean white clouds, whose shadows darted over us like gliders.

She, back then, held the cat and said, very suddenly, and out of the blue—"You love me, don't you?"

"Too much," Harold answered.

"I know you do because you put up with everything. You give like no man I've ever known. Sometimes I try explaining to people just how wonderful you are but it's impossible. And you just go on encouraging me. The only thing I wish I could do would be to show you how much—I feel for you," she said.

"But you can't," Harold answered. "We've talked about it. If you can't, you can't." In the meadow, the salal was everywhere, holding out its blooms like tiny opal lanterns. In a few months, Caroline would win this place as a park, an appropriate commemoration for this still moment, which would be recollected in the mirror when they would make love.

Harold kissed her, felt her soft and delicate frame. Is there anything more arousing, inflaming, than asceticism? he wondered. Her face turned towards him, then in profile; he was almost ready to pass out from the way the wavering light fell upon her cheekbones.

"We best stop," she said, "or our cat will get away."

And now, in this other memory, less remote, she handed the cat back to Derek. She didn't insist this time that they keep him. And then Harold reflected that now he was the one who could not express his love. He had become blocked like her.

"Yes," Harold said, "you better leave him here, so he can find his masters."

In the car, Derek took in the remoteness between him and Caroline; later, Harold would remember that a white cat had dropped in on Joanne and Sonya, too, Was it then that Derek had begun to remove himself from them? It was as if, then, he could envision the time he would be separated from him—the world outlined in purple and the begonias burning red and yellow in their beds, as constant reminders of the strangeness. It was a world such as some of his parishioners had talked about, when they had been ill, exiled, divorced, fired. Yes, Derek sat there and watched their silence, perhaps already with smoked-out nerves.

The light from the Western sky was now a perfect peach color—or imitating those roses that could be called neither orange nor pink but were exactly, delicately in between. All the tentativeness of their family held him bolt upright in his driver's seat. They went through a low-rent district, reminding him of Caroline's mother, who had been a real estate agent, and he thought about the days following Brenda's death; he could only look at Caroline in the bed from the mirror—for it would have been too unfeeling to look at her directly—day after day in the mirror, scrolled by her father, the one-time carpenter. The animals raced around the glass or drank from the pool, or seemed to, and she had gone on crying for days. And he had not been able to tell her of his grief, anymore than she could tell him of her love.

◇

Harold's sermon got finished on the Saturday before Columbus Day. Was the last rally just a year ago? he wondered. It seemed a millennium.

This time they had a No on Nine banner, which they marched down the center of Arden against all orders, over to the 1950s part of town, around and around the Arden Balboa Inn as a picket where Samuel was rumored to be showing up, and then back to the Renaissance Fair, before joining their affiliates up in Capitol City. Monday night, they were to have their "No on Nine" Benefit Concert at the Arden Dome. Appleton, in fact, was still in Washington, D.C., trying to nail down some particulars on it.

They assembled under the awnings of the building which had all the copper emblems. In Isabella Circle, because they were blocked from Columbus Square. Through the glass, they were watching a TV set in the lobby.

"There's the ad for the Oregon Protection Alliance."

In it, two boys were waiting to be placed with their adoptive parents, who turn out to be two gay men. "But where's our mother?" one of the boys asked, near tears.

("She's not there—deal with it," Derek said on the side.)

"Don't let this happen to Oregon. Vote Yes on Nine," the ad went on.

A hiss went up. Harold could scarcely hear the

133

dialogue, but knew what it said, he had seen it, read about it, so many times before.

"Your 'father' Appleton should be home tonight," Eleanor told him. "Here, take a flower."

Somehow she had rounded up some purple dahlias, and somehow she had started calling Appleton "your father." Years ago, when Harold used to dream of owning a roll of color film, he'd promised himself the first snapshot he would take would be of a flower like this. With a butterfly on it. He put the dahlia behind his ear.

"What's the occasion?" he asked her.

"I'm proud of you," she said. "And don't ask questions. Proud of Joanne, too. But I wonder where she is."

Eleanor looked into the lobby but the reflection stopped him—with a crash. There he and his mother were, along with his stepson—as still as porcelain figures, shot back by the mirror of the glass. The undersea copper rust gave a rich accent above.

Someone beat a drum.

Tambourines shook.

On the edges of the parade, some people in premature Halloween costume scampered about. Harold held up one side of the "No on Nine" banner, and they were setting off. Eleanor walked on his left, Derek on his right.

"On our way to the Balboa Inn?" Eleanor asked. "Well, it's been thirty years since I've been there. At the one in Seattle. When it opened, I remember the TV station sent me down to do a spot, as if I were a reporter. I believe it came out in color, back in the days when you had those huge consoles in the hazelnut where you mix your own colors like in a paint box. Everything in that Balboa Inn was light blue, at a time when offering a pool for the guests to swim in was really something. And that Saturday in the 1950s we had parachutists jump from an airship—one, two. It was so beautiful at early dusk, it was almost beyond description."

And she continued about the day when Joanne was suddenly over her depression, and they were driving her home, past the lovely iris gardens, on the outskirts on the eastern side—thousands and thousands of gold spears, like an acre of argonauts coming up from the ground, under a purplish shadow, as the horizon bent down, toward another field, and the sun made clouds seem like they were taking leaps, with Appleton's DeSoto going stretching out ahead of them, emblem first. That was 1950s territory, too. They passed another park, and the wrought iron was as delicate as doll's furniture, above the river that looked like a blue satin ribbon—as if that whole part of the city was a young girl's birthday present. And there, in the distance, were Mount Hood and The Sisters. And as she sat there, with Joanne beside her, she thought—My daughter's back! My daughter's back!—holding her hand for the first time since she could remember.

"Harold," she then said sharply, "I understand that Carey has left you."

A cheer went up. He waved to the onlookers. Derek tossed dahlias.

"Yes, that's right," he answered.

"Well, all for the better. I never liked him anyway," she said in her usual decisive manner.

"He wanted out. And the job at the bar wasn't working," Harold told her.

They had gained sight of the river. Blue herons flapped up out of the water, in Rodan-like shadows. Their wings were the same colors as the clouds. Someone switched on "I Am What I Am" (Gloria Gaynor). They had a phalanx of dancers, briefly attired. The unison of their muscles was intoxicating. What a distance from that time, not long ago, he tried to dance with a man at the Fair, and had gotten into a fight. At last he had stopped apologizing.

Finally they reached Riverside Park. It was as if Nature, after weeks of rains, had lifted the glass cover of the mists and presented them with this pristine day, in full sun, with all of autumn preserved. A Columbus Day birthday present. The oak trees were lined with a spotless yellow mail, and further off, light spiraled through the closely woven evergreens, resting at random on the planes of an eccentric maple. Everywhere there were bowing red squirrels.

They crossed the river, and Harold thought of old hymns.

"Did you hear the polls?" Eleanor asked.

"Which ones? They seem to change every hour on the hour."

"We're neck-and-neck. Something's got to give."

Was that why he was so tired—why there had never been any let-up, any reassurance, after days of canvassing, calling, fund-raising, speechifying? There never was that sense of elegance or eloquence which comes from resting on your laurels, in a place of safety. Sometimes he just wanted to sit in a corner and stare.

Maybe that was the reason. But, no, it had more to do with the campaign giving him an ultimatum. Stop hiding from your flock and come out.

They were above the river. Walking on water. Or at least above water. Beautiful drifting willows were reflected in pools of rain—in grass—that bordered the river. The retinue from their local Allegro Theater bounced and exploded; multi-colored, they were like confetti.

> *One, two, three, four*
> *Cut the measure*
> *To the core!*
> *No on Nine!*
> *No on Crime—*
> *The Crime of Hate*
> *In our State!*

The ferns parted; the willows seemed to wear their golden drapery a little off the shoulder, and the still-life carnival of 1950s Arden—preserved forever in the northwest sector—appeared suddenly at the end of their path like the Emerald City, only this time, even on a sunlit Saturday, it was all neon blue, its crown, its center, its marquee being the Balboa Inn and "Welcome Oregon Protection Alliance."

They circled the place, scaring up some pigeons, who wore collars of shimmering turquoise. The manager and the president of the alliance stood behind glass, worried, consulting, waiting for the first $200-a-plate guest to pass through. Somebody had said Samuel was slated to speak, but as usual with him, you could never be sure. They thought—having the facilitator of the whole Columbus Day Celebration (and candidate for your next state senator) would tilt the scales of the election in their favor. Was he really going to show his hand? The distant but sympathetic feature speaker.

And as cars started pulling up, and people began crossing the picket lines—all those Harold expected to see in some church tomorrow—the news went up that Samuel was on his way. KILT turned its cameras in their direction, was surveying the crowd, all in anticipation. Therefore the volume was raised.

> *One, two, three, four*
> *Hate is something*
> *We deplore!*

Then all of a sudden, Harold saw the crowd being parted and here was Joanne, a bit breathless, even misstepping a bit, wearing her "No on Nine" button.

"Sorry I'm late," she said. "Hope everything is O.K." She was taking out some sunglasses, which had a hint of sky in them.

"Where were you?" Eleanor asked.

"I was talking to Samuel."

"Is he coming?" Eleanor asked.

"No," she answered, bemused, smiling, "I don't think he's coming."

He exchanged a glance with Eleanor. "You mean you talked him out of it?" he asked.

"Let's just say he's indisposed for the time being."

"Where's Sonya?" Eleanor asked.

"She's down on the corner finishing a long distance call to Appleton," she answered.

"Isn't he going to be flying back today?" Eleanor asked.

"He's still in our nation's capital finalizing down the concert for Monday. He was trying to get straight what songs Sonya wanted the rock band to do. I don't know—you've got me."

So the Balboa Inn was not going to have Samuel after all; droves would be seated, waiting for the keynote luncheon speaker, and there would be only be an empty podium. Who could they dredge up at the last minute? Reagan, perhaps? Still giddy, Harold found himself in the marching ranks again, and as they went back over the bridge, everything turned to streamers; the cones of the sumac and evergreen climbed the air, and there were flashes of jewel-colored bottles in the low-depth October water. Samuel had denied them their space for the Columbus Day Rally, but they had gone ahead and planned it anyway. Yes, Harold thought, we have planned it anyway.

So everything turned back full-circle to Samuel's Renaissance Fair, with its jugglers and flowery gowns and jerkins, then took a turn around Columbus Square, past the main statue of Columbus, whom someone had dressed up in paint and drag in the dead of night, and in memory, for Harold, they never stopped, because they were an exploding nova, new born, inexorable, for within the same wing beat, they went on to do their other rally in Capitol City, where at the banquet Joanne spoke and brought the house down; went on the next morning to Harold's church service in Arden (for he was not to be outdone!)—a procession, where he told everybody who he was.

Afterward, when the sermon was over, Eleanor was beside herself. With pride. They were walking toward the church parking lot, which, like the sanctuary, had been scoured of its graffiti. The trees were like golden lanterns. "I really don't think I have ever felt—I can't express to you the overwhelming sense I've gotten in the past twenty four hours—it's just beyond imagination, the pride I felt listening to my children"—she walked between, linking with their arms—"to think I could ever live to be so blessed, to have the two of you show such courage after all that you've been through! My God, it's safe to say last night and this morning have been the happiest days of my life, and there's no doubt now that we will win!"

But they were still waiting for final help to come through from Appleton, their man in Washington, D.C. and elsewhere.

"Let's just wait and see," Joanne said.

PART THREE

Appleton

OVER THE SUMMER MONTHS, APPLETON HAD GOTTEN many papers together. On Samuel.

There had been this little matter about Samuel possibly being a cross dresser. Appleton actually held the receipts for some stockings. And he kept them, along with the other clues and evidence in a special small suitcase with an "aeroplane" emblem on the clasp. For emphasis he had put a pink triangle on the outside. He imagined now, exactly when and where Samuel might have dressed himself in long fishnets, put on lipstick, and looked before a mirror in a blonde wig. Ironically, this might have been in San Francisco, in the sixties, not far from the place where the fabulous Sylvester, the gays had told him, had gone out hoofing on six-inch heels, heading for Castro. Perhaps it had been at exactly the same moment, just below his window.

The incident had come at nighttime, the one which had prompted him to say, "All right, this is war." It had also jettisoned him into going out and getting the goods on the man. Just the day after the family had reconnoitered at Eleanor's Castle. It was autumn, and they were finishing up at the No on Nine Office in Capitol City, and here a woman asked if he would walk her to her car.

"That's a good idea," the broad-shouldered facilitator said, overhearing. "No one should leave this office except in twos, anyway."

"But you don't mean to say," Appleton said, "that even I'm not safe, either. That in provincial old Oregon an old man could be jumped."

"Bashers don't discriminate on the basis of age, dear," the Facilitator said.

This sounded slightly condescending and Appleton didn't like it—especially coming from this cherubic young man, who couldn't have been a day over twenty-five, and was one of those let's-drop-into-Capitol-City-and-organize-a-protest types. And swishy and swarthy to boot. From California, no doubt. Appleton nevertheless escorted the woman into the street, a young lady who was attractive indeed, and who Appleton wished would take his arm. Good luck, especially these days. Still, they made their way down the night avenue, chatting amiably, when Appleton was aware they were being tracked by a truck the next street over. A four by four. Appleton pointed to it— and the driver immediately roared off—but the exit made them all too hasty to get to her car and say goodnight. No kiss, either.

They shook hands.

Appleton had just turned to cross to the Over-park, gathering enough wind into his lungs to make it, hopefully, up to the fourth floor, when the four by four, materializing out of an alley, rushed past, showering him with "Faggot, Faggot, Faggot."

Needless to say, Appleton didn't pause to shout back, but got himself up those Overpark stairs, jumping in his DeSoto with no time to lose. He went freewheeling out, first down one ramp and then another. On Level Two, however, he heard squealing behind him and in his mirror, saw the thugs full tilt on his tail and wished, for a split second, for a James-Bond torpedo to blast them all dead from behind. Straight off the fucking planet. Maybe these were the hoodlums who had jumped Derek. Their car edged forward and menaced his fender—all right, fuck you, too—for they were flipping him off and turning gladiatorial thumbs downward. An underground-looking bunch of young toughs. Appleton could see them mouthing the Big Fours, as he finally crashed through the toll gate, letting the atomized boards fly into their windshield and take out one of their headlights. A few neon traffic cones were added like a sprinkling of bowling pins or confetti.

Screeching halt—a blinded truck.

Appleton roared off.

He didn't stop until he reached the Castle. Ellie, unfortunately, was still out at another No on Nine meeting. Panting, he turned on all of Ellie's restful lamps—with the fringed lampshades—and sat down. Steadied his poor heart, in her Victorian rocking chair. Let his pulse catch up with itself. Called the cops, who said come down and file a report first thing in the morning—and don't worry about sweeping up the board and glass.

Oh yeah? That's big of you.

Sitting down again, he glanced through the newspaper. Oh, no. A guest column from Professor Samuel T. Hollingsworth. "Let's Keep Cool During this Hot Election." Right. Samuel, you've just written your last editorial. Sanctimonious closet OPAer posing as chatty liberal professor guest columnist for a minor Northwest newspaper. Accomplice! Accomplice! Try that on for size. For at last I think I've got the goods on you. Your ass is grass.

◇

But, really, getting the goods on Samuel went all the way back to three years ago—just before the arrival of Eleanor into his life—with the formation of what became Measure Eight. Appleton had been sleeping in as usual in the Rosium Rest Home in Seattle, when the phone rang. He had been dreaming of clocks. It was the Governor of Oregon.

"Appleton, what the hell do you think you're doing, sending me a confidential postcard? You may as well publish your message in *Willamette Week* and hope by chance I'll read it. If we're going to talk gay and lesbian liberation, you're going to need to come in here and argue your point. And argue well."

"What do you think of the idea of an Executive Order as a means of protection?" Appleton asked him.

"I don't know, I don't know," the Governor said. "I don't know. For just state employees in the work

146

place? It sounds awfully limited. But I want to hear. I want you to say more. This Proteus Precedent you've dug up is interesting."

"I'll get my show on the road," Appleton answered, rubbing his eyes.

"I'll get some committee members to join us so we can have their feedback." Then the Governor hesitated. Appleton remembered he hesitated. Because already the Man in the Mansion was probably planning to bring in An Opponent for a little consultation and debate. I want to get both views. He was that way. "And one thing you've got to keep in mind," the Governor went on, "is that these guys will be from the Legislature, not the University. So no long-winded speeches. Just the facts, Ma'am. And also—" Cough, cough.

"Yes?" Appleton asked slowly.

"Do something about your appearance. Last time you were down here, you looked like something the cat dragged in. You looked, in fact, like someone straight out of a rest home."

"I am straight out of a rest home. Still straight in one," Appleton said. He realized, however, that the word "straight" these days was not friendly.

"Well, you don't have to appear to be straight out of a rest home. These men and women are legislators. Clothes make the man. Or the person, as they say these days. Now I'll hand you over to my secretary to set something up."

Making the date and with that on the calendar, Appleton could feel the hastening again. The clocks that had been in his dream started picking up speed. He remembered Billings, his son, visiting him at his bedside when he had been at death's door two years back, and he said, never again. No more Death's Door. Death's Backyard, maybe. Death's Park, Death's Playground, Death's Stadium, where you drop dead sliding into home plate—but only in front of thousands of devoted screaming fans. But to lie down on the back porch and expire—fuck that shit.

Getting dressed, he went down to Go, Inc. (franchise health club and delicatessen), and bought two containers of high protein powder. The label promised him lungs of iron in three months. Ah, the deep-lunged Menelaus. Appleton before, Menelaus after. And he remembered a mural he had seen while in the railcar, the Proteus. How the gods and heroes had flowered on that ceiling! Such beautiful blue robes as you would imagine angels wearing and such grandly formed muscle—reaching and gesturing and flying— and at the center is that mystery man Proteus, changing shapes in spokes, while the shadows from the shifting landscape outside flickered on him— earth, air, fire, bird god, over and over, as in a child's magic lantern show. That's what he wanted—to be a part of that.

For now, however, at Go, Inc., he must ask the simple question about "getting in shape."

"An aerobics class for septuagenarians," the owner suggested.

"What about hikes for septuagenarians?" Appleton asked.

"Yes, absolutely"

"Are there many groups like that?"

"Many?" His voice went up, and he pulled out a volume as big as a phone directory. "The Rosetta Stone Exchange is so specialized it can get you aerobics for overweight male restaurateurs over fifty."

"O.K. Sounds promising."

Meanwhile Appleton was getting distracted by this makeshift foyer. The health food store reminded him of a Witch's Kitchen. Appleton could imagine an old crone—and her friends—flying down at him on broomsticks, giving him the mystic signs, just grazing the iodine-colored bottles.

"If I take all this stuff and I do my workouts, can I build up tissue even at my age?" Appleton asked.

"You bet. Think of Jack Lalanne. You know what he does in his free time just to keep his neck and jaws strong?"

"He chews sponges," Appleton answered. "And suppose I do double workouts?" Appleton went on. "Am I building up tissue or just tearing it down or some darn thing?"

"Depends on how you go about it," the owner said. The man had a kind of eagle-like agility. Seemed ageless, really. In a white tank top.

Appleton got himself in front of the full-length mirror. "I want to go kind of broad at the shoulder and narrow at the hip. To impress the Governor." But in the mirror there was also some weirdness behind him. A sudden, creepy-looking creature in a fishbowl.

"That is the strangest fish I have ever seen," Appleton said, looking over his sort-of-sloping shoulder.

"Pet piranha. My wife says he looks like the lead in *I Was a Teenage Werewolf*. When he looks at you, head on, look out."

"As you were saying—"

"Follow this schedule," he answered. "If followed, we guarantee results in thirty days."

"And what about"—Appleton flipped his wrist, but in a Marlboro sort of way.

The owner flipped his wrist back. "That's the best part. When you're finished with our program, you'll want to do it with the gals anywhere from one to three times every twenty-four hours."

"Want to do it? I've got a corner on that market already. There's a difference between desire and delivery."

"Desire is delivery," the owner answered grandly and metaphysically. "But that's something you've got to learn."

Well.

Even though Appleton had moved out of range of that mutant fish, he still felt spooked. This was a good start. He felt especially well armed now to meet the Governor.

And so the next month saw him in a motel room in Capitol City, with some hard rock and roll shaking the walls from the next room over as he got dressed. Usually, in such cases, he would pound out "fuck you" in Morse code as answer back. But this time it was different. The music was all wonderfully about some lady's man who always looked so sharp he had women running and screaming after him. "Starched shirt," the song said, "polished shoes." (Appleton put them on.) "It just drives the women folks wild. Oh."

Appleton stood in the mirror in full suit and tie, looking (sunlamp-) tanned and twenty years younger from Go, Inc. "They go wild, 'cause he's so decked out—Wow!" And as the guitar lit up again, Appleton lit a cigarette for effect, and cleared out of the room. In the hall, he nearly collided with the janitor, who was doing up the hall.

Whistle. "Look mighty sharp. Who you seeing today?"

"The Governor," Appleton answered.

He actually believed him. "Well, good luck!"

One macho puff. Over the shoulder. Still, it ended up like Bette Davis. "Thanks."

And now, if everything were perfect, he'd have "Marlboro" tattooed on the back of his hand, like a rare stamp. But there was nothing there but veins— still, as he drove away and got to the Capitol, he felt the Witch's Kitchen had—zap!—turned him into something as powerful as Menelaus. Or an atomic bomb.

The conference room was arranged according to the Governor's close designs, and all were waiting for this Professor Emeritus of Law (which he was) to arrive. The place was furnished like the inside of the famed Proteus smoking car—it was all posed damsels (in this case in marble) dropping their bath towels in about 1890. Some of them lit themselves up with the orange, coned-shaped lamps they were holding; all pointed toward the mural on the ceiling. A Phidian (Praxitelean?) George Washington with abs of steel clutched some thunderbolts. Yes, Appleton could remember the dip in the railway car decades ago and the image on the wall presenting the Libric scales (much like Washington here), and she seemed to hold her blindfold askew, while all the while the zodiacal signs raced in a circle, with Cancer opening and shutting his pinchers. And then the steward was bringing in cups of coffee and the card game of Shakespeare, all on a platter—the trump is the one of King Lear. Outside the hollowed out landscape shimmered under the touches of lightning, as though under the carefully wrought bolts of Zeus himself: one touch and a crop of green land suddenly appears, as one spot upon the landscape, flourishing under the following rains—two more strokes and there are more islands of trees (birch, aspen, and evergreen) and as the islands gradually join, Appleton realized, way back then, that that juncture was the mossy rock of Oregon, with the irrepressible Columbia going through, with the still steady swiftness of Ocean. A land to take your breath away.

The Governor came in talking.

"I'm ready to sign," this Man in the Mansion said. "We've drawn something up, based on your suggestions. But I wanted to hear one last pro and con before we lurch forward."

With that, Appleton saw the Governor's interlocutor. He looked a little like his own son Billings, but he knew that was not being fair. He resembled him in his salad (bar) days—scrappy, appealing, querulous,

and impossible. Appleton used to remember a college professor saying, "She has about as much irony
in her veins as Florence Nightingale." Well, this man
was just the opposite—he *had* so much irony, he could
give transfusions. And in seeing him, he knew the
Governor had set him up. To fight. Instead of being a
pro-forma consultation, this was going to be a show-
down. Thanks, Gov.

The man—introduced as Samuel Hollingsworth—
said, "I want to make it quite clear I'm not here to cut
down Dr. Appleton Romney's proposal. I just want to
suggest some problems it might raise."

Oh? Sophisticated and definitely not born again.
Yet. And he appeared to be speaking not just to him
and the Governor but to a woman who was present—
who seemed to sit as though behind a veil, and not
at all at the table but in a row of chairs against the
wall. Libra.

"Well, what sort of protocol should we follow?"
the Governor asked, trying to be as winning and
boyish as possible. Days when The Man in the Mansion was in a good humor like this, Appleton thought,
he could bring us, state-wide, paradise and winter
apples and country dances, but let him get sour on
something, and you had disastrous eclipses, sunspots
and global field burning. All the way from Portland to
Courtland. The wages of having a Renaissance man
as your Prince. "Perhaps," he went on, "our eldest
should speak."

"No thanks," Appleton answered, and almost
added, "Sire." "I can tell Mr. Hollingsworth has some

things he's burning to say. *So let's go in order of need.*" Besides, how could he speak before figuring out that weird veiled apparition at the back?

"What I have to say will only take about a sentence," Samuel Hollingsworth said. (Famous last words.) "An Executive Order barring discrimination against homosexuals in the workplace will be instantaneously challenged."

"Anything of value almost always is," Appleton answered.

"I'm not finished—. Petitions will be circulated and a ballot measure will arise specifically designed to strike it down. We understand it will be called Measure Eight. The overall public foment could prove to be far worse for gays and lesbians than if we had done nothing at all."

"This is pretty thin stuff," Appleton replied. He had his number even from the beginning. "Such things don't just occur spontaneously. What makes you think there's the machinery in place to create such a groundswell?"

"You've never heard of the Oregon Protection Alliance?" The Governor asked.

"Never."

The Governor threw himself back and gave him a heavenward look that was more like a whistle. "They're a group that got started by a Baptist minister and the chairman of the State Republican party," he said. "They're a fountainhead of conservative causes, including Truth, Justice and the American Way."

Oh, that way. Suddenly it seemed to Appleton that

he remembered meeting their leader somewhere—a man with long, lousy sideburns. And as he made that connection, instantly doubt and "horror chill" stole over his bones. The California handoff. Appleton was sure, he was tragically sure, that this was a group he had inadvertently donated to at one time.

"Let me put it in plain cash register English," Samuel said. "If you put this Executive Order through, be prepared to go out and raise half a million dollars to counter the Opposition. Because that's what a political advertising campaign will cost you come November."

The Governor looked at him. "Are you willing to do that, Appleton?"

"I don't see why you're asking me," Appleton answered. "I only want to plant the seed. I'm not responsible for the Noah's flood that follows." In the pause, there was also the Proteus Precedent. What would Dr. Wren—the black man who had taken the case to court—say? He could see him, in that precedent, demanding his tea in the dining car, and then the train coming to an unscheduled stop, and the crew ejecting him through the back door. But somewhere in the Oregon legal system, a suit was being filed somewhere, a judge was ruling in his favor, and a precedent was being set, which They had immediately hushed up. Only to crop up again through the vines, the silt, like fruit or treasure. Where a minority is concerned, the burden of proof is on the blocker.

Now Appleton looked at that veiled statue, that female unknown who was sitting toward the back and listening. He was willing to do just about anything now to get her attention. "I don't like the choice you're giving me," he answered at last. "It's like the question we used to ask when we were kids—would you like to be dunked in a privy or have a shit pie in the face?"

"Let's stay on the subject," the Governor said, smiling but making a sour taste at the same time.

Samuel answered with a wry grimace. "What we're saying," he went on, "is that half a million could go to other essential causes. Besides, gays and lesbians are protected in the workplace under the laws of our Constitution. If we invoke an Executive Order, we're essentially giving them special rights."

"But that's of course what we must do," Appleton answered. "That's why I came down here. I have a legal interest in this case. There are special groups such as blacks and women who do need additional protection against discrimination because they are vulnerable."

"But gays and lesbians are not born into a minority status like those others," Samuel countered. "What they have is a lifestyle, not a condition."

"And you're sure about that?" Appleton asked. "Your tin-can phone to God has given you this useful piece of information?"

"Gentlemen," the Governor said, "please." He was much delighted in being the serene pocket in this uproar.

Nevertheless, Appleton had made the Apparition smile. She had drawn back her veil. "Don't tell me," he said, primed, "I have to raise a half million dollars just to support what's right. Whatever happens in the wake of this Order happens, and perhaps the price will be sky-high. But don't sit there saying that that money is just sitting waiting to be rechanneled to more cost-efficient causes when it hasn't even been raised yet."

Their wild and wooly governor looked even more elated. "Appleton, you're just sitting in that Proteus dining car again, aren't you? Still thinking about your major research project."

"In a manner of speaking, yes," Appleton answered.

Samuel was much cast down by this opposing sunlight. He whipped out a paper in retaliation.

"I just want to leave you with an outside reader's opinion," he said. "A person highly qualified but who shall remain nameless. He says, 'There is a distinctly fine line between protecting homosexuality and sanctioning it. Who a person sleeps with is nobody's business and constitutes a right to privacy. However, if the Governor were to forbid discrimination in the work place, he would send out a strong message that there was more to being gay and lesbian than simple sexual behavior. He would, in fact, be saying that it is acceptable, and beyond that, preferred, since he would be singling out one group for exoneration. State agencies would be particularly susceptible to this message and might, for example, start placing more and more foster children with gay and lesbian couples. Because of this, I ask the Governor to seriously reconsider the action he is about to take.'"

A few Zorro counter-swishes from the old gay blade, if you please. Thank you. No, Thank you. Gay? It was so obvious Samuel had written that opinion himself. Swish, swish. He'd take care of that *tout de suite*. 'Cause the well-dressed man just drives the women folks wild. Wow! The apparition was looking at him, Appleton. "Governor, may I respond?" (How he loved those days when they talked about foxy ladies and those days, older still, when women jumped out of cakes, and those days, ancient, ancient, when Carmen, secretary in one of their offices, danced on the desk at the Christmas office party, using two staplers as castanets—*Ole!*)

The Governor looked at his watch. "You've got forty-five seconds, Appleton. Talk and talk fast."

"The Proteus Precedent says it all," he said. "The burden of proof is on the majority. We need to show cause that there isn't prejudice, and since no proof has been submitted, we have to offer protection and amends where appropriate, even at the risks mentioned in the 'expert's' letter. Besides, suppose a few kids are placed with gay people—coupled or single—I can think of some cases where this might be of enormous benefit. To everyone concerned."

"Time's up," the Governor said, and seemed to be Groucho, suddenly, on *You Bet Your Life*. "You've both been mesmerizing to listen to"—eyebrows flipping—"and I could go on talking with you all afternoon, but it's time now to move on. I want to thank you both for coming, and now I just need the time to do

the necessary worrying. I'll let you both know what
I decide."

Appleton stood up with the rest. Hear ye, hear
ye, the Governor is leaving the room. He did, in fact,
look a little like Groucho. Appleton glanced up again
at the Phidian George Washington presiding over
them all, Schwarzenegger pecs in perfect accent. Now
he would have to wait to see where the lightning bolt
would be striking.

◇

Well, he won the argument, but lost the war. The
Governor was persuaded to launch his referendum,
but then Measure Eight passed and struck it down.
By then he had met Eleanor and was living with her
in her castle. And then along comes Measure Nine,
and after the incident in the Overpark, yes, indeed,
Appleton was out to have Samuel's ass on a golden
platter. Nevertheless, in the months to come—with
Measure Nine on the rise, Samuel's star also began
rising with astonishing and frightening speed, and so
Appleton decided to take the bull by the horns and
go see his son, Billings, down at Arden University.
Appleton knew he knew plenty about Samuel, and he
thought he could get it out of him, under the guise
of burying the hatchet, while giving him that tour
of the renovated St. Christopher's College—the one
Appleton had helped establish and the one which
Billings had "revamped" all on his own. Shit.

St. Christopher's had *once* been a Great Books college within the University and a model for the rest of the country.

Once. So much for that.

"Now, Dad," Billings said, shaking out his keys to the building so they could go up to his office, "I want you to try to keep an open mind."

Since last time, Billings had become very meek, almost hangdog. The iron grating, so once familiar, now reminded Appleton of Rodin's Gate of Hell. It swung past them, and they were inside. He turned on the lights. Wax dummies appeared in military uniform. "How nice," Appleton said. "Visual aids."

"This floor has been taken over by ROTC," he said. "Don't pay them any mind."

"So you gave a whole floor of my college to the Military, Billings. Would you like to explain yourself?"

"Everything," Billings said, "will be explained once we get to the computer."

The next floor, however, had no computer and was even worse. For they were now at a bunch of friezes. Rorschach blocks in stone. Evidently some mix of psychology and sociology.

"Normative Studies," Billings said.

Appleton felt like turning on his heel. It occurred to him that all of this was the reason he had signed into the Rosium Rest Home in the first place. This immense heart failure. Not his but his son's. This belief only in Fashion and the foreseeable future. What, Appleton wondered, had been on Billings' mind when he had taken over—the thought that his father was going off his rocker or the thought that his father was outdated and ought to be in a rocker? Or maybe for him as well as everybody else these days they amounted to the same thing.

"Two down and one to go," Appleton answered. "What can we expect on the third floor, Billings? Dinosaur eggs?"

"I told you we were going to have a look at a computer."

"Is that what St. Christopher's is now?" Appleton asked. "A computer?" Nevertheless, he got to the top of the stairs feeling, as they say, strong and able despite himself. Maybe because of lots of workouts at Go, Inc. For Appleton was delighted to find, even now, that he was still breathing easy. He was wearing a polo shirt and jeans—something he never would have tried in his non-program days. He guessed he could say he was dressed to kill. He was ready to take on Samuel again, and he was ready, he guessed, to witness, even, St. Christopher's do-over (fuck-over?) in post-modern attire. He had been dreading this day since he didn't know when—and you know what? He was doing all right. And it was because he was still after Samuel's ass. While Billings fiddled with the keys on the second set of double doors, he looked out the window. The campus was filled with pink lines of emerging ornamental plum, and here and there the little paths were dotted with white and purple lilac.

By now Billings had turned on the lights. They were going inside.

"I guess we should start with the basics," he said.

"The college has been reduced by two-thirds since you left."

"Did you do that or the University?" Appleton asked.

"The University doesn't even consider us reduced at all. ROTC and Normative Studies are component parts of our new combined program. In their eyes, we're much bigger than ever."

"Check. And how much room does that leave for arts and letters, math and science?"

"That depends on whether you are taking the military degree or the normative one," Billings answered.

"The military degree leaves more room for the arts?" Appleton asked with a decided edge.

"Dad, cut it out."

"And what's next?" he asked.

"Our series of specialized courses which substitute for the liberal arts."

"Such as?"

"Interpretative Sexual Dance."

"And?"

"Recipes and Embedded Gender Coding."

"And?"

"The Minor Films of Alfred Hitchcock."

Great. Five weeks of *Blackmail* instead of *The Aeneid*.

"And," he added, "*Letters of a Disillusioned Androgynous Gardener*."

"Isn't that the author that helped us on No on Eight?"

"Right."

"But the book's only been out a few months. They study that in college already?"

"It's a whole course."

Billings pressed the exit key, looked guilty with a Gioconda smile, if Giocondas can look guilty.

"You mean the whole four-year classical core curriculum has been scrapped?" Appleton asked.

"Basically. That's the bottom line. Basically, basically. Everybody was saying that everyone in the core was dead."

"I should be so lucky," Appleton said. "Let me have a go at that thing. For practice. For something I really want to ask you about. Ellie's taught me how to work one of them those."

With some effort, Appleton conjured up the old-time curriculum. On a disk that was a back-up to a back-up to a back-up. In his mind, in a mirror, a spook came in and smiled. "By crackie" (the spook said, gap-toothed), "we've done it." It was just like playing pinball with Derek, on Ellie's Cymbeline machine. You hit buzzers and niches until a whole garden of red and yellow roses lit up. But unfortunately in this game there was no garland to be won. He kept trying to put a generic student through the one-time standard set of liberal arts courses, and he was getting blocked every step of the way. "Metabolic Intervention" kept coming up and "History of Equitation." There was no Shakespeare, either. The machine finally buzzed, exited, and gave him a dozen smiley faces.

"Pretty bad, huh?" Billings asked.

"I think you better count yourself lucky that ROTC and Normative Studies will still have anything to do with you. History of Equitation? I heard that was short for Old Horse."

This hoary chestnut flew straight past Billings. "Does it help to say it's this way in most liberal arts colleges all over the country?" Billings asked.

Appleton gave him an Armageddon glance. "Don't you see—the loss of critical thinking in colleges is one of the reasons the OPA can flourish."

Billings nodded. "Samuel authorized all this years ago. With his special Quincentenary Projection Plan. Educational Updating for the State. But now some of us are beginning to have second thoughts about all that we've lost. Dad," he said at last, "what the hell are we going to do?"

"There are two things we can do." How, Appleton wondered, did I get hooked into "we"? "*You* can either let St. Christopher's run its natural course—that is, into a nonstop descent into an academic salad bar— or you can call Jeremy."

"Jeremy? But Jeremy got thrown out years ago," Billings answered.

"Exactly. That's why you're going to have to light a fire under the Administration's ass to get him back."

A contemplative Billings. A new look.

"But Jeremy doesn't like all the ongoing educational fashions," Billings said.

"Right."

"Jeremy doesn't like Normative Studies."

"Right."

"Jeremy doesn't like ROTC."

"Right."

"Jeremy doesn't like high school credit for college—"

"Right, but—" Appleton said.

"Yes? But what?"

"Jeremy is an educational genius," Appleton told him.

"What does that have do with anything? He doesn't cooperate."

"That's all I've got to say about it," Appleton replied. "Because I really need to talk about what I came for." Mentally, Appleton had to mount a podium before getting on with this. "Just exactly what is your relationship to Samuel Hollingsworth?" he asked. "Who is Samuel Hollingsworth? And what's his function here at the University?"

"Samuel Hollingsworth's spot," Billings said, "is what they call a 'created position.' His degree is in General Education, but when he got into Oregon, he was made a City Planner for Capitol City and later Arden. He essentially built the whole Arden Dome by gaining pull from the legislators. Then he was hired on as adjunct faculty here to teach courses on psychological balance in cities, in a program called PICK-WICK, and then not long after that, he was made dean, where he got this humongous grant to redo St. Christopher's and project a four-year program leading to the Quincentenary Celebration of the 'New World,' in diversified form. I think he's going to call it the Arden Renaissance Fair, come this fall."

Appleton now had to think back—to terribly

painful territory. But that was the reason he had come here in the first place. And that mental spook was cracking that fucking smile again! "Do you have reason to know anything about his personal life?"

"Much reason. We were army buddies going way back. How do you think I got this job?"

"Did you know a former wife of his—Gloria?"

"Yes," Billings answered. "Actually I knew her well. A sort of saintly woman who went down early."

"Did you know she died (and dove) from a diving tower?"

"Yes, I was there."

"You were?—I saw it in the newspaper," Appleton said, recalling.

"Everybody," Billings said, "read about it. That Aqua Cavalcade was the jewel of Seattle at the time."

"What did he say when she died?" Appleton asked.

"That she was no longer his wife but that he had tried to take care of her but failed."

Appleton had to stop again. "What were you doing with him when Gloria Hollingsworth did her terminal dive decades ago?" he asked at last.

"We were ex-army buddies, catching up," he said. "We bought tickets together."

"Later to both become college administrators?"

"Does that sound so strange?" Billings asked.

"No. They're quite parallel, really. Was Samuel big on the Republican Party then?"

"Absolutely. The young Republican's young Republican," Billings answered.

"But later he became an ardent liberal."

Billings paused. "Yes. Somewhere in the grant application process. In the 1980s. I can't remember the change exactly, but it was very smooth. It happened when we were redoing the college."

"No doubt it was smooth. Ever known him to be a member of the OPA?"

"Dad, don't be ridiculous. Samuel's not stupid. One word about that and he'd be hounded clean out of the Oregon Academic System and Oregon Politics itself. Especially as a hopeful for state senator."

"Maybe now. But not necessarily ten years ago. And maybe not in the future. Anyway," he said, "let's try something. Let's try to call something up on him. You know all the back alleys and crotchets of these programs. Can't you dig up something on his history?"

Billings stared at his father. "But why would I want to do that?"

"Because," Appleton said, "I suspect you'll want, very soon, to clear yourself of all past associations with him. And at a very crucial time. To dig this up now might give you security in the bank at some future date."

Billings did not say another word but went straight to his work. And like Santa Claus, he did not take long to come up with something out of his pack. He stared into the computer screen, reminding Appleton of Ellie. "Sure enough," he said, "these closed files tell me that there is a whole confession, on disk, which Samuel wrote."

"Eureka," Appleton said. "Where? Where?"

Billings typed again. And again. Even did a little program on the side.

His face. "My God," he said, "it's in the files of the OPA."

"But where?"

Billings tried again. "It doesn't say. You'll have to track that one down yourself."

Eureka, still. Appleton slapped his son on the back. "Doesn't matter, doesn't matter. We're really in business now."

But Billings stopped him. "But this doesn't mean he's a member, Dad. It may mean the opposite."

But Appleton had him on that one, too. And he recalled the debate back in the Governor's office. "My dear son, the OPA habitually requires a confession from everyone before he or she enters their membership. I've found that out since wrangling with Samuel in front of the Governor. That's the way they keep them in. That's inside knowledge, too."

Billings smiled. "This is all quite bizarre."

"You've just described the entire state of Oregon, my friend. Anyway," Appleton said, by way of leave, "that'll do nicely for now. I'm off to find me an OPA vault somewhere. For now, thanks, thanks much. I'll even forgive you the destruction of my whole academy."

"We're rebuilding. We're rebuilding. And meanwhile," Billings concluded, "I'll keep trying to track down the files from here."

Appleton started down the stairs, seeing spring vistas at every landing until he was out the door.

Was there anything more wonderful than a Saturday campus? So many stretches, of light and shade, of leisure. It reminded him of a book he once owned, *A Guide to Excellent Picture-making.* One photograph showed a parasoled woman leaning over a rose bush with a latticework at her back, and the caption read, "Poise is essential to pose." That was the way it was on a Saturday campus; people did not run around; they posed. And in the same book many interior shots of 1920s French doors or fluted window glass. That's what he had seen from inside St. Christopher's, although he had been too distracted at the time to reflect on them. Now he'd like to have Samuel hanging upside down. By his bootstraps. Accessories are essential to the pose.

He found Ellie back at Harold's.

"Just look at this," Ellie said. She was pointing to the TV. "Moira Shearer. She has just about perfect features."

Whenever you walked in on Ellie at anything, it always seemed like she had just ordered up something special—not only for herself but for anybody who was lucky enough to join her.

The screen seemed to be all silver. Clark Gable crossed against a diaphanous curtain. Flash. Accessories often—

"And there's that child of theirs," she said. "That boy." She put her two bags together and switched off the set. "Well, that does it for me. Find out anything interesting?"

"I find it interesting that Samuel made a complete

political switcheroo somewhere in the 1980s. That's a start. And there's some files somewhere. A confession. We could well dig that up."

He put his arms around her.

She kissed him. "What are you planning? A heist?" she asked.

"Yes, let's not waste any time," he answered.

◇

Two months later, he had a new appointment with the Governor (now ex-Governor) to follow up on the next step. He knew he had a "cabin" on the coast, so he arranged to see him there—he'd heard the OPA had offices somewhere about. Ellie went on up ahead of him on the bus—he was to join her in a few days. She was to hunt for more collectibles.

When his morning finally arrived, he found himself travelling a long road out of sleep even though he was waking up early. And in the car, he kept reminding himself I really must watch where I'm going. After several slow hours, finally, up ahead, Hamilton came up out of the mist, and he felt proud to be getting there by seven. He felt bold. And how else did he feel? Brassy. Wide awake at last. Like Ray Anthony on his horn. He remembered when Ray did a street solo on television. It was night; he was carrying his trumpet and he got captivated by a young lady on a theater billboard, and so he played a hot "Birth of the Blues" to her. Just the way he felt about going to see the Governor again—a hot solo.

The sunlight was taking over. He turned off his

headlights. Everywhere the outskirts of Hamilton seemed to be reflected in puddles within a green depth of fern. It was what he would call flamingo weather—plashy, with alternate glares and rain on the sidewalk, with perfect surfaces for orange webbed feet. He remembered how the rain came down when they arrived there eons ago! Basic training. The whole place seemed to be one shaded, wet grove of ferns. The squalls rose out of the West, battered the ocean until it became a chaos of tempest and loose-connected lightning, and then rolled over them, trying the walls, newly hewn, of their fort. Everywhere there was the smell of lumber back then, and everywhere the sound of voices like the pattering of drops.

"Too full up. Some will have to go to the hotel," one of the officers had said to him. Oh for those old forting days!

"Not enough serving dishes to go around. We'll have to scoop the mess out garbage pails."

The rain dripped and poured, flowering into puddles, the grand rhododendrons rising just outside the hotel window back then, their magenta fuchsia blooms flourishing under the storm. Beyond, through the parted red curtains of the hawthorn, he could see, as a frightened young private, the breakers dashing themselves upon the beach, in timed avalanches of water.

In the window of the Hamilton Hotel, a bowl of magenta and white variegated dahlias was framed, and beyond, there was the fortress, where he marched on guard duty, night after night in the rain—who would have believed that all this marching could have come from a boy who went back home every night to a vase of magenta and white dahlias?

He had kept up his march, watching the loads of cedar being brought into the lumber mill. He kept thinking of the night before, when he had awakened from a dream in iambic pentameter; he had been full of lines to rival Shakespeare, but before he could write them down, he had fallen asleep again. On the walls of the fort, he could see the winds out on the ocean, driving the clouds in; the glassy face was lost and the surface became indented with rain and reflections, much as a pool at the base of a waterfall becomes indented when visited by someone who wishes to drink or behold an image.

The clouds clattered and crashed. The rhododendrons were stripped of their blossoms in pink and red ribbons, even while the beautiful maritime hydrangeas stayed intact, composed in their blue and purple reflections of the sky. Below, the Hamilton Opera House opened its green awning to keep its ticket buyers from getting wet. There was a pause in the storm; they were besieged by gulls; then there was a flood of water.

He remembered feeling cold and damp, as if he were a bulb in the spaded green earth, and then he could remember becoming red in the face.

The doctor (a black man), checking the men over, took one look at him after he got back.

"Send that man directly to the infirmary," he said.

He couldn't be sure how he got there, but the next

moment, he recalled waking up in a bed, with other men with the same malady (influenza) beside him.

It was time to get up. How long had he been there? Time had passed. Someone had put a bowl of yellow dahlias—huge, almost as big as sunflowers—on his night stand. He opened a window. The smell of the sea was different. The salt burned in his nostrils, reminding him that he had almost died.

"Attention." His commanding officer came into the room. "Good to see you're better, Private. Here are two overnight passes."

"Thank you."

"I'm taking you off the wall and putting you inside the lumber mill."

"Thank you, sir—may I ask something else?"

"Yes."

"Where is Dr. Wren?" Appleton had asked.

"Dr. Wren? There is no Dr. Wren."

"But he's the Negro doctor who saved my life. I need to see him."

"There's a whole team of doctors here who pulled you through, but he's not one of them."

But he remembered distinctly—a black face bending near, offering him medicine, his body going chill suddenly, when water—from his hands—was pressed to his lips.

The commanding officer left. Appleton felt destitute. There is no Dr. Wren. As he headed out with his two passes, everywhere the gold ocean created maelstroms of reflections—on walls, on roofs—and above, the sky opened into mirrors, which reflected back these weather patterns of solar storms. In town, all the shops had stacked roses and chrysanthemums, and in the dime store window, there was an array of paper kites. It was his secret hope, as he walked past the roadsters of Marine Boulevard, that Dr. Wren would reappear one more time, as a miracle of the spring. Because for some reason, he feared he was dead. Appleton wandered and wandered until the boardwalk lights came on.

There was nothing left but the Opera House—and inside, suddenly a great tone sounded from the organ as it rose from the underground and with it was revealed the Magic Garden of Ozma, then later the meadow of Persephone, where a blue-gray Hades snatched the maiden away, overturning the paper tulips and daffodils gathered in her lap. Lost like Dr. Wren. The hills and vales on the poster-painted walls were a deep sea green, punctuated by small lights that were to represent roses and crocuses (purple clustered with candle flames for stamens). The onstage Persephone was like a scarf being borne away in the wind, with her mother following soon after, in a chariot drawn by dragons. Ceres, advancing, was the color of hay and corn stalks, and where e'er she walked, garlands seemed to spring up behind her.

And now the whole opera house seemed to flower and change, like those racing shadows on the walls of the Proteus dining car. Ceres now was gathering poppies and, being offered food and shelter by an old man and his daughter, was being taken to the sick bed of the dying son. Miraculously, she was putting her lips against his and the vitality was shooting through him again. (At this moment, the walls of the house fell aside and the meadows were alive with lights once more.) She then rolled him into a bundle and placed him in the fire where the fumes of mortality were purged from his body, and at last he stood up, whole and cleansed. That was himself—Appleton—touched by Dr. Wren!

He stumbled back to the barracks. He broke into the fort secretariat. Dr. Wren's address at all costs! And there it was, all right, at the back of the roll-down desk. And so, in total secrecy, he wrote him a letter.

That was the important moment—his. Acknowledging being saved. Even though, later, a letter came back with the word "deceased" written rudely across it.

So where is my spring miracle now? Appleton asked, still driving. I'll tell you—Wren was the one who established the Proteus Precedent! And he was thinking about it once more.

And now the landscape up ahead was the promise of yet another new life, as the town arrived, even while it seemed one 1950s Roman brick rambler rambling to at least the tenth power, oh yes rambling rose, with all the little bathroom fixtures being put out—as concrete novelties—on the lawns; the pink of the plashy flamingoes matching the pink of the wild rhododendrons lining the boulevard named, quite placidly, "Ocean Shore Boulevard," "Wave Crest Drive," with "Elysium Place" perhaps being a new avenue recently touched by Ceres. Yes, the parks were so carefully laurelled—here's one now—so arranged with clusters of pruned roses and the domesticated cousins of their wild maritime sisters—those rhododendrons again, that you expected at anytime to find fine ladies at 1950s tea tables eating baked avocados, cardinal salad (beets, among other things, mind you), and slices of grape juice pie.

He went right for the Sputnik Motel, where Eleanor had signed him in. He opened the morning door quietly with his own key, and was pleased to find again the turquoise kitchenette whose every corner he remembered from olden stays.

Ellie, lying on the bed and stirring, had heard him come in.

"Had another migraine, honey? he asked, reading her face.

"Yes." She laughed and propped herself up. "But I'm better. I loved taking the bus here. The few days to myself were perfect."

She got up and drew on her robe. By the mirror, she had to steady herself. "So we should leave soon— to see the ex-Governor?"

"Yes—you're sure you're ready to get up?" he asked, still watching her closely. Ellie had opened the window, the ocean swooping its way in, like a crook-necked swan, white and elegant. The sun was still dodging the mist, with the unlit moon fading more and more above the water. The sum total effect of all this pastel was—you guessed it—he wanted to jump Ellie's bones.

"Yes, I am ready. You still seem rattled," she said. "And not just by the ex-Governor."

"I feel like I'm losing my memory," he said. "You know those times when your computer has a disk failure and those smiley faces come on and the sign says, 'for subnormal functions, strike any key'?" He didn't wait for her to answer. "Well, that's the way my brain gets sometimes. I have this hideous suspicion that sometime back I accidentally ended up putting money in the coffers of the Oregon Protection Alliance."

"That's awful—I'd stick with amnesia," she said, laughing.

She smiled and got dressed, his lust still the worse for wear. How strange. When he had first come in, her face on the pillow had reminded him with such easiness of stone sculptures he had seen in Italy— ones which Michelangelo had perhaps carved upon but never finished, the portraits still asleep in the stone. But now she was all motor skills and motor power; she was right behind him, riding his tail.

They had until two before he was to see the ex-Governor, so they took a small tour up the coast, viewed the barracks and the yellow tulips again and spun back, for a visit to every souvenir and antique and collectibles store in the county. The ghost of Dr. Wren was following them, he was aware, while Eleanor was doing a little comparison shopping to psyche out the competition even more. Meanwhile by himself he climbed up an ivied cliff, reaching the locally famous Moss Mansion, headquarters for the Oregon Coast Archive Society. There was a sign in the window which said, quite whimsically, "Excellent

Editor Wanted." The snow from the trees drifted down the bluff.

"I've been working on a little something," he told the attendant, as long as he was there—and honoring his recollections—"which might interest you. A memoir of my forting days in Hamilton. When I almost died of influenza. And the black doctor who saved me."

"We've been looking for something like that," the attendant said, who was at least as old as he was. That old? "Send us some text and we'll see what we can work out. And by all means send the complete manuscript." He gave him his card. Degas.

Staring, Appleton, of course, was deluged with thoughts of paintings. But the canvases became something else. Stairways. Shadows of wrought iron railings. White silk rustled by wind machines. A woman with a name like Veronica holding up her hands in sudden fear on a lobby card, while her lovely white gown rustled.

"I think I know you," Appleton said. "Didn't we meet in Hollywood? My name is Appleton Romney."

"The dramaturge in *She's Working Her Way Through College!* You're the one who punched out Ronald Reagan, bless your heart." The skeletal man laughed and lit a cigarette.

"Those aren't times I particularly like remembering," Appleton said, taken aback. "But did I punch out Ronald Reagan?"

Surely this man must be given to whimsy.

"Sure as hell did," Degas answered. "Punched his lights clean out."

"Oh, no. That can't be right. I really wasn't a dramaturge, you know, but a more-or-less stand-in legal advisor to the show."

"Obviously it was more," Degas said.

"And you? What about you? Aren't you a famous director?"

"I am now what they call a cult classic," Degas answered. "Sometimes, having that title, I feel like I should dress up like Boris Karloff's Monster and hide out in these coastal hills and conduct strange rites." His smoke went straight over Appleton's head. His smile was a firm crease of wrinkles. "Back then, however," he went on, "I was simply a creator of B films for RKO. They weren't building any churches in my name back then."

"Then what were you doing on the set of *She's Working?* I don't recall the reason," Appleton said.

"They thought the director was going to walk out any minute because of Reagan problems—remember how he hated his job—and they were going to have me fill in, just in case. I'm surprised you don't remember."

"Oh God yes, Reagan was a professor. Now I remember. I was also there to show him how to act like one." Appleton made a face.

"Not exactly a congruent role," Degas said. "I thank my lucky stars Humberstone the first director hung in there."

Now the Wren Memory was pushing him forward into another. A grand fundraising dinner. With

Ron and Nancy. Other horrors, which would no doubt be unearthed if they ever tapped into Samuel's Confession.

"Gargoyles, gargoyles!" Appleton heard himself say suddenly.

"Come again?"

"That's what I always say whenever I get bad memories. That punch-out is coming back as we speak. Although I talk a pretty big macho story, Reagan is the only man I've ever hit in my entire life."

"To me, that's talking a pretty big macho story indeed."

Degas was smiling and seeming to levitate behind his desk. All mixed in with the gargoyles was a moment Appleton remembered where he was going down an obscure hallway on the Warner Brothers set, and he passed between two mirrors and parted palms and there he found both of them, Ronald Regan and Virginia Mayo, the female lead, decked out on couches. Ronald, stripped down to his BVDs, was wearing Virginia's emerald headdress. Virginia, holding her stomach with laughter, was also clutching a football.

"I guess," Appleton said, "it would be fun to speculate on what would have happened if you had taken over on the set. Imagine that whole glitzy musical that was all co-eds and burleycue queens being changed from the vision of an ex-fullback studio director into interiors with shadows and subtly cat things everywhere, even in the conservatory with the possibly Venus fly traps. Imagine Virginia Mayo in a white nightdress rustled by a wind machine."

"Imagine Ronald Reagan in one!" Degas put in.

"Now that *is* grotesque," Appleton answered, laughing. "But, in fact, I saw nearly that."

A little clock chimed one. Shouldered by a mini-Atlas. Through the window, beyond the drifts of the snowball trees, there was a big street scene in the parking lot of the huge Balboa Inn across the way.

"Well, I have to go," Appleton said. "About this editor's position which you have posted in the window—"

"Yes?"

"Would the editor necessarily have to live in Hamilton?"

"Not necessarily, since arrangements could be made for the manuscripts to be sent elsewhere. However, he would have to be present for board meetings, of course."

"She. I'm thinking of my stepdaughter." Appleton said. " Could I have an application?"

He nodded, dismissed his cigarette.

Taking the sheets of paper, Appleton felt a premonition, as if there was more to this than mere job searching. He said, "By the way, do you do any more movies? I haven't seen any around."

"The last one was in 1959 with Richard Carlson. But I still do shadowy novels. Under a pseudonym, of course. In fact I'm doing one now sort of on the OPA."

"Really?"

"Yes." Degas had gone to the window. "As a matter of fact, their coastal convention is going on here as we speak. Actually, it may take some patience getting through all that when you drive out. They're just now breaking up."

"Well, I'll be ding-donged," Appleton said. "This is like meeting a French chef on Monday and hearing his name three times by the next day."

"I suppose you know one of their offices is right upstairs."

"No. I knew they were somewhere around here, but not this close."

"It's our friend Reagan," Degas said, "who inspired this whole thing in the first place. Years ago, he and Nancy had a little supper at the White House for just the grassroots conservative organizations from all over the country, including Oregon, and he told Rev. Hanshaw not to sweat the small stuff anymore but pursue major moral-political issues for conservative victory. That's how Hanshaw landed on scapegoating the gays and formed the OPA group when he came up to Oregon."

Oh no, oh no, oh no. You mean, Appleton said to himself, you mean I, feeling guilty for punching Reagan out, gave money to the man who, thirty years later, planted the seed which formed the gun now held against the temples of my Joanne, Harold, Derek and maybe even Billings along with all my future gay grandchildren? As he stood there, he was sure there was more than a little shock to his face, and he started to sweat.

"Thanks again," he managed to say.

"Be careful going out," Degas told him, by way of

leave, "as I said, their headquarters are right upstairs. Don't take a wrong turn on the stair." And laughed again.

Oh, no. And Appleton had a brilliant idea on the staircase, which, magically, on its own, did take a wrong turn. The stair was perverse, if you will. It went straight to a door at the top of the tower-like edifice, with no one home yet, because no one had come back from the Balboa Inn. Nevertheless, and with great decorum, Appleton knocked! Knock, knock. Who's there? Appleton. (He opened the door.) Appleton who? Appleton-stepping-in-and stealing that's who. Without a word and with a Go, Inc., heart ticking inside full-tilt, Appleton wound his way in, went straight to a back room as though he knew the place by rote, went to a file cabinet (he'd seen such places before, which operated by blackmail and terrorism—cult specials), pulled open a drawer and found back files where the confessions always are. He found Samuel Hollingsworth under "H" complete with computer disk attached to the inner sleeve.

Now I *am* a thief, he thought, and ran the hell out. In a minute he stumbled back toward the antique store, but he hardly saw it. His soul felt as if it were breaking down, going biodegradable under the stress. It was excited and implicated at the same time. He had grabbed the file to make up for what he realized he had done in the past. Even this file wouldn't be good enough to outweigh that. He felt at one with the street scene full of honking, rattling automobiles. All in the parking lot of the Balboa Inn—clearly visible now from the antique store across the way. The little money that he had invested in worthy causes—and so far back it wasn't worth remembering, was it?—had become an avalanche starting forward from 1952. From a sweet little musical where they sang in front of dormitories and violently green Technicolor lawns to a collection of switchblade Christians meeting on the coast of Oregon, all to hunt down his kids. On the set back in Hollywood, they sang wistfully that "She's Working Her Way Through College" but whatever knowledge she gets she's never going to use—a familiar refrain on campuses off and on this soundstage, Appleton was there to say, now and then. Still, there had been something so beguiling about that soundstage campus, with its sparky green trees and scarlet roses, set out carefully so as not to appear to be in pots—with its statue, hastily poured the night before, which looked like a cross between Chief Seattle and the Statue of Liberty. There had been such an inexplicably protected and stagey beauty there—accessories are essential to the pose—with some emerald fireworks going off and resting kindly in the trees, how he could be led, finally, to punch out the President-to-be, the star of the film and feel compelled to give him money?

Meeting up with Ellie without a word and walking down a street, full of the OPA, was not fun. As they got into the car and he touched the brake and inched forward, touched the brake and inched forward, brooking the traffic, he had the most unsettling feeling that maybe he was more like these people than not, that he could have walked straight into the lobby, hung with palms and Spanish arms, hung up his hat and started smoozing, perfectly at home. Except now he had the file.

"What is it, my dear?" Eleanor asked.

"Guilt," Appleton said. "That's what. I just figured out" (the ex-Governor's retreat was not far off; it would be coming up soon), "that I inadvertently sunk money into OPA years ago."

Eleanor looked over. "You said that before. Are you sure?"

"And I've just"—holding it up—"stolen a file from them to set the scales of Justice right."

"Stolen?" she asked.

"Yeah. Robbed. Ripped off. Thieved. While their little conference was breaking up."

"Take it back then," Eleanor said. "This instant. You aren't setting any scales right by doing that."

"It's the goods on Samuel," he answered.

"Really?" she asked.

Still with his right hand free, he fished out the disk. "Complete and total goods," he answered. "We've got what may be called the lowdown."

At the ex-Governor's, they waited in the foyer while Appleton's arcane mental camera flashed and flashed at the garden. Shadows of a red-winged blackbird. A wisteria which had been coaxed up a trellis and was threatening to bloom like spring thunder. Accessories are essential to the pose. He could see it, plain as day, what his parents had worn when photographers still used flash powder. This will be a quick quiz, Appleton. Name the scene which got deleted from *She's Working her Way through College*. Forget that you accidentally donated to a cause you now loathe, have committed highway or at least stairway robbery. Instead please step into our TV studios. Think about trivia, please. And now he could see the lights dimming around the $64,000 isolation booth and he could hear that tick-tock music starting that's a cross between Bernard Hermann and Leroy Anderson, because no kidding, he really was on the $64,000 Question at one time—General Categories. Well, after Reagan's "Right to College speech" in *She's Working her Way through College* and his great defense of Miss Mayo's right to education, even though she was a burlesque queen, the crowd up and carries him on its shoulders right down to the beautiful quad. (This is still in the film.) Getting over-exuberant, however, they accidentally dump him into the fountain, and he has to be taken to the gym to change his clothes, which have been sent for. There he meets the muscular Gene Nelson, the romantic lead, who, sweaty from his wonderful "Is This Love?" solo in the gymnastics room, and, having removed his singlet, hugs Ron in gratitude for saving his girl from expulsion.

"I can't tell you," he says in the deleted script, "what this means to me, Sir."

Ronald in his undershirt hugs back.

Afterwards, Ronald, vulnerable from the take, had decided to relax a little with Mayo, and that's when he found them in exchanged costumes, Virginia with a football, Ronald in parrot green headdress. They were impersonating everyone on the set.

"You're killing me, you're killing me," she said between bouts. "But do it again, do it again. Do our director one more time."

And Ronald crossed the room with Humberstone's round-shouldered gait. "All right," he said, and then added a lisp, "'I want all of you to listen up.'" He cocked his head. "'And if you think you can direct this show better than I can, you've got another think coming.'"

"If you don't stop," she said hysterically, "if you don't stop, you're going to have to outfit me with ribs of steel! Now do Appleton."

"You do Appleton."

"Oh shit," she said. "I don't have the courage to do that sourpuss." She started heading, with a bump and a grind, over to their impromptu wet bar. All sodas. Also, Appleton could see now that she was still carrying a football. To see himself as a cross between the Gipper and a burlesque queen was not something he fancied, so he started making discreet, Tarzan-like noises to catch their attention.

They both looked over and started laughing.

"Well, here's an even better improv of Appleton. Himself."

"Except he needs the headdress," Ronald said.

"I hate to disturb you," Appleton called over acidly, "but I thought you might like to know that you have strict orders to get back on the set and to follow your lines the way they were written. You haven't yet given the speech on Free Speech." And he was looking at Reagan.

"Oh is that right," Reagan answered in a high Lulu voice. "'You have strict orders to follow your lines the way they were written.'" His voice dropped an octave and he squared his chest for dramatic emphasis. "And I'm telling you that if you're not out of here in ten seconds, you're going to be tasting a knuckle sandwich."

"I'm not leaving until I can give the director an answer," Appleton told him, flaming all the way to his forehead. He was aware Virginia was watching them as if she were rolling down her stocking. Holy smokes.

He didn't answer.

"And another thing," Appleton said. "You better get yourself into some clothes."

"Miss Mayo," Ronald asked, circling the room in ellipses, "do you think that Appleton looks more like a penguin or a puffin?"

She let out another belt of laughter.

"You know I'm not going to stand here and argue with the testiness in you," Appleton said in a furious and high-and-mighty way.

Ronald put his hand on his hip, adjusted his head-dress, "'Well, you know,'" he said, quoting Appleton with a coquettish turn of the head—"'I'm not going to stand here and argue with the testiness in you.'"

Virginia rolled onto the sofa. "Ribs of steel, please! Ribs of steel!"

"I am going to knock"—Appleton couldn't say "balls" in front of Miss Mayo, so he used "No. 2" on your hit parade of fifties male threats—"your head so

low and you ass so high, you're going to have to tip
your hat to take a shit!"

Reagan, who had grabbed his football, pointed to
his chin. "Come on, I dare you. Come on! Come on!"

Appleton went for him. Sock! Biff! Whomp!—
connecting directly to the kisser. Reagan went cart-
wheeling across the room, over a Salome couch,
crashing into an arras, which dropped on him, making
him look, for an instant in his headdress, like a music
hall Queen Victoria, just after coronation.

Later, he found money on the set and gave it at
the fundraiser Reagan had invited him to.

Flash.

To alleviate the guilt.

Relief. Saved by the bell. The memory was over.
Give the man a cigar. Give him $64,000. The Silver
Screen. The powder went off—and, as he and Ellie sat
waiting, the ex-Governor entered the library of the
stately seaside home.

"Well, Appleton," he said, "we lost. Got clobbered."

"It's a tough thing," Appleton answered, as he was
shown a seat.

"Excuse me," Eleanor said, not to be pushed to
the back wings, or daunted, either. "I'm Eleanor Rose
Towning."

"Sorry," the ex-Governor answered, "I didn't see
you."

"Time you did," Eleanor answered ironically,
making Appleton wince as she sat down beside him.

"I have no problem with that," the once-Renais-
sance Prince of his state replied—for he was not to be

daunted, either—"I am, in fact, delighted to have you here, and know exactly who you are."

"So who am I?"

"You are the daughter of Lucinda Rose, the woman who engineered the great patroness to give us two Isabella Squares—two for one in one state."

"That's quite so, and quite true," Eleanor answered, mollified.

"We're quite grateful."

Nevertheless, in the pause that followed, Appleton felt all his static at once. Desire to conspire with the ex-Governor to get the next job of anti-homophobia done, so that he and the ex-Governor could save face—and, along with righting the wrong of the past, pay for (Eleanor's compunction had to be acknowledged) his act of stealing.

"So what are we to do, Appleton?" the ex-Governor asked at last, "now that they've trounced us, and are more likely to come up with another initiative by fall— the busy little bastards are circulating those damned little petitions, hither, thither, and yon as we speak."

"Torpedo their credibility. Mud sling."

"We have no mud to sling. They keep themselves pure by watching our every move. They enforce confessions from their membership to keep them that way."

Appleton waited. Here goes. "Tell me, once and for all, how long has Samuel Hollingsworth been a member of their circle?"

The ex-Governor hesitated. "How would I know that?"

"Because," Appleton said, "he's been busy, busy,

busy on every commission you've ever named. Besides local and federal government, too. And for one hell of a long time. He looks younger than he actually is. Much. You two have been in the same coach together for over thirty years."

The ex-Governor consulted the wisteria, and seemed to see flash powder, too, on this sixty-four thousand dollar question.

"Even if I tell you the truth, what would you do with it? Who would you tell?"

"Most likely everybody, I suspect," Appleton answered, "if the time was right."

"But I don't know."

Appleton lost all patience. "Oh for crying in the night, Jackson. It was as obvious as a gravy sandwich that he was a member from the time we met for that little tryst in your office. Let us please not be coy. All I need is a confirmation of the length of time, so I know what to do with the sudden information I've got."

The ex-Governor turned. "Sudden information?"

Appleton had expected this. "No, no. You first."

"But I don't know. Based on what everybody can see, I would say yes. But I have nothing secret to offer even if I was willing."

Appleton took out the disk. "O.K., so let's posit that you don't know. Then we just take this, and we add to it at least four years of secretly recreant behavior, and we also add he's been playing liberal all this time, and we explode the OPA support by showing his hypocrisy. I'm sure we can find many,

many statements he's made in the past in favor of gay rights."

"You do that," the ex-Governor said, "and you may have exploded the OPA, but you also destroy his Renaissance Fair—which means the loss of millions and millions of dollars to the state, come this fall. And the loss of a major display case in general for the state of Oregon. Our wonderful Quincentenary, 1892-1992."

"That's a chance we've got to take," Appleton said. He could only think of Joanne's suffering, Derek's. "We simply don't have a choice."

"I'd think twice about that," the ex-Governor said, "if I were you."

"That makes perfect sense, Appleton," Eleanor said. "Waiting, I mean. Thinking things through."

"You both don't understand," Appleton heard himself saying, "I'm not asking for permission. I'm going to do it anyway."

The ex-Governor turned, seemed to retreat into the nineteenth century of the sea garden. "Then you must do what you must do—what's on the disk?"

"Probably Samuel Hollingsworth's confession."

"You think long and hard about that," he answered. "Before you share another man's private life with the public. That kind of slinging has become standard in this country, but somehow I never associated that with you."

"He's not associated with it," Eleanor put in, "and he will think long and hard about it. It crossed my mind for a while there, too. I even wrote letters against Samuel to Family Services in Arden. But not this—this goes too far."

◇

The night Appleton was chased through the Overpark and had vowed revenge on Samuel, he sat up to all hours still wondering if he should leak the OPA confession to the press. While all the while waiting for Ellie to come home. By then he had broken the code on the file, and read it, from first to last. So that Reagan now had reared his spooky face into his thoughts a second time. Samuel *had*, as Degas had said, gotten his many ideas for advancing the OPA from a fundraiser at the Gipper White House. Beyond that, all that the file really did say was that Samuel had been liberal once and was an OPAer now. It also said, "I recognized I need to join you, because I felt my lesbian wife was neglecting my daughter. She left her alone during a Pride March."

It seemed at this moment they were poised on a knife blade as far as the Election was concerned, and the best bet would be to go to Samuel's office and force him to resign from the organization. He'd confront him with his hypocrisy without having to do a smear campaign. Samuel'd be cowed, especially now that he had autumn designs on running for state senator on a Democratic ticket a few years from now.

Eleanor, however, arrived with the same ideas as before.

As Appleton listened, he saw that the dawn was breaking, and he considered that today would be his

Columbus Day—that is, the day when you rallied yourself when all hope was gone. Maybe he ought to look at his Columbian Commemorative stamps again—look at a few sets and sell some for the cause.

"Well," he said, "like I was telling you, I could just try confronting Samuel in his office. Get him to step down."

"Better," she answered. "Better. He's in his Portland office this weekend—I know that because Joanne said Sonya and her friends are visiting up there for a football game. He dropped them off at some parents'."

Appleton did have an idea. Another Columbus Day idea. "Then if it's Portland where we'll be," he went on, "we can stop in and sell some of my stamps and coins at that weird mall. After seeing Samuel."

"You're not thinking about that again?" she asked. "Certainly you don't want to touch that beautiful collection until it's absolutely necessary."

"It sounds like it is, my love, absolutely necessary, or at least you drive a pretty persuasive argument."

"Think really hard," she said. "Do you really want to give any of those stamps up?"

Later that afternoon, after a long sleep with her, he did drive her up to Portland. Appleton knew they were pressed for time—another emergency planning potluck that night, as soon as they got back.

"Do you want to see Samuel with me?" he asked Ellie.

"No," she said. "I'll wait in the car. If I go in, I'll go for his throat."

As he approached Samuel's Portland offices, he

felt surrounded by the autumnal day, as though it were a brick courtyard. The light shone obliquely in anticipation of October, and he looked nostalgically down on Ellie visible through the windshield two stories below. She was in a kind of circle of light. Minor, but distinct. The precincts. And over in the distance of skyscrapers was another Columbian wall, with the emblem of DeSoto—the drapery of sun cascading over. He thought of Joanne, too, and her poetry reading. Her poetry cast a glittering shawl over everything. He remembered her saying that she had come up to Portland one time, and the city had swirled in front of her, like a vortex.

"Yes?" Samuel said at his desk, looking over his reading glasses at him, from top to bottom. "What can I do for you?"

Appleton tried to shake hands but Samuel avoided him. Never, never until that moment had Appleton appreciated what Joanne had been through—must have been through. And Appleton remembered what Harold had said about all OPAers. They were motivated by their fear of being prone to other men. And that's what he felt, standing there—and the fear was in himself, too!

"Look," Appleton said, "I don't want to get nasty. But I'm fully equipped to disclose your close connection with the OPA. We know you're giving them power and advice."

To his disgust and fright, Samuel smiled. "What would you tell them? I'll tell you. That I went to a Ronald Reagan dinner in the early 1980s that helped get the OPA started and that I contributed to their campaign, and that I stood there in the Governor's office, with you against me, urging him not to advance his Referendum? Is that what you'll tell the newspapers?"

Appleton didn't answer. He couldn't mention the confession. Not yet.

"And I can tell you what I'll tell them," Samuel went on, "that I was duped. Because my original understanding was that they were to keep all political causes out of education and the workplace. That's the way I signed on—the way you did, Mr. Romney. Your name's on the original contributor's list, too."

"Mine?" Appleton heard himself asking disingenuously. How could Samuel know this?

"Yes, absolutely. I have it in writing that you made a contribution to a let's-protect-education fund, which ended up in the bank accounts of the OPA, too. You wanted to make sure Diversity did not rip education apart—save your beloved Plato."

Appleton found himself seating in a chair. "But I didn't stay on for the hate ride," he answered, almost instantly on the uptake. "My contribution was an accident—through Ronald Reagan. I'm not a member of the OPA—like you."

Samuel settled back. "And so what if I am? Who will believe you if you say so? I'll simply say that you're spreading calumny."

"There's still that moment you argued with me in the Governor's office," Appleton answered.

"There's isn't anything in it I would unsay on a

state-wide or nation-wide basis. It's on the platform of my bid for State Senator. From my humble sociologist's point of view, orientation is a practiced behavior, not an inborn predisposition."

"I have a copy of your confession," Appleton said at last. "What do you say to that."

"If you do have my OPA confession," Samuel told him, "you have it on record my heartfelt worry that my own daughter was being slighted by her own mother. Do you want to go public with that?"

Check. For one split second, Appleton's hands fanned out, ready to go for the throat. He felt too prone. Isn't that what they mean when they say you're fucked? Then he turned on his heel, and was almost out the door when Samuel added over his glasses, "It's almost as though I had written all of you into this myself. You're like improvisational actors who keep getting up to try again and end up doing just what I wanted anyway in the first place."

This kind of omniscience was enough to make Appleton speed up and slam the door after him.

"We lost," he said to Eleanor, once he reached the car again. "The campaign is over. He's got the perfect answer for even my confrontation. Oh"—he said, clapping his head, King Lear style—"shit."

"We'll find some other way of dealing with him," Eleanor said. But she was dejected, too.

Soon on this vague autumnal afternoon, that didn't even belong anymore to poor, disavowed Columbus, or even October, they went looking for a stamp store in the Building of Beaux Arts Boutiques.

"My heavens," Eleanor said, "the title's absolutely shameless."

They were on the escalator in a moment. The hanging jungle (imported, in design, all the way from L.A.) under the solarium reached out to touch them.

"The malls are such a wonderful experience," Appleton said, still insisting on his blasted mood, and nearly being hit by a hanging plant. "You need a goddamn machete to ride up to the third floor."

"Never mind."

En route, they passed a bookstore where two life-sized cardboard mummies, advertising the latest blockbuster, spat plastic coins at each other. Beside, there was a nostalgia shop which consisted of nothing but bottle caps. Two doors down, the stamp store proved not really to be a stamp store but a boutique within a boutique within a boutique. It was a sort of closet—or better a junk drawer, Appleton decided—in a shop full of miscellaneous geegaws.

"I have a little shock for you," Appleton said to the man, trying to muster up some enthusiasm. "Something you probably haven't seen in a while." And he pulled out a used copy of the 1865 American Commemorative of the Columbus Landing—with inverted center.

The man nearly fainted on the spot.

"Here," he went on, without waiting for him to speak. "You take it and verify it, and after you have, phone in how much you'll give me."

"If it's authentic," the man said, "it could be worth up to $25,000. But let me give you a receipt now."

Eleanor was still speechless as they drifted back out into the mall.

"Well," Appleton answered, showing her to the escalator again, and feeling much better. "I've been thinking about selling it for years. My father brought it back after visiting Chicago in '92, along with a clock that chimed, Columbian Expo silver dollars, a full-tinted portfolio book, stereoviewer cards, and enough stamps to make anybody independently wealthy at this very moment. I've been just waiting for a worthy cause."

◇

He found that the arrangements to fly to Washington, D. C. had been made for him. He was the only one available, really, to nail down the rock band fundraiser at the Arden Dome. That had the name of Zig-Zag, no less. And now imagine me, he thought, a rock ambassador! The day before he flew out to Washington, they had the No on Nine Fun Run, organized impromptu by Harold. Then they were to leaflet the football game and some outlying neighborhoods afterwards. That morning, the dew was everywhere, and the maples and poplars were reasserting their autumnal magic, like a mantle, over the town. Standing there, congregated on the starting line, they got drive-by horse laughs, cat calls, giraffe whistles and zebra jeers, Appleton considered, all from the hidden Oregon Protection Alliance and their allies, those goddamn gutless wonders. All of which Appleton had to say the Steering Committee had anticipated last night at the planning potluck.

And so that day, with the runners, many of them crowned with glitter, tiaras, and last-minute flowers in their sweatbands, Appleton felt personally and verbally assaulted from the sidelines.

"Faggots! Would you look at that? Whew-we! Even an old queen in shorts."

"Ah, take a flying fuck on a rolling donut," Appleton yelled back.

Harold, who was in the six-minute-mile section, turned and looked at him askance.

What the hell else were you expecting? Appleton wondered. It was eight in the morning and cold enough, in your shorts, to freeze the balls off a brass monkey. Or the nuts off a bridge, as they say. My joints feel like peanut brittle, Appleton decided, just as the gun went off, and he found himself hightailing it for the first butt and butte in sight.

And everything, in fact, went O.K. for the initial mile. In fact, he even passed his friend Jeremy. Gaining in the first part of the second half, he flew by a willowy wind ensemble fluting itself away on a street corner for them and then a hard rock band playing at another.

(Later he learned that Jeremy, while running, that educative genius who would save his St. Christopher's, stopped cold and did a showstopper the moment he could make out the tune of Johnny B. Goode, dancing his little butt off, much to the thrill of the crowd, the dismay of the performers, and even the bemusement of the reporter who happened to be standing there.)

The problem came when Appleton realized Jeremy was passing him back, tit for tat, and that meant that he and this woman from out of nowhere were vying for last place. Almost unconsciously, he had known she was there and had found her to be getting on his nerves almost from the start. Glancing back, he caught a glimpse of the Elysian town—the priceless golden arches of the trees—and could see that all the landscape was warming up.

Which warmed him up. So he poured on the coal, and the crowd, seeing this old fart trying to finish, let out a cheer. They were subtly divided. Should they be ageist or sexist? The woman, large and attractive, but obviously not in shape for running this far, got miffed and pressed on ahead. They only had one more street corner before the finish line on a school track. Up and off a sidewalk. They were doing a three-miler. But as he came down from the curb, an ankle gave way, and the woman triumphantly sprang off. At least a hundred people must have jumped in to save him, as he went down. A tank of oxygen materialized out of thin air, so to speak.

"Everyone clear away," Appleton yelled. "I'm going to be all right."

Seeing Harold in the crowd—he had gotten done long, long ago—Appleton signaled him to be his prop, and together, step by step, they walked it in. As they crossed the finish line, everyone went wild seeing this underdog. Appleton must have been kissed by a limitless throng of screaming beautiful lesbians. Wow!—let's start the race over and try again for the other ankle.

They patched him up and put him in an unnecessary brace, and they went back home to get their leaflets and signs for the football game.

An hour later, he was standing showered at top of the basement stairs with his ankle, miraculously, intact. It was Go, Inc., at work. Looking down, he could see that Joanne and Derek had the stationer's supplies all over the floor and were finishing up the last of the signs.

As he went down the stairs, Ellie followed. "If we're going to go out canvassing," she said, "let's do it before it rains."

"It can't rain," Harold said. "There's a game today. Are you all packed, *doctorvader*?"

"Yes, yes," Appleton said, feeling irritated. "I'm way ahead of you."

"I remember," Harold went on, holding up a crayon, "when I was a freshman at Leighton University in '63 and we all went over to this guru's house, way out in the back hills and I knew something strange was going to happen, when the guru said, 'Let's color pictures—choose the crayon that leaps out at you.'"

Derek made Twilight Zone sounds.

"What does the crayon say to you?" Derek asked, in a spooky, satirical way.

"Turn on and tune out," Joanne said dryly.

"Not anymore," Derek said, putting the last of the flags on his bicycle.

They all went out into the October afternoon, complete with a pug puppy, who looked like a guinea pig on a string. To Appleton's mind, she barked at everything. They passed the Fairgrounds. They had talked the county into letting them have a "No on Nine" booth there, and in the later afternoon, Harold would be spelling the other volunteers so they could go to dinner. In the distance, Appleton could see the Arden Dome hovering, with its huge replica of the *Salvatore Mundi* on top.

Ahead of them, the stadium looked imposing; people were well on their way into the expensive game. Appleton felt abandoned as everyone dispersed, posting themselves at different gates, having planned for a reconnoiter back at the park in the neighborhood targeted for their leaflets.

Left to his own devices at Gate B-7 of the stadium, Appleton was nearly bowled over by these autumnally dressed citizens who didn't give a fuck what he was offering.

"Be sure to vote against Measure Nine," Appleton said, "against discrimination."

"No thanks."

What was it he was seeing, amidst all this hurry to get to the gladiators?

He thought these were people he had seen before.

At St. Christopher's College, some of them, several years ago.

"Leaflet against discrimination?" he asked.

"No, thanks. It's almost time for the kickoff."

They could have just as well been wearing

buttons—that was it—of Culture with a slash mark through it. None of their education was giving them a basis to care.

The football game started. You could hear the kickoff. Suddenly Appleton felt completely alone.

So he waited, knowing the roars from the game might indeed vote in Measure Nine.

But had he done any better himself when he had been their age? When he had been busy screaming at Billings from the sidelines to tackle harder? Where had his Plato been then?

Rejoining the group at the agreed park, Appleton watched while Ellie went up to leaflet someone in the neighborhood. Afterwards, the woman watched them from her porch. Appleton guessed that as a group they looked pretty strange.

"Interesting," Ellie said, "she's got those old sepia photographs on her piano. Remember those?"

"Remember those? At the Rosium raisin ranch, you were counted odd if you didn't have them. Full color? What's that?" Appleton asked.

Derek stopped his bike. "Oh, no, look what's coming." The pug was barking like crazy.

For immediately they were being joined by two refugees from a Prom Night (thirty years ago), turned Halloween Ball. Halloween on wheels. Now their party really looked strange. A couple of passing cars slowed down. It was then Appleton realized that the woman was in the tux and the man was in the taffeta. He had a gorgeous beauty mark.

"Why haven't I seen the two of you before?"

Joanne asked, looking at the additional flyers they had given her. Clearly they were ambassadors from No on Nine in Portland.

"Too busy," they said together. "We just want to give you these personally and to remind you—no stopping to talk. You might scare people off."

"Good advice to give," Ellie said, giving them each a pat.

"I'm co-facilitator of the Volunteer Committee," Joanne said rather haughtily, and with some emphasis. "You don't have to worry about us knowing the guidelines."

"Just here to offer support, dear," Ms. a Go-Go said. "And to deliver a message." She stared at Appleton. "You must be the emissary to Washington, D.C."

"I think so," Appleton answered. "I fly out tomorrow morning."

"Good." She pushed her hair back. "We have a message from Central Office. To request donations from the Auxiliary Society when you reach Robert T. Tate University."

"Where would I find such a society?"

Bored, the rest of the troop went on ahead, leaving him high and dry in uncomfortably non-ironic territory.

"The Auxiliary Society is the Mother's Club for the University. Their main function is to raise money for Persian rugs for the various student lounges. But they're also interested in our cause."

"Really? I thought I was pushing it even setting foot on campus."

"Didn't they explain—Robert T. Tate University is not like other gospel colleges—"

"I'll believe it when I see it."

"Well, give it a try. Everything counts now. We're so close."

Appleton watched them depart, and then headed on up the street, feeling defeated by his reflections at the game. But just as Appleton passed the next house, he was awakened by a dozen mental snapshots, all falling on him at once. One was of a sepia-tinted two-story bungalow with a picket fence, and a growling barking German shepherd in the yard wearing a red bandana. The leaves came down from the poplars, and the scene became, very suddenly, Color by Deluxe. Another was of Ellie running at him suddenly, pointing to the two second-story windows and yelling, "Give me a quarter! My kingdom for a quarter! Give me a quarter before the inspiration goes!"

And all the while the rest of them were yelling, and the rust-colored shepherd and their pug puppy were getting louder, and Appleton heard himself saying, "I don't have a quarter! Jesus, a quarter, what's so important about a quarter?"

"A telephone. I'm inspired. I've had a brilliant flash for a campaign commercial, the one they're all waiting for, with time running out. Oh where are Tuxedo Junction and his/her boyfriend?"

"They just left."

"Shit."

More barking and general chaos.

"Here, Mother," Joanne was shouting from up the

street. She was standing on a porch and was holding a receiver, with the cord going all the way back up the steps and back into the living room.

"Eurkea!" Ellie yelled, stealing Appleton's word. "I have found it!"

◇

The phone ringing. Appleton thought he had missed his flight. Still dreaming, he imagined himself out on the night airstrip, stumbling over sapphire lights and trying to grab the plane by the seat of the pants. Somewhere in the midst of his take-offs and landings, Billings was hanging around, reminding him of his failure with St. Christopher's. Awake, now, he was feeling for the dresser and running into the wall.

"No, Honey, no," Ellie said, out of the dark. "We're at Harold's, remember. Arden. So you can fly out. The dresser and the phone are over there."

Total blackness. "Now you tell me." Nevertheless, Appleton found the phone.

It was Jeremy. "Jeremy, if you've called to talk about things academic, there are better times you could have chosen. My plane's due out at six a.m., and you've got to remember you're talking to an old man."

"I was just down here—"

"Where?"

"Guido's Bar. I was just down here doing what I always do—discoing my butt off on just seven-up and coke (and I don't mean the other kind of lethal skeletal coke, belonging to the horrors of voodoo and other miscellaneous ravages, like on the old Signet cover of *Heart of Darkness* with the bare-chested Swede and enticing Negress, doing the bottom-to-bottom hootchy-kootchy before the African bonfire.) But ever since my wife died you know I have come here every night and danced on the dance floor alone without alcohol or other stimulants and brought two bath towels to dry off with. So imagine my surprise—when your semi-stepson comes in looking like he's fresh from the prize fights, followed by his boyfriend, who's getting madder than hops at him until he vanishes into thin air?"

Appleton found himself slowly coming up for breath. "Who vanished? Harold or Hops?"

Ellie was immediately coming up beside him in the partial dark.

"Anyway," Jeremy went on. "Harold's in a heap over in the corner right now with this Billings fanning him. Billings just sort popped up out of the blue."

"Does Harold need medical attention?"

Ellie flew out of the room at the sound of that. Looking, no doubt, for the first aid kit.

"I don't think so."

"Well, then, why don't you and Billings just drive him over?"

"Because he won't budge. He wants to wait until he's strong enough to go back to the Fair again and dance and fight—whichever comes first."

"What time does he think it is, anyway?" Appleton asked.

"I don't know. He's pretty furious. Anyway, the bar says it's going to call the cops unless we get him out of here. And they've already taken his name down once. Wait a minute—" There was mumbling and some clatter.

Appleton waited, still feeling in the middle of *Walpurgis Nacht*. Time now to be the Sharp-Dressed Man again, who knows how to make suave plane change-overs and how to rescue his poor "stepson."

Jeremy came back to the phone. "We've got him to his feet. We'll be right there."

"Thank you very much indeed."

"And by the way," Jeremy said. "Billings tells me you want to do a try on revamping the St. Christopher curriculum by having me do my gig on the computer. If that's what you want, I'll do it."

"Sure you can spare the time away from the bar?" Appleton asked, not too sleepy for sarcasm. "I suppose we could bring some dance tapes into the office while you're working—"

"Never you mind about that," Jeremy said. And hung up.

"Who was it?" Derek asked, coming into the room.

"Something about your father," Appleton said. "He just had a little trouble over at the Renaissance Fair."

"What kind of trouble?"

Ellie stood just behind with the first aid kit in hand.

"He got into a fight and ended up at the bar."

Derek closed like a cobra lily over a hapless fly. *Walpurgis Nacht* for sure. Stay away from Derek.

"Well, at least he did something original," Appleton said. "Usually they go to the bar first and then get into a fight."

Derek spun, dervish-like, and left the room. Ellie put down the useless kit. "Remember this gives you no excuses. No excuses at all!" she called after him.

Witches' Sab—

Slam. Appleton started thinking about Neptune. They said that planet is encircled by a hurricane as big as the earth. And that's what this earth seemed to be getting like. Just try to catch up and immediately you're whirled off.

In about five minutes, Billings walked Harold in. Appleton considered that his son looked like one of those miscellaneous monsters on the lobby cards of the 1950s, carrying the supine girl. Or even one of those cardboard mummies they'd just seen, about to spit a plastic coin. Jeremy led the way. He pointed to the television, which Derek had left on. TV always got weird past midnight.

"You know I learned to dance that way," the testimonial said. "Those glow-in-the-dark footprints that show you how to dance are just out of this world. Not sold in stores, so hurry."

Billings laid Harold gently on the couch. Immediately Ellie started patching him up with mercurochrome. Appleton couldn't tell if he was aware of anything or not.

Derek came back. "All this time I thought you were on my side," he said to his stepfather. "I thought you were part of the solution," he said. "But now—you're just asking me to go back out."

"Derek, I'm sorry," Harold answered.

"You promised you wouldn't go to the bar."

"O.K., I did go but let me explain," Harold said wearily looking up. "I was just looking around at the Fair with a gay friend, and everyone was dancing. Straights with straights and some women with women." He was leaning up from the couch. "But the minute we joined in, some farm boys jumped us and we got into a fight. Why couldn't we dance? We had a right. There was a skirmish. I was so depressed with myself—for fighting—that I went to the bar to get some support. That's when my friend jumped ship."

"Some friend," Derek said. "Just about as loyal as my other father—or you, for that matter."

"Look—I got beat up a little bit. So what?" His eyes were getting defiant now.

"It'd serve you right. You promised me you'd never go near that place again. You were so damned self-righteous about Dad working there, but look at you now"—but he stopped himself, because Jeremy was making for the door.

"I'm just going to go right straight from here to St. Christopher's," Jeremy said, "and start in on doing the Curricular Shuffle; Billings has given me the key. I plan to be there all night, because I can't sleep anyway—"

"When do you sleep?" Ellie asked.

"—and you can call me there if you need me again."

"And I plan to stay here," Billings said. "I can sleep on the couch where I'm available—"

"No, you're not going to stay here," Appleton said. They must have order on the planet Neptune, even if it is surrounded by a hurricane. "It's too complicated as it is. We've all got to get up at four if I'm going to seal this deal, so we're all going to sleep in our own beds for the rest of the night—what's left of it. Everybody—either get the hell out or march to their room."

Harold didn't exactly march. He put one arm around Billings and another around Derek, who decided to help despite himself, and they walked him down the hall.

◇

Appleton came back from Washington, D.C., to plenty of news.

At the airport, local headlines were screaming the blunders of the OPA.

And boy were they blunders. After Harold's talk show, Rev. Hanshaw had gotten brassy. He was so sure that what had caused the TV hostess to blush was truly God's word, he went ahead and out of defiance submitted the whole hate-package for printing in the Voter's pamphlet. That is to say, graphic descriptions, provided by the OPA, of "unspeakable" male unions eventually appeared in every mail slot in the state.

Well, the jury was in on that one. For even the most homophobic were now saying this could have only come from a political cult gone-mad. No one, not even the hyper-religious, believed anyone could have the temerity to print such an outrage upon personal privacy in a voter's pamphlet except—Verily, Verily—the Deranged.

Then Sunday evening something happened much closer to home. One of Derek's bashers confessed. Appleton was sitting with Ellie in the Community Center, waiting for their next drop-in ("talk with parental figures"), when a man in his twenties rushed through the door and virtually dropped to his knees. He had felt haunted all this time, he said. He was one week away from being sentenced, but not for a hate crime, and he had to confess that was what he had actually committed. Derek, in the room and hearing this, picked up a handy broom handle from a corner for the side of his attacker's head, and while Appleton and Ellie had the presence of mind to stop him, the young man got up and ran out as quickly as he had come in. Next thing they knew, the boy had rushed to the local paper and told all, with a "profile" hitting the front page Monday morning, linking him through his parents to the OPA. This basher had grown up amidst the various types of hate material similar to what had appeared alive and direct in your local friendly Voter's Pamphlet, and the Arden paper sensationalized the hell out of every last word. Appleton felt most privately pleased with this, although he certainly didn't say so aloud.

But that wasn't all. Something hit even closer to home Monday afternoon, just before the Concert. Sonya, in the middle of the turmoil, and still not, like the rest of them, wanting to write her father off, asked, just like her mother had done, where her diary was—it had been lost somewhere in the original shuffle between Capitol City and Arden.

It became so important to her that at last Appleton drove her down to Samuel's apartment building to check for it in the storage unit.

The manager got a key and took them down, and there they found a bin filled for sentimental reasons with 1950s and 60s memorabilia, with the *piece de resistance* being, no less, a picture of Samuel and Gloria standing together in upstate New York. Holding hands. The framed photo was lying on the floor.

But for Appleton, there was no time to think about it. He had to move on. To the Arden Dome. Concert night. Columbus Day, getting ready for the band and the big fundraiser.

"Appleton," Alice said, approaching him the moment he got to the benefit concert, "we have problems. My God, do we have problems." She was dressed in black again—she was the same woman who had been in Joanne's house that night he and Ellie had been called in on an emergency—and her voice seemed deliberately funeral, as it had been before. All that evening and all that afternoon, the backstage rule was—the higher up you were, the more high-and-mighty and put-upon you sounded.

"I certainly hope they're not serious ones," he answered, still trying to listen and concentrate. "The lighting is so balled up now, the diagram looks like a crow's nest."

"No, it's no problem at all," Alice said sarcastically, "just a little matter of the whole lesbian community threatening to walk out in the middle of the show. The co-facilitators saw the Zig-Zag rehearsal today, and the whole thing is sexist from top to bottom. Here they are, about to go on in two hours, and we have women threatening to tear up their tickets in unison and stage a mass exit."

"You mean they'd buy tickets just to tear them up?"

"You bet your sweet personality they would."

The only answer Appleton could think of was Jeremy. Jeremy, Jeremy, Jeremy.

"I don't need a man to fix this," she said. "That's the problem in the first place."

"Shit." Appleton tried to contain himself. "This is no time to talk Affirmative Action," he said, "when there aren't enough women to go around. Besides, I'm not going to be asking Jeremy to tell you what to do. You give him orders and he'll implement them. But here I go all the way to Washington, D.C. and Virginia to get Zig-Zag to perform for us, because Robert T. Tate University has a special claim on them, and now every single female is going to walk out on their show. Talk about ingratitude!"

Without so much as kiss my foot—Alice was burying her face in his shoulder. "Oh, Appleton, I'm so tired, so very tired. Everybody's been getting on my case—"

But before he could offer comfort, he turned and found the two of them straight up against Ellie, who had come in from behind. Who was also holding a

Zig-Zag promo book and giving them disapproving glances.

"Thank you, Alice," her glance said, "and now your parking time on my 'husband's' shoulder is up."

But, actually, she had no time to get worked up about it. "My God!" she said, staring at her watch. "We must find a television set! My kingdom for a television set." Instinctively, backstage, the good-humored warm-up band was getting out of Ellie's way. A set was found in the central dressing room. "Mind if I switch for a moment?"

Appleton saw a football game tumbled into the salad dressing and lettuce of a commercial.

And then came the spitting image of the German shepherd house they had canvassed just at the moment of Ellie's grand Annunciation. Only this time the two second-story windows had silhouettes—the left one labelled "hated," the right one labelled "hated." The music of "This Ole House" came on, like a nickelodeon—louder and louder, with the shakiness and infirmities described. Meanwhile shingles and shudders and downspouts were avalanching off in cartloads.

Ellie beamed from ear to ear. "Now get this. Other people thought this one up."

Appleton was startled by a stroke of lightning, and the silhouettes and labels on the screen toppled also, and in their place were two beautiful people each framed in a window of a transformed house, an Adam and Eve if you will, holding "No on Nine" signs. At the end, the clouds parted and the sun shone and the garden filled with blooming flowers, opening in 4/4 time. On the screen: "Hate is easy, but the rights for all of us take work. Work No on Nine. Vote No on Nine."

Everyone, including the band, broke into applause.

"That really is something, Ellie," Appleton said. "No wonder you were saying 'Eureka!'"

Harold appeared just as Appleton was testing the lighting. "Zig-Zag won't go on when they said they would. They're saying now they've got a plane to catch—a midnight engagement in Boise—the Boise Dome, no less—so they'll have to go on first."

Alice looked ready to sit down on the floor. "But what about the warm-up band—the whole crescendo we were supposed to build up? Woodsong was supposed to get everyone worked into a minor frenzy, so Zig-Zag could finish them off."

"I don't think Woodsong could warm anyone up in the first place," Harold said. "Not even if they reinvented the Beatles on stage before our very eyes. They're not very—well—charismatic."

"They've got something worked out on the checkerboard," Derek said—meaning the mammoth screen which, in back of the stage, presented, among other things, moving cartoon characters. One hundred and forty feet high. "I helped them."

"Good for them," Ellie said, "but that's not frenzy. I suggest we just cut Woodsong altogether, and put Zig-Zag on solo—even if it's just one opening and closing number—so there's no sense of let-down."

"That may sound right," Derek said, "but that's not the way we're going to do it. Not when I busted my butt to get Woodsong to do the board and this rally in the first place. We can't screw our own people over. They're local queer—let's just see Zig-Zag as the warm-up to *them*."

"Now you're cooking," Alice said. "Just rewrite our program notes accordingly. We're just going to have to risk anti-climax."

Jeremy appeared. Appleton felt that true help had arrived at last.

"And while you're at it, you two," he said, "get Zig-Zag to get the sexism out of its act before it goes on. That means in the next few minutes."

Alice and Jeremy ran off.

The ushers arrived. Little bow-ties and bare chests. Appleton was restricted to views behind the curtain. The huge checker screen lit up as a test, pumped light, and then was quiet again. Joanne arrived with Sonya and Richard and Olivia, and the light man supplied them all with "Sirens brand" ear plugs. The set-up was getting more and more elaborate, with the handymen forever blowing into the dozen microphones. They were putting down miles and miles of electrician's tape, when the doors burst open and the throngs came in, swathed in neon buttons, stickers, t-shirts, and chic black drapery. There were muscle men, muscle women, and some mighty goodlooking drag queens and drag kings to boot. The ex-Governor sat down toward the back, along with some supposedly unseen spies from the Oregon Protection Alliance. But Appleton had learned to spot them a mile off.

Alice stepped out into the spotlight. She had

added nice long white evening gloves and a big, black floppy hat from the sixties. When she announced that Zig-Zag would be playing first, Woodsong second, she got applause, and everyone seemed to move in closer, sympathetic. Brightening with surprise, she stated the objectives of the "No on Nine Campaign," thanked everybody interminably for working so hard, and then announced an anonymous single donation of $25,000.

It was a few moments before Appleton realized the Coliseum was cheering and stomping its feet.

Without further ado, and exactly on time, Appleton saw everything go black, and the stage filled with three bearded hoodlums (you could tell a tobacco company was one of their sponsors besides Robert T. Tate University) in cowboy hats along with three go-go girls, who stepped on to elevated platforms, each with her own mike.

Instantly Appleton sensed the hostility in the audience. The cheers died. Well, we definitely went wrong on this one. Why hadn't Jeremy and Alice stopped this at the pass?

Nevertheless, the band played three atomic-bomb strokes, and immediately the whole stage split apart, with the beat driving full tilt and the pink ladies swaying back and forth. Why, I remember, Appleton reflected, a moment when Walter Winchell hosted Roberta Sherwood on television, and she sang a few bars of "Up the Lazy River," while beating the hell out of a cymbal, and Walter just went nuts with the beat—lost his hat. So the same for me. And these ladies. Because he just drives the women folks wild!

Carry me, carry me, carry me down! the song said. But not so the audience—it was definitely not being carried. For sure it was the pink ladies that caused the block. Great, Appleton thought, the whole p.c.squad is going to get up any minute and walk out anyway, and then we're up shit creek, including yours truly, the Well-Dressed Man. Appleton looked around for Alice, but she was nowhere to be seen. Maybe she'd jumped ship while the getting was good.

Ellie came up and took his arm. She had seen his face.

"How about that $25,000?" she asked, smiling.

"What about it?" Appleton asked back. "What good's it going to do now? Just look at the faces on that audience. It's up in smoke."

She put her finger to her lips. "Just wait," she said. "I happened to bring Lucinda's scrapbook with me."

"What?"

"Just wait. Mother's scrapbook. The clippings from her cigar box. I got Derek to put the pictures in the show."

Back to the three atomic bombs again. Utter darkness once more. Three more strokes. And then, when the stage suddenly broke into light again, an uproar of applause. Appleton had to look twice. The pink ladies were on the guitars and drums, and the hoodlums were in bikinis doing the backing vocals. Overhead, the checker screen was now alight with a colossal photograph of Virginia Woolf. A riot of cheers. The guitar struck again, Virginia changed into Walt Whitman, and then again into Virginia and then into Martin Luther King, and then finally into an exclamation point! The stage was almost rushed.

Frenzy. The band came into the home stretch and dropped them at the finish line. Storms of applause. Yells. Appleton could hardly catch his breath. It took many minutes and all the security guards to calm things down. By then, it was too late for Zig-Zag to do another number. They had to leave for Boise.

So Alice came back and explained again why Zig-Zag had disappeared and then said, very simply, "If you are lesbian or gay or gay-lesbian supportive, please stand up."

One row after another, after another stood up— until the whole dome, 25,000, was on its feet, with applause and cheers which could have raised the roof into outer space. Some struck matches, some opened lighters, so many that Appleton thought the fire marshal would hit the ceiling.

The houselights came back up a little.

But poor Woodsong, Appleton thought. As the warm-up band, they had only three songs anyway— and the two previous acts, Zig-Zag and Alice, were impossible to follow. The ultimate thankless job. A one-joke comedian following up on Bette Midler.

Nevertheless, the houselights went down again, and they played. And the first two songs, folk in nature, were graciously but somewhat tepidly received. Certainly they were performed with charming shyness.

But when they were through, Appleton noticed the

leader looking assertive all of a sudden, and she came forward and announced that the group was changing its name to the Jean Teetor Band. Oh, you're Jean, Appleton thought. The band then switched instruments and wired themselves with plenty of state-of-the-art equipment, adding a drum deck and drummer. Accessories are essential to the pose. And as though part of the switch, Jean, a black woman, took off her denim jacket, revealing a white halter top. (A storm of cheers, especially from Appleton.) Then added jet-wing white glasses (an even louder storm), and she introduced her lead singer, Mr. Achilles T. Grant, a white boilerman in tank top with wire-rimmed glasses on a Roman nose.

Their final song, "Nutbush City Limits," was dedicated to all their friends in the Oregon Protection Alliance, who were presently barricaded behind bullet-proof vests in their Adamsville headquarters, just up the freeway.

The song began in a peculiar fashion, and Appleton at last detected what the sound was—a locomotive. It was then that the colossal checkerboard behind them told the story: once upon a time there was a town named Nutbush. It had a church and a bar. It was just off Highway 19. When you went through, whiskey and romance were hard to come by. And if you ended up in jail, look out—only salt pork and molasses. Things never changed there. There was always a picnic on Labor Day; otherwise you spent the weekdays working the fields. Friday you went into town and then Sunday back again to church.

While the board beat time and illustrated the people and town, the band turned into a double locomotive. The audience, initially stunned by the return of light and noise, began, slowly, to warm up. For now sweaty Achilles, in the motion of the train silhouetted on the darkened stage and lit screen, mentioned a small *Northwest* community, and with that, a shout went up.

"It's very quiet. Not much happens there," he said, speaking out in the middle of the song as it still roared along. And the board started showing frowning faces floating above the town. "You better come out when you're going through Nutbush. And you better watch out for the *OPA* when you're driving through Arden!" And with that word, the place was on its feet. "Watch out for the OPA when you're driving through Arden!" Just then the board filled with smiling faces tagged with pink triangles. Another locomotive of guitars. "You can hear the grass grow as you're walking through Arden. You can hear the homophobia grow as you're walking through Arden!"

In the instant, an explosion split the stage again. The singer pulled off his tank top, Jean took off her glasses, and the band plowed straight on ahead: Achilles sang, and the pink triangles engulfed the frowning faces—"Biff!"—all the frowning faces were instantly transformed into hearts—"Right!" A huge No on Nine symbol filled the board encircled by a heart. "Yeah!" Muscular arms straight up—and the whole town was whisked into an exclamation point and then a flash-powder explosion with a phoenix rising from out of the top of the screen, which presented the words "Peace" and "Love" and the pictures of Woolf-Whitman-King below. "Arden. Arden City Limits!"

"You've got it! We've won!"

The explosion went off in the audience. And in Appleton. People were rushing the foot of the stage, tossing money and pledge cards. The ushers didn't know what to do first—push the enraptured crowd back or pick up the money. Appleton struggled to find where he was. On stage, the band had joined hands with the organizers in triumph. Appleton found himself and Ellie and their family running out to join them. It was then that he saw Billings, bringing up the rear as might be expected, and Appleton remembered that it had been his signs of possible gayness that had helped depress his mother. And just then the whole place burst into a second barnstorm of lighters and matches, so many that Appleton couldn't help smiling that at just about this time in the Rosium Rest Home a male nurse would have be asking, clipboard in hand, "Mr. Romney, have you sometime today, well—you can just say—"

"Crapped?" Appleton would ask.

But he wasn't at the Rosium. I'm on this stage with the multitude of the heavenly host. And, forced to bow one more time, he saw, oh no, the re-tank-topped Achilles making his sweaty way down their row, as though in a wedding reception, hugging each one in due order, making no exceptions. O.K., Appleton, Appleton thought, just stand your ground, Appleton.

You've got what it takes. You can take a sopping hug from this approaching giant. Ulysses T. You've been through worse. Stand tall. Close your eyes and think of Oregon. Try to think of something positive. Well, that tank top he's wearing is a nice shade of green. At least I think it's green.

"Hey, Pop," he heard Billings yell, as he clasped the sweaty boilerman—Appleton could glimpse his son between Harold and Derek—"good work. Congratulations."

"That's right," Ellie said, turning to him and taking his arm again. "And I think it might be safe to say we've won."

"The question is," Appleton heard himself saying, turning and taking in the stage and the entire resounding coliseum, "does it matter?"

PART FOUR

Samuel

A FTER THE ELECTION, SAMUEL FOUND HE COULD CER-
tainly pick up the pieces. His life had never been
easy, and certainly one defeat like this was not enough
to set him back.

As he walked through Arden the next day, with
Measure Nine roundly squashed in the newspapers,
he couldn't help—and only for a moment—but see the
Renaissance Fair/*Salvatore Mundi* banners as ensigns
of a great loss. The troop of Shakespeare players were
also packing up and pulling off, and Samuel had
something of a sense of a carnival or circus leaving
town, going down, and that he was the janitor left
behind. Specifically hired for clean-up. The "new"
Shakespeare lines he had found had been proven to
be bogus. All the scholarly journals had turned out
against him and Richard.

But now, even with Measure Nine defeated, the
course of the past was helping him out, even so. As
he left the Arden Dome behind, finished signing the
forms which put the Renaissance Fair to rest, made
apologies for not appearing at the Balboa Inn, he saw
that Caroline must be ready to go with him. All he
had to do now was approach her.

For things were readying themselves into place.

In fact, it had even occurred to Samuel that they could draw away that boy—that son— right into the family. These memories were helping. If Harold does adopt him, Samuel now considered, some way or other they could pry him loose, and make him a part of the new unit as well.

Walking straight downtown, he made his way to Caroline's apartment, hoping this was not Derek's day to visit. It seemed, with these thoughts, inevitable that he should go there now, make his declaration, and find her ready to take him into her life. Now that she was free, entirely free of Harold. Where had her loyalties and interests been all these years anyway?

But when he got there, she was very busy with some environmental group, and asked if he could wait just a few minutes. It was clear they were making headway on some recycling project, as well as a campaign to abolish cruelty to animals. Samuel, feeling vulnerable and impatient beyond belief, only caught snippets of what was being said. It seemed that she and her ecology buddies were also out to prove how much of a certain toxic substance they could find in the average citizen's garbage can. And they were planning to go through thousands of receptacles before they made their report! All over the country, this was to go on, he surmised, people nosing their way through back streets and alleys, picking through and sifting, evaluating trash. Samuel sniffed a little. He began to be aware of faint scents of urinals and abandoned train terminals. To him at this moment, full of his need to declare himself, these people seemed nothing more than blue jays that shat and squawked all over everything. Didn't anybody believe in privacy anymore?

"At last," Caroline said, coming up to him after the last of them had left. "Sorry to keep you waiting."

But now that Samuel had his moment, he didn't know how to begin. "Caroline, you know we've always respected each other?"

She looked quite solemn, hearing that. "Of course, Samuel. And by the way, I'm so sorry to hear that the Election didn't turn out for you."

Samuel realized later he should have picked up on "for you," but in this instant, it passed right by.

"Thanks. And I can't help but think of all those times we shared in Cornell, and the research we did, and then now, how we've both lost people who mattered to us the most."

She looked up, quite pert and upbeat. "Well—"

"I mean," he said at last, "could we perhaps start seeing each other?"

Once again, she did not follow—just as she had not back at Cornell. "Of course, we do need to check in every now and then. In-laws just don't dissolve with the marriage, do they?" She smiled.

"I mean," he said, "see each other seriously."

Caroline's face fell at last. "Samuel—you don't think that I would—you can't possibly be serious."

Suddenly Samuel saw that painting by Gloria— *The Sea Nymphs of Prometheus* hanging on the south wall. He had given it to her. "Of course I'm serious. Why not?"

"Why not? Samuel, I was Joanne's, your own ex-wife's, friend. Even counselor at one time. Do you think I could breach a personal trust, and beyond that, a sense of sisterhood, even if I did have feelings for you? Joanne trusted me. And I'm still trying to make amends for giving that opinion at Family Services."

"But I thought you did that for me."

"For you?" Caroline asked. "No—for Sonya. Back then, I felt as you did, concern for the children, but I didn't do it for you. Of course not! And now I've changed my mind."

Samuel felt very suddenly that he was at the edge of a cliff.

"Samuel," Caroline went on sympathetically, taking both his hands, "I can only have the strongest concern for you as my 'brother-in-law' who lost a vast election. I am very concerned, of course. I know it must be hard. But you must understand from where I sit the last thing I need in my life is another man." She smiled again—that disastrous, impossible smile. "I've got Harold to deal with—and Derek, who prefers his company, even while I still have reason to believe Harold is not as responsible as he could be. You saw it—the man seized me by the shoulders, even though he's since apologized. Harold and Derek are more than enough men in my life."

The Sea Nymphs of Prometheus. Now what was he to do? The painting yawned open in death. Gloria sitting nestled next to him in Ithaca. The loving, beautiful artist who needed, required, his protection.

There was no replacement. He was getting a final no at last.

What could he do but thank her for her honesty and leave?

On his way out, his memory went back to San Francisco, when he had gone down to see Richard. Before he came back on the plane, he had not been able to reach Caroline for a little solace on the phone, so he had gone into a women's shop with the idea of buying Joanne or Sonya (whom he had left in the children's playroom) or somebody, anybody a little gift (the shop girl understood), but instead, after buying something—a whole outfit that he could see Gloria glowing in—he ducked into a dressing room when no one was looking, and held the dress against his own body. Mentally dressed himself into Gloria.

Just once, then, so she could come back to life.

He imagined kissing her in the glass in that dressing room.

And then the San Francisco shop-girl, who had seen him, came by and knocked on the outside, as though dozens of men that afternoon had done exactly the same thing.

"Tell me when you're ready, and I'll be happy to answer any questions."

Suddenly Samuel felt himself caught. She knew that many men who put on women's outfits. This was routine.

So he called out, "I have no questions!" and a minute later, he slunk out, with the tried-on clothes left behind, with the girl—who looked like Gloria, too—having her back turned.

◇

When he had been a boy, after his mother's death, his father's friends had swooped down and rescued him, the way he wanted rescuing now. Pre-Stonewall faggots, with himself somehow feeling to blame for all of this, perhaps because he had been the one to find his mother dead. He had opened the door and seen her in the mirror first. The sight of her! What if he had seen her at first head-on! In the mirror, his father's friends arrived, grieving, along with his father's sister, Anna, who had a set of keys on her belt and arrived along with his father's "friend," Carroll, who had deep veins in his neck. They whisked him and his father off to the outskirts of town, where he, Samuel, rested, cried and rested, and his father's lover Carroll would go out to the garage and make bedroom furniture for him. How many bookcases had he made for him already? Ten? Twenty? And while he rested, Anna, the real estate agent, with the keys to the kingdom, would unlock houses all over town, pulling back glass and sliding doors to balconies and gardens—those million dollar twenty-year plantings—to peace roses, ideally shaped and full blown, as if dropped from heaven itself, pink, yellow, at sunrise—all her possibilities for his father and his lover. Until finally she found for his father his famous estate—all flowers and all closets. Because he never, never came out. Just smoked and drank himself into a tree stump. And had sex on the side, once Carroll dumped him.

The stump was reflected in the mirror. Later, at his grandparents' home, safe from his father, he lay awake listening to the children shuffle through their recesses at Our Lady of Fatima. Normal children. The icon's shadow shifted, with every period; he could hear Virgil pronounced through the window. At 3:15, everything folded down; the children disappeared in whistles and hoots; he remembered what it was like to hold his mother against his breast.

Through the door, down the hallway, he could hear Grandmother talking to his father on the phone. "No, I don't know how Samuel's taking it. Why don't you ask him?"

Carrying the phone on a long cord, he walked to the sunroom, looked at the tulip tree, flowering and opening in the evening.

"I'm doing all right," he said to his father. But inwardly, secretly, he blamed him. Mom must have known! All his terrible secrets. And now his father wanted him back in his life, after neglecting Samuel's own mother.

Meanwhile, while Samuel waited for him to answer, he thought about the sun, about all the explosions, which crossed all the millions of miles on its surface, and what an unlikely thing a tulip tree was, growing in his grandparents' yard.

"You hang in there, you take care, now," his father said. "And when you come home, we'll be like pals, you'll see."

Oh yeah? he thought. Oh yeah? We'll see about that.

Meanwhile, after dinner, his grandmother might drop a white rose in a vase and then sit and read *Masters of Deceit,* nodding as she went along, refusing always to tell anyone her own private history, which went all the way back to Stalinist Russia, labor camps, and a telephone call which had saved her and her sisters from instant death. Samuel knew hardly more than that, except there had been a house they all had lived in in Chicago, and a cousin who had come to visit them bringing a coffee cake covered with nuts. And the family had never ceased laughing about the time he had left the cake out in his bicycle basket and the squirrels had gotten the nuts—every last one of them.

But that day of waiting in the darkened room did not lead to a trip back to Seattle. Not right away. Instead his father came in and swooped him off even further to Orcus Island, to his "friend's" summer home. It was a place which the man had built himself, through long summer days when the sun had hung suspended and tentative between phosphorescent clouds, when it had poured gold upon the water. Here was this man lifting their pipedream high up over the water. The windows—the windows were the marvelous creation facing the bay—set in a triptych, each arched. But Samuel knew what they were doing—the two of them.

He lay upon the bed and heard the banging—they were now renovating the boathouse. In the mirror—also scrolled—he saw the far corners of the sunset, and he remembered the time his grandmother had told him about her girlhood.

"Every October, Samuel—and I'm never sure why October sticks out in my mind, but it does—the sisters at the school would have us put our heads down on our desk and ask us if we'd been having any evil thoughts or if we had been looking or touching where we shouldn't have. And then after going to confession we'd come back—and I remember this distinctly—and Sister Angela would read to us about the death of Columbus. It was very distinct: the three ships at rest out on the Ocean at sunset, and the men slowly lowering his body into the sea. I think of there being a glow upon the orange waters and I think of the man as being St. Columbus."

In the mirror, he could see the snow of the blackberry blossoms, and beyond, the wintry acres of the loganberry vineyard. In the late summer, the grounds would ripen to purple, matching the bloom upon the Olympics at sunset, all framed in his father's lover's windows. Was it there that he decided—if I ever get a project in my life, I'll never let it go? Was it then he took out his Globetrotter Stamp Book, and contemplated the Columbian Exhibition? An escape from those two men down at the boathouse, one of the ones who had abandoned his mother? And a place of refuge (like his grandmother's memory) at last?

"Samuel, is that you packing in there?" his father asked, coming in. In every corner of the room, there was a fragment of the sunset, floating upon the water.

"Yes, Father, I'm just putting a few things together."

"We won't be leaving for a few days yet," he said, bursting into tears and holding both of Samuel's hands. "There's just too much of this grief—"

Grief. With his lover still continuing to bang.

It was then he took out a handkerchief, handed it across and, smiling with slight acid, said, "Quiet, Dad, or you'll rust your hammer."

Which he was still holding.

There was a beam of light—rose—upon the dresser his lover had carved. Samuel left his father standing there. For some reason, Samuel was reminded later of some green skeletons that had been on the cover of the issue of *Novum Ironum* he and Caroline had edited at college. They had radiated outward, as if from under a deep sea emerald. Because from that day forward, Samuel was on his own and free of him.

Many, many years later, Samuel was entering a Conference Room on the Arden campus, just as liberal as he could be, listening to a report from the nation's capital, delivered by a woman who just happened to be his sister-in-law, Caroline Towning, presently Grants Liaison for the state. Conservatives still dominated the legislature, but the new minorities were on their way up.

At that moment in the Conference Room, Samuel had his whole life in view. For decades, he had been getting ready for this. No one else in academics back in the sixties or even the seventies had shown even remote interest in what the Quincentenary might bring—like a bonanza of funds galore—no one, no one, except himself.

In a crimson notebook, he had kept projected a constellation of workshops, seminars, conferences, be-ins, art fairs, and grand parades plotted in the manner of Grand Opera, all slated for this distant *annus mirabilis*, 1992, arriving on the horizon with glacial slowness. Of course, in preparation for this, Samuel would need seed money, seed time, seed grants, seed frills, seed expenses, to make the next years affluent and easy, cushy and prestigious. The next morning, according to plan, he would fly down to San Francisco, with Caroline's report under his belt, to negotiate a deal with the House of Leonardo, run by his uncle-in-law, Richard, who held exclusive exhibition rights to the *Salvatore Mundi*, the so-called da Vinci painting of Christ, as well as the lines of the disputed Shakespeare *Passion*, the prospective jewel in the crown of the whole shebang.

Suddenly all sat up to polite attention when Caroline entered the room ("all" were mild-mannered but top-gun male academics and civic leaders). *She* opened *her* crimson notebook and had only one thing to say: for the Quincentenary, gentlemen, the Federal Government would only be giving out money to racial minorities, gays, and women. Any questions? If you were thinking about Columbus-Columbus—that is, Renaissance-male-quest-exploitation-rob-the-wampum-from-the-Indians-rape-the-wilderness-Columbus, think again. Forget Shakespeare, forget Dante, forget Virgil, and certainly forget Leonardo. Kiss that goodbye. The Western world as we all know and love it has dropped off the face of the earth.

Samuel was so stunned, he couldn't move, not even after the meeting broke up. He just stared at his crimson notebook. Crimson. One of his father's words. Gloria's. Joanne's. Harold's. Diversify, diversify, diversify, was all he had heard. What, on God's green earth, did that mean? Instead of promises and an early sign-off, he had been given a little envelope of buttons. All with pictures of Columbus' Nina, Pinta, and Santa Maria with slash marks through them. He heard the Columbus song they used to sing in second grade, off key. And all of this coming from a woman he had seen as his safety net.

He was so shocked, he hardly noticed, when he got home, that Joanne was even more off her rocker than ever before. She was with her lady friends. One night, not long ago, he had watched her exit in the company of yet another Amazonian-grandmother-type, and he had thought, "You have stolen my wife!" And that had been it. The rest was history—the history of their marriage, their love and passion together, with him turning, firmly, to the comfort of this slowly, very slowly arriving Quincentenary, and his plans to be eventually free of her.

One night he had gotten a call from a friend in the legislature. "Do you know where your daughter is right now?" the man asked.

Samuel was in the back bedroom, getting ready to change out of his clothes, so he could make dinner for him and Sonya. "Yes, I know where she is. She's in her room."

"She's also on television. Crying."

Samuel dropped the phone and ran to the set. It was an OPA commercial about gays and lesbians. It showed a little girl crying her eyes out beside paraphernalia for a Gay Pride march. She had been left alone. It was Sonya.

Later he confronted Joanne about it.

"We got parted by the crowd. I ran back as soon as I could," she said. "It was only ten minutes. I had a friend watching her."

"Ten minutes!" he shouted. "This is unthinkable!"

But now. What was he to do? And just as he was asking himself that, he received another surprise phone call.

"Samuel," Richard, Gloria's own father, Joanne's own uncle, said over the receiver, "I know I shouldn't be calling you like this."

"Why not?" Samuel asked. "You want to talk to Joanne?"

"No. I want to talk to you."

For the second time that day, a torpedo hit. Never, never, since the death of Gloria, had Richard spoken to him privately. That was their silent agreement. Richard must always remain known to him as Joanne's uncle, without the least hint of Gloria, or as his prospective business partner.

"I know it's awkward for us to talk one-on-one like this, but there's an opportunity coming up which you simply cannot miss."

"Which is?"

"I've got friends in the art world. I can help you

when you come down to negotiate the *Salvatore Mundi.*"

"I know we talked about that, " Samuel answered, "but forget it. Everything like that is down the tubes. Leonardo ain't p.c. no more. It's all for fags, queers, dykes, spics, niggers, chinks, and, and—women." Samuel was beyond fury.

Richard grumbled. "See here, Samuel, this is no time to get nasty—just clouds things. Joanne told me you're slated to come down here to the House of Leonardo tomorrow. Meet me there. I'll drive over. We'll think of something. Are you listening, Samuel? You can't afford to get depressed again, the way you did before. Gloria's death depressed me, too, but life goes on. You can still become the most powerful man in Oregon, if you play your cards right."

Samuel hung up. For some reason, he knew Richard was on the money, and at the back of his mind, he concluded that he would feel so much better flying down, if he took his Sonya, snatched her out of the clutches of lesbian heaven, if only for a few days. Who knew when she would be abandoned again? He asked Joanne, and she was very amenable of course, and so, for the first time in recent memory, he felt as though he had somebody with him who loved him again. He continued to feel that way as they flew down the next morning.

At the House of Leonardo gallery, they compared notes, Richard and himself, as though they were mariner's charts for his Discovery of the New World. And the sample prints of the Leonardo almost made his hair stand on end. There must be a way out, he thought, there must be a way so that this can see the light of day. There absolutely has to be! He could get the world to accept Leonardo again.

But all around, treading those slanted hills of San Francisco, were the feet of the emerging Disen-franchised—as was true in Capitol City and Arden and indeed all over the fucking country. Not just the usual Castro clones and fags you always see, but the little cigarette butt ends of people in wheelchairs, little sanctioned black kids allowed to run screaming through the supermarkets, lesbians who looked like they'd beat the shit out of you if you looked at them sideways, people in walkers, people with canes, and above all, the New Women, nothing but the New Women. They could be dressed any which way, but you knew exactly who they were. They were the kind who demanded orgasms in bed, but who would knock you straight through the ceiling if you didn't help with the breakfast in the morning. The equal-timers. The egalitarians. The ones who were out to get even with history. 50-50. Five-o, five-o.

And out of this, somewhere on the streets of San Francisco, Samuel found, to his amazement and disgust, that his heart (for certainly he had left it there once) was coming rolling back upon him—on wheels—down a steep hill, in a wheel chair. Gloria. He was looking out the window of Richard's car when it happened—Sonya beside him paging through one of Gloria's old fairy tale books. Gloria was wheeling herself back into his life, a ghost he had ditched because of her accidental death and later through his marriage to her look-alike long ago, a cousin who was being lost to him yet again in exactly the same way, through that fucking mystery called Diversity, which had drawn a slash mark straight through his life and his Columbian sails.

Suppose, he thought, getting back on the plane the next morning with Sonya in tow. Suppose, he gave the OPA his nest egg. (For he had a little political capital put away.) Five thousand dollars. Suppose he gave them his understanding of Oregon politics, headed them in the right direction, even joined the party himself. Tried to change the political climate.

Suppose, if he did all that, such a measure should pass well before the Quincentenary? And it was very likely with the conservatives still in office.

The Funds originally earmarked for things gay and lesbian would flow right back in his lap, into his program now called the New Diversity.

Because he wouldn't be so stupid as to be Old World again. Never.

He would be the Czar of the Renaissance Fair, post-modern style. The seed money I'll apply for, he thought, will be earmarked for nothing but Androgyny Workshops, Curriculum Experimentation, Revision of Traditional Colleges (like St. Christopher's), Equal Opportunity Field Studies, Investigation of Minority Museums, Restorations of Totem Poles. Slash mark buttons? You bet! We'll buy millions, and sow them like wild oats.

The seed money would place him in every major

city in Oregon in the next few years, you betcha. They'd just leave out the lesbians and the gays, who were busy doing exactly what his father did and Joanne was perpetrating now. Neglecting children. And, still, while crying many tears of liberal rage over the OPA Ballot Measure, he would see the voting population successfully steer the funds straight into the coffers of his Leonardo and Shakespeare gold mine, thank you very much. No one would really give anything to the queers now. Only the safe minorities, who you can't push around anymore anyway. And everyone would be grateful, grateful as could be and would express themselves in votes—for his upcoming candidacy as state senator.

Suddenly an extraordinary weight was lifted, as though he had once been Atlas himself. The ghost of Gloria wheeled herself backwards right back over the hills seen from the plane—over the hills and far away, right out of sight. When he got home, he found it possible even to be civil to Joanne. His jealousy flickered into indifference. For the impending political world would soon hunt her down.

September found him secretly in Hollywood with Ronald Reagan, who, holed up with Nancy for a visit, held a special dinner for members of all those in the OPA and similar groups nationwide, dining them lavishly amidst cactus and palms, while he, the President of our country, spoke of not sweating the small stuff, men, but targeting the real moral foes of Family Values. Center on the gays, folks, they're our one last target, and they're like a magnet. Yes! People will muster behind that banner like no other. Just say no to gays.

Before the night was out, Samuel and an ex-video maker had gotten on famously and found themselves amongst the charter members of the OPA. He had his picture taken with Ronald, again, both of them fondly remembering the time many years before when Samuel had been an officer in the military.

He signed $5,000 over.

Wrote his confession for the OPA.

The burden of seeing his daughter crying on television was lifted.

For quite some time thereafter, the connection never gave him cause for alarm. He even told Joanne about it, in a roundabout way. The group was never in the papers, so how should she know what it really meant? Who the hell wasn't for protection? A deal was struck with a land development operation to build the Arden Dome, in exchange for several acres of protected grounds which eventually became the OPA Headquarters up near Adamsville just south of Portland. The Arden Dome grew magnificently under his hand. Like the marvelous global bubble in *Forbidden Planet.* There were beautifully landscaped gardens and a full-scale exhibit hall previewing the Columbian Quincentenary to come. Visitors, passing through, nodded and smiled and made mental notes to reserve motel space in Arden when the golden week five years away finally arrived. His whole civic master plan was emerging.

But then the first glitch came. Things until then

were humming like a veritable sewing machine. The first ballot the OPA started pushing was not the one they promised. Far from it. Instead of blocking state funds, it simply tried to stop the Gubernatorial Referendum, which Samuel had tried to muscle away through talks with the Man in the Mansion privately. Argue as he might about premature starts, the members outvoted him, and Ballot Measure Eight was on its way to the polls before you could say Jack Robinson. They were to spend all their time torpedoing the Governor rather than blocking funds.

Nevertheless (Samuel had to be flexible), there were two bright stars in the crown of this apparent disaster. One was, with the Measure now at large in the state, he felt sure the grant-giving climate would be so resistant to these gays and lesbians, it would have to divert its moneys.

He guessed right. For—for whatever its actual reasons—the Board funded him, not them, to the hilt, and two years in advance.

The other star was—with the climate rapidly turning in favor of Measure Eight, throughout Oregon, Samuel knew it was time to strike while the iron was hot as far as Joanne was concerned.

For Samuel was thinking back, with the most sickening sort of envy, on all the times he had been hosted in the private homes of the OPA, with their wives bringing roasts piping hot out of the oven and setting them amidst plates of jellied yams and sweet potatoes—or how these ladies, still living to be sure in the 1950s, snuggled up against their men in their husbands' cars—even rubbed their knees, when apparently no one except Samuel was looking. Or he thought of his friend, the toy store owner, also a clandestine member of the OPA, who had a wife so dumb he probably fucked her every night if he wanted to. Sometimes when he saw her, he wanted to sink his mouth upon one of her ample breasts.

It was time he had that again. So he souped things up politically, and he schooled himself to nod humbly to women's objections to the entire male race, past and present—in all those committee rooms where he was getting power but being repeatedly told that he and his gender had perpetrated the most vile sorts of things on the second sex, and that he was responsible. Whenever he raised the least semblance of a protest, he would be admonished severely and told that he could not possibly understand anything, because his methods of writing and speaking and even thinking were completely different from theirs—and since he did not know what it was like to be a woman, he would please to keep his mouth shut.

And although his muted clout continued to grow via these negative residencies in these potentially powerful planning sessions, he would sometimes find himself running straight for the car at lunch break, speeding far out into the country, and in the first clutch of wilderness, rolling down the window and screaming, "Bitches! Bitches!" at the top of his lungs.

Sometimes, too, coming out of Arden late on a summer evening, he would be overpowered, just as he had been in San Francisco, by a sense of its belligerent, begrudging, bullying alternative life. Ex-hippie women in silk hats snatched from the Salvation Army bins would whisk by him in the crowded bike lanes, just daring him to pull out. And there were the grand-mothers in their bike helmets, pedaling their hulking thighs away with their jeans rolled up, taking their own sweet time—women who ought to have been home, serving cardinal salad and grape juice pie to their bridge clubs or at least to their retired husbands behind sheer curtains. Or there would be the female thugs in their pea-jackets and colorless backpacks with their hair rolled into shapeless knots on the tops of their heads, slumping their way down the street with about as much gait and sexiness as a load of potatoes rolling down a chute. It seemed to him that, ironically, feminism and the Sexual Revolution had done nothing more than conspire to drain all the sexiness out of life.

So he was getting ready for Caroline.

Driving along University row in Arden, back toward the Freeway and eventually home, he won-dered if he might find in it still a semblance of the exis-tence he had known in the Fifties, before his mother had died, one isolated home still safe from Diversity, and War and Feminism, and—and—Homosexuality! Maybe that gabled house, now turning on its lights for the evening. Where there was still room for life, real honest-to-God spaciousness, rather than a constant vying for an ever-shrinking space by greedy little here-tofore midgets that were breeding faster than germs in a kitchen sink and that had gotten their start with his father, that liar!

When he would finally reach Capitol City, he would breathe a sigh of relief at last, for he was back on conventional soil again, and free of that vermin-like, underfoot activity, governed by crawl-space intelligences.

But at home, there they would be again—in the form of lady poets and politickers who talked about artificial insemination. Joanne's circle. Women who didn't bother to shave anything on their bodies, and who, accidentally seeing Tina Turner live on HBO one night because it was Sonya's choice, talked about what a no-talent stereotype she was—walking down those some thirty stairs in a sheer dress on to that great stage in her opening number in Barcelona, one high heel at a time, six inches up, breathing raw sex. Sure, Samuel thought, she's a no-talent stereotype. Sure, she's got no beauty, no gift, no spark. Sure. She's only got great legs, great tits, great voice, great artistry, great lyrics, along with millions of dollars and screaming devoted fans and music which she even wrote herself. Sure she's got no talent. She just happens to be a musical genius, still, at fifty-two. She's only the sexiest thing on two legs on the planet mesmerizing seventy thousand people. Sure, it's an outrage to watch her going down those stairs singing "Nutbush City Limits," backed up by a line of dancers hot and sexy enough to detonate all of Western Europe with some of the Middle East maybe thrown in the bargain. It all has to do with some arbitrary standard set by white heterosexual males. Sure, it'd be far better to have one of you, in your pea jacket and your butt two axe-handles wide, come waddling down those thirty stairs to the open arms of some feminist support group, and hear your sickening female cant!

And Sonya had run to her room with her choice of Tina Turner being criticized. Samuel went to her, and held her.

"Don't listen to them," he said. "You've got a perfect right to watch."

He returned to the living room and told the herd to leave.

"But why?" Joanne asked, dismayed, and still starry-eyed from all the talk.

""Because we have a right to our own television set!" he yelled.

Two days later, Joanne made her confession about Clare.

That night, he moved out and took Sonya with him.

But then something happened. They won with Measure Eight, and he gained custody of Sonya.

But then something happened again, and he suddenly felt the most overwhelming nostalgia for Joanne—just like before—after she had gone into Woodland House.

And he admitted he was a member of the OPA.

And then Measure Nine failed.

And then Joanne told him No. And then Caroline.

◇

A few years back, they, the four of them, Harold and Caroline, himself and Joanne, were on their way to Sylvester's Bar—reached by a back road, among farms—and indeed they were a sorry sight—clergyman, counselor, professor, college administrator, all the crown of years of education and good breeding and culture, and they were going to a place where they had no business going. A gay bar. But still it happened. As they drove straight into the spoked sun, the straw of the wheat fields was lit up. Here and there, there were the flames of the field burning. Small birds darted among the telephone wires. And over beside some bundles of hay, was a shirtless boy racking up the last of it. Sometimes when the sun hit him right, he looked like a man—great shoulders. Then the angle changed—and the barn in the distance altered also, turning mellow yellow, and this farmhand seemed to belong to boyhood. Samuel saw Harold take one look at him, and he knew that Harold was attracted. Holy God! Another one.

"To be out there and looking like that," Harold said. "Could there be anything better?"

For you, no, Samuel considered.

And he began to see that night that he could grasp how these people thought.

Because they were nearing the bar at last, as night drew on, and he could see Joanne's face changing now that Sylvester's was coming into view, with its neon sign of Sylvester the cat perennially trying to grab Tweety in his cage.

And then they were inside. A dance floor. Some multi-colored lights. A strobe. A DJ's booth. A box of records. A few tables and a bar. It seemed more than it was, because the music was loud, and the lights seemed to spin, like a Ferris wheel lined with many colors. Everything attempted to be upbeat and urgent because the people had no other place to go. Yet— the magic was rough indeed; the sleight-of-hand scarf really had nothing on the other side. The song being played was really about whores and dice, and although at the bridge—if you could blow an alcohol reading of .15—you could imagine the female disco singer putting fifty dollar bills in her bosom, you could also see, maybe, on the morrow, the faded tracks around her heavily made-up eyes.

They sat beneath some apple boughs painted on the wall. It was only now that they dared glance at anybody. Slummers that they were, the waiter already had them sized up and done an instantaneous pounce, so they ordered lavishly. Caroline and Harold went off to the rest rooms.

"Samuel," Joanne said, "my department head is here. I didn't know this was her place."

The department head's profile was presented to them perfectly in the winking Christmas lights of the dance floor. Sometimes her features seemed deftly penciled; at other times, they seemed heavy, as if her name should be "Julia." During the lighter moments, he thought of both minuets and switchboard operators.

"What's her field?" he asked.

"Creative Writing."

"That seems about right." And it did.

The waiter brought their drinks.

"The Men's Room," Harold said, just coming back, "is covered from floor to ceiling with pictures of naked men, cut out of magazines, showing everything." He was sweating.

"Just see it as the Sistine Chapel," Samuel told him.

He didn't bat an eye. "The pictures show everything. I mean everything. It even shows some men in bed together."

"Harold," Caroline said, temporarily liberal with alcohol, "tell them what you told me about Carey."

Harold looked sheepish—"I just said—that I have a friend whose body is so beautiful I enjoy looking at it as much as I do a woman's."

"Really?" Joanne asked. "You never told me that, Harold."

"Yes."

But then it was Caroline who spoke abruptly.

"Let's all get partners," she said, out of the blue. "Joanne, you go ask a woman, and Harold, you go ask a man, and then Samuel and I will try the same when you get back."

Nothing could match the sense of betrayal in Joanne's face. She simply stared at her in disbelief. Her stare was like a flash of blue across the table. Someone opening a box with a sapphire ring in it. His father's words. Someone using Ophelia as trump. Suddenly Caroline realized the cut and looked terrified—Joanne had obviously confessed something to her?—and stared appropriately down at the tips of her shoes.

Caroline's eyes got teary. "That was so stupid of me to say. Forgive me, Joanne."

But to his total surprise, Joanne answered, "Well, never mind. I might in fact go and ask Clare to dance—who knows."

And when he was alone with Joanne, she said, "I was thinking about what Harold said about Carey's body. Clare and I went to the mountains once, and I got to hug her afterwards. To think of her body with all those ice crystals outside. And I hadn't even known."

She waited.

At last she added, "Would you mind, Samuel. Would you mind very much, if I just went over there, and spoke to her? After all, she is my boss."

"I wouldn't mind at all," he answered.

Left alone, with all in perfect order, he just concentrated on Caroline out on the dance floor. Suddenly she seemed terrified—trapped up by the mirror, right by the reds of a tree painted on the wall and ceiling, half fruit, half blossoms, as it waved itself in front of her, and the blooming side spread itself in a Johnny Appleseed fan. A curtain was being parted and she was being tapped on the shoulder. One of Clare's friends was asking her to dance. Therefore the terror. Samuel laughed out loud. And in being tapped, and in the sapphire light—like a bulb blinking and blowing out—she was smashing through the reflections and getting lost on the other side. It was all panic underneath the boughs.

Breathless, she returned to the table.

"Did you see that?" she asked. "That woman asked me to dance. She actually thought I was lesbian."

"That's what you get for being such a good dancer," Harold said. "No one can resist your choreography. Don't you remember *It's Jane*!? Way back at college? Half the female cast fell in love with you after your Sequoia number."

"Besides," Samuel added, "not two minutes ago you were daring all of us to go out and ask them. What's the crime if they return the favor?"

"You don't understand," Caroline answered. "She thought I was one of them."

But Samuel was looking in another direction. Because now he could see Clare and Joanne together. The moonlight of the momentarily empty dance floor fell upon the two. All the points of their jewelry were accented all at once. That seemed a sign.

"Clare's such a poet," Joanne said, coming back. "Just to talk to her is like going to one of her readings."

"But she's your department head," Caroline said. "You've heard her talk before."

"But not here. She talks differently here."

At just that moment, there seemed to be a glitch in the lights of the bar. But in defiance of something, he was getting up and whisking Joanne off to dance without asking her, and the place, having looked like Christmas, was seeming more like the Fourth of July. A giant blue cape settled over the room. He had gone green with jealousy. For all his resignation, he didn't want Joanne to have Clare now. All of a sudden, she was the one who allowed him to think these flashy thoughts now—in vocabularies he didn't understand but loved and he knew where that love and fear came from, too.

Oh my Christ to think of the emptiness of the house after his father had left, now that he, Samuel, was trying to dance here in the bar. He felt for him then just as he was feeling for Joanne now. As he went absolutely insane, in madcap and bells, throwing himself all over this dance floor, looking at Joanne knowing he was losing her, he was thinking about his father. This was coming up. Jumpin' Jackflash. That's me. That's him. He was getting ready to order her out of his life, the way he had ordered his father out. But he didn't want to lose their words, their presence, their crimps in nature. Like the tree he had seen falling suddenly, cracking at the base. Just like that. In a storm. And he didn't want to lose his father's poetry—those beautiful phrases—beautiful until he became cynical and something else. These points of light. He didn't want to lose her poetry—those lovely images of the mermaid and the sea beach, which the dance floor resembled, with its sapphire pebbles, rolling around from the mirrored ball.

But he had to lose her. He couldn't live with these curveballs thrown at him, which struck and left him for dead. He must vulcanize himself. Must eventually marry someone like Caroline, who was just like him. He must have continuity! That's what he was thinking, seeing her dance. Because it hurt too much having someone not able to care for him (not in a million years!) the way he cared for her, when she had this special way of thinking or talking which was a realm apart.

So I must have protection, Samuel thought, seeing that someone, back at the table, had put his hands over Harold's eyes. Harold's boyfriend, Carey.

He went back with Joanne to the table.

"Are you up from Courtland because of your son?" Samuel heard someone ask.

"Yes," Carey answered. "But he's back in Arden with his foster parents. In fact"—looking at Caroline and Harold—"that's what I want to talk to the two of you about. I wanted to know if you'd consider being his foster parents next."

Samuel couldn't concentrate on what was being said. But Caroline was sitting there, looking like a black queen holding Harold in checkmate. "This isn't the place to be talking foster parents," she said, turning professional.

"Curious thing," he said. "I had no intentions of ever seeing Derek again after he was born. He was the one who tracked me down after he was old enough to get into the orphanage. But once he found me, I started to get involved."

Caroline's face was laced with indignation. The blue hue died on the dance floor. A new light was reflected in her face. "That was big of you," she said.

"It's what I had to do," Carey answered.

Suddenly they were aware of Joanne and him, listening in.

"I'm sorry," Harold said. And they were introduced.

So you're a gay father, Samuel also thought, looking at Carey. I had me one of those.

"This is my habit," Carey said, looking at them. "Bring my private life wherever I go. I have to. When I'm looking out for good places for my son." And he turned back to Harold and Caroline. "Whatever you may think, you have to admit both of you would make wonderful parents."

The remaining light heaped Caroline's lap with treasure. And now Samuel saw, as a concentrated point among the dancers, the figure of himself, like one of those figures that touches a bell (with a sickle?) in a Viennese timepiece. Under a shower of gold. "Have you ever," she said, "considered raising him yourself?"

But he could see she was picking up on his cue. Setting exactly the same trap for Harold. Via Carey. Who had been "in the works," apparently for a long time. All that jogging together—which Samuel now remembered. All that white river rafting in Colorado. White river, indeed. Soon they'd be paired off, and she would be free, too.

"That's what Derek wants," he answered, "but that's not what he's going to get. I've got visitation rights, but I don't live the kind of life that can be of any good to him. Besides, Derek is starting to show gay tendencies, and the agency doesn't want me to encourage that side of him."

Harold look scared. "I don't know," he said. "We've never talked about a child."

"And this is certainly not the place to start discussing it," Caroline said.

"Well, think about it"—and in leaving, he put his hand over Harold's under the table. Samuel saw it.

"I could have gone all night without hearing that," Caroline said, when Carey was gone.

"Just consider it," Harold answered her. "You don't have to make up your mind now."

"You know what it's like for me when someone suggests we have kids."

"We need to think about it," Harold repeated. "For my sake, we do."

At this moment, Samuel began to feel how decayed everything was. He wanted to say to Joanne at last, "Everything is going dead. I looked out the window today and everything was like ash. And what's it like when you and I touch? Your mind is off somewhere, just as it is now. And the same is true when we're home. When Sonya is with us, it's as if there is a presence in everything. But when she isn't, there's nothing. Only my memories of Gloria." And as he thought of her, he saw the blooming rose of Sharon tree holding up its branch of cup-shaped flowers just outside the bedroom. He could hear Gloria breathing.

Caroline said, "We need to put this on the back burner until I'm ready. Please no more."

"I heard say," Joanne said, trying to ease the conversation along and sound positive, "that the Governor is going to try to sign a bill which will protect gays and lesbians in the workplace."

"That's years off," Samuel answered, drawing up

his chair, still tingling with the sight of Clare as well as other things. "And, besides, if it ever does get off the ground, I'll see to it personally that it's stopped."

He glanced across at Caroline, who seemed to understand.

PART FIVE

Joanne

AFTER THE DEFEAT OF MEASURE NINE, JOANNE FOUND herself going for walks near Isabella Circle. She was to leave in a few days again for Hamilton on the coast, to proofread and edit not only the forthcoming issue of *Oregon Coast Review*, but also a little volume of poetry (her own) which she wanted to get published. And she was to see her once-partner Clare—at Star of the Sea—who was in treatment for drugs and alcohol.

In all these weeks and months of electioneering, it was only now that she had come to the full luxury of her own thoughts. The thoughts, when they had first come, had not been of herself. Which was typical. She and Harold had even talked about this. About themselves. They were like transparencies. Became other people.

She, in fact, on her walks, sensed herself becoming Gloria, imagining what it had been like to be Samuel's first wife. Perhaps it was also because the volume of poems she had been planning was to be about her cousin, as well as her grandmother. The volume was to prove—or perhaps disprove—something, that Gloria had been the truly strong woman she had been—not the mad Ophelia of family story. Instead of there being just a handful of poems, such as she had read at the rally, there was to be a whole sequence, showing the deceased woman in all her strengths—as separate from Samuel! And the same was to be true for Lucinda, her, their, grandmother. Vindicated as sane.

And Joanne also knew that she was holding out on herself—that she was thinking about Gloria so she didn't have to think about Samuel. The triumph of the election. The tradeoff. Did not have to think about what was to happen to her own grief. They may have won, but she was so lonely!

And her thoughts turned to Gloria. Her best friend, at one time. Lost, as well as her husband. At least there would be a refuge in Hamilton, where Gloria had spent so much of her time.

Gloria's grandest painting had first hung in the gallery of the Century 21 Exhibition; it was like sunbursts on the wall or ice caves, causing the onlooker to tunnel in. Its colors, its prisms belonged both to the West and to the East—of the United States—showing mantling vines, crisp with the frost of autumn, or permanent snows, freezing on the trellis for winter. And also—from the West—a madrona on a cliff at sunset; the sky poured into its branches, and below, the sea dashed in—aquamarine. Somewhere beyond this silhouette was a shadow, not on the ground but in the sky, as an attending ghost against the crimson. She had even seen this painting (or perhaps it was another) also hang in the Windermere Museum, next to a strange rendition, two dwarves at work on a picture (grotesque), with a head of Apollo—classical—at their feet.

And in that painting, too, there was rain dripping from eaves, of fog crossing stone, stone recessing above bay windows, and of firm lines of rain striking glass above labyrinthine alleys, which suddenly opened to a vista of the sea and dashed rocks. There were interior views of tearooms and antechambers, with silhouettes—as though lit by candles in the background.

And let's not forget the latticework in the park, the roses blooming in the fog, as the sky lowers, and for moments at a time, the gazebo was lost and the leaves of last autumn were blown away. One opens an umbrella while bowed above the beds, hoping to fight off the impending mist. And what else was there? A persimmon tree, in full leaf and fruit, standing in a stone courtyard; it seemed to be hung with golden lanterns. This painting rested at last in the Stanford Museum, the very small sandstone building, laced tight with shadows and the boughs of eucalyptus. It was there, standing before her own work that Gloria met Samuel, dressed in his ROTC uniform, Joanne supposed. It was the power of the green uniform that must have drawn her cousin, the sense of the power of the man that must have kept her quiet, always listening. He said, "Second Lieutenant" and "Quincentenary," and Gloria must have been convinced she had met her Renaissance man at last. She had been up numerous nights studying *Chapman's Homer*, and in those texts, the shape of him had emerged. She wanted a hero who could sack and shiver down the world, someone who could send a directive which would turn an empire. She gave him her painter's card. The overarching tree on the wall seemed to shade them.

It was her year of glory. Joanne had learned that about her cousin. She went off to Victoria, Canada, and came away with crystal gardens in her mind. She stretched canvas in Hamilton and set up her studio above the boardwalk. Her view of Tillamook Head brought old lanterns flying into the room and evergreens capping white sands. For a moment she was reminded of a split second when, in Switzerland, the sun had glazed a mountain, its peak opening like a flower in the morning, and it was that simultaneity which had made her capable of creating the entire crystal palace series, with flashes of fern and flamingo, orange carp in blue underwater, and the purple lances of water lilies lighting up the foliage. The sun slanted down from the crystalline room, and as she surrounded herself with canvas, you could almost smell the consummate humidity—a transferred herbarium.

Evenings, Gloria would meander down the beach to a place where there was a turn in the cove and she could swim in a forbidden backwater. There Gloria would practice all of her strokes for the Aqua Cavalcade. The waves would break up against her, forming a soft lace at her feet, and the evening would create a silver afterlight moving west, toward the Orient and the interminable constellations. Was it at this moment, of getting out of the water, of pulling off her bathing cap and revealing her blonde hair, that she met up with Samuel again? What could be said about him except that he was like the annotated page of

Holinshed—the one from the history of Richard III—whose marks are thought to be Shakespeare's own. He was like that page because his presence suggested, in the margins, authenticity and sincerity and even genius, while the rest was merely raw material and history. Gloria, creator of lithographs of madronas, read only the marginalia. She allowed him to follow her to Seattle and the Aqua Cavalcade.

But not only to the Aqua Cavalcade—to *A Midsummer Night's Dream*, which it played on the side. She was the mermaid in Oberon's speech, singing beneath the fireworks of the stars in the open-air theater, while the orbits raced to find the direction of the music in the summer night. During the day, while her time was her own, they walked, she and Samuel, the laurelled paths of the city, stopping at the Windermere Art Museum, where there hung the painting again—an orient pearl on waves—the one Joanne would later call *Lucinda*.

"Just look at these hydrangeas," she said, once they were out in the gardens again. "They're called 'Lace Cap.' How beautifully that suits them."

"I can show you a whole garden of them," he said. "Acres and acres."

And he took her there. To a precipitous mansion in the north part of the city. There she found hydrangea fields as in a dream, their pinks and salmon reds flashing out like ocean waves, under a changing sky. Or if all of Shakespeare's rainbows had descended upon the garden in various forms, the effect would have been the same.

Gloria must have gone up the stairs just as she, Joanne, had done later, with an old man, Samuel's father, talking as they arrived at each landing, and as they paused at each window, Gloria must have parted curtains ever so slightly, watching a castellated city roll in in the form of clouds, watching the granite boulders below, whose soft brown was accented by the sharp green of the hydrangea leaves and the rising dots of the unopened blooms. All of this to be caught perfectly later in one of Gloria's last paintings.

"That belonged to my wife," Robert, Samuel's father, said. "It's the highlight of this final landing." And Gloria could feel its magnetism, for the view shone purple and white with pearl and amethyst, too.

They reached the library, and it was there that Gloria must have taken Samuel's arm, the way she, Joanne, had taken it so many times so many years later. She was shown a poem, then a second, a third. The clouds returned; water dropped in arcs. Outside, the sun, toiling with a storm from the sea, shone in the room like a fitful magic lantern. In a single instant, Gloria imagined she saw a greenhouse go up in flames. It was more terrifying than a stable fire; stems and stamens set ablaze—rhododendrons this time—glass shattering in sequence in the heat. In the next instant, she knew this poet had taken something to get these effects; he was a man riding high on chemicals. Perhaps that was why she felt she was being walled up.

And that was all. She moved with Samuel to upstate New York and set up housekeeping in upstairs rooms.

Squirrels raced over the roof. Downtown, she knew the equestrian rose every day at noon, its shadow conquering the whole central square. For Gloria, in the spring, there were whole breakers of blossoms, and she imagined an entire town lifting its lamps in the rising mist of pear blossoms, in Courtland, where she had seen *A Midsummer Night's Dream* once, where there had been no mermaid sequence—no song to rearrange the heavens—only the explosion of a star shell to represent the meteors. For her, the stars became the blossoms; the trees held them out in front of them like a string of fish, above the still green ponds of grass. She saw a cascade of bridal wreath. (Sundays, she would dress in white lace and go with Samuel to the Episcopal Church, and afterwards stand in the warm courtyard of alcoved statues, the shadow of the stone Joseph falling across the flowers like a gnomon striking the face of a dial.) She saw the pear trees in an orchard—they were nearly vertical fountains of white. And there were apple, cherry, and crabapple—all pink dots—that formed arching bowers.

But while she painted through this maiden spring, something was disturbing the surfaces of these trees. A green parrot flew through. It settled on boughs, jabbering and screaming, its feathers like green flames. Her father arrived for a visit, and as he stood with his back to the fireplace—the afterlight climbing his suit at noon, he asked her if perhaps she had made a mistake.

"You were at your height of glory," he said. "Paintings hanging in galleries. Diving for the Aqua Cavalcade. You left everything and everyone in the lurch."

"It had to be a new direction for me," she answered. "Samuel, that is."

"Even if that's so," he said, "please come back to see us. Perhaps in the fall. Having been through a summer here, you'll want a change."

And still the parrot screamed, ruffling the leaves. Outside, she knew the whole landscape was on the verge of something. She was reminded of her own moments of springtime panic, scattered among the arborvitae.

"I have a commission to do an opera set design," she said. "That's why I haven't come out. It opens soon."

"Then do come when it's over," he said. "It could be your triumphal run."

She knew he saw the restlessness in her. The loneliness. The longing to be an athlete again. And how she wanted, sometimes, to be standing before hundreds of people once more, concentrating all of her being into the knife blade which was to be her one self—turning into the water.

With the splash, she heard the parrot. It flew over jewelled moss, through an opalescent rain.

"Let's go out for a walk," she said.

Taking her father's arm, she went out into the square, seeing the ghost of ships in the windows, as the clouds tumbled into arched ceilings overhead, looking like the spring bowers of cherry blossoms.

"Is he attentive to you?" Richard asked. And for a moment she could still see the reflections from the midday fire climb his back. "Does he help take care of your illness?"

"He doesn't know about it."

"That's what I was afraid of. You should tell him about it—and all the precautions."

The leaves flew at them in the street, reminding her of paper ones she had colored bright red in first grade. She could feel the crayola in her hand. For some reason, she knew this would be the last time she'd ever see him. Her vision cleared instantly, and the bird sailed into a grove of azaleas. She was on the coast, watching the breakers come in like momentary earthquakes; she was in San Francisco, pausing at her favorite street signal—behind the opera house; she was in Portland, waiting in a rough end of town for a cable car to come around the bend and disturb the lamplight.

"Don't worry," she said. "I'll take care of myself. Very good care of myself."

After Richard left, Gloria began the sketches for *The Marriage of Figaro*—and she dashed out a set for a scene embowered with song; the musical staves seemed to entwine flowers together—a perfect Mozart garland. She lifted her coffee cup, looked for Samuel in the street below, and instantaneously, she could smell lilac like a heady gardenia perfume, and she could see the bushes in profusion converging on a cottage—deserted—out in a field: purple, pink, white, violet. It was a storm of blossoms, and as the riotous spring filled out in her sketches, she could see the orchards of pink and white dogwood, forming

alternating variegated floral displays like floating
clouds of color. There was a chorale on the horizon;
the different tints were like keys striking against each
other, all momentarily marred by the green match
flames of the threatening, screaming parrot. And
what was this? Windows were opening—better, they
were doors—to a courtyard of camellia and sounds of
the city streets. It was a restaurant of white linen and
hanging plants. There were individual roses at all the
tables. She could smell lilac again and Scotch Broom,
and she knew there was panic just under the crushed
blossoms. The sweeping view which cut across the
fog-gray landscape of impending winter held in it like
an unstable potion the auroral dogwood, the ram-
pant lilac, the high-pitched azalea, which might at
any moment explode into a vortex of color. She sat
concentrating, looking for the way of carrying forward her next line of flowers—the red dots of parrot
tulips—into the developing spring of her sketches.

Samuel came into the room. He had files under his
arm. Gloria hid her sketches in a sheath. She wanted
to say, "If you would only let me inside your life just
an inch—an inch—I would give you all."

And he did; he took her in for a moment. He said,
"Half the men in my unit are gay. I don't think I've
ever told you. I've never seen so much pain. I'm going
to have to call someone in to see what we can do."

"What do you mean, what you can do?" she
asked. "You can't send them all to the psychiatrist?"

"They would never change anyway. There's something in the air," he said, frightening her. "Things are

different now. They're not going to apologize in the future."

"Who will you bring in?"

"I don't know yet." But he knew! He knew! It would be Caroline. "Maybe I'll start with a researcher. Come up with a plan of mainstreaming them, but keeping them closeted at the same time. Meanwhile I'll work on a physical fitness program to get their self-image back up. I've never seen anything so depressed."

"You're very kind to do this," Gloria said, kissing him.

"There is very little I can do," he answered, putting her off ever so gently.

Now Gloria felt the presence of his cold father once more. The greenhouse shattered again. She sought again the voice of Lucinda, and she saw the two of them together once more, but this time her grandmother was dressed the way she had been in a studio photograph. The sun set through the colonnades of the Palace. It was as if she could hear the bells her grandmother heard tinkling from a church tower back in Texas. "If we have God in our hearts, dear, we need never be afraid."

"I need to tell you something," she told Samuel. "I accepted a commission to do a set design for an opera. Secretly I've been doing it all this time while you've been away. It opens soon."

"We've been through this before," he answered. "I thought we were going to give this art up."

"I've decided I can't," she said.

He answered, "You know I can't hold you back. Anymore than I can keep you from swimming."

"Swimming I've given up," she answered. "It'll never come back. But this set I have to design. And maybe others."

Gloria finished out her sketches. The world opened up. Gloria watched the vernal furor take over the hills, while the sun bloomed, creating tiny rivulets of gold, like the lake streams viewed from a plane, or long watch chains. She could see irises cracking open, as though out of the chrysalis, opening out into the damask wings of the most glorious purple. She put the brush to the canvas and stroked out the hydrangeas and rhododendrons belonging to Samuel's father and to her grandmother, and in that unison of the oils there arose all the gardens she had known since she had arrived in the fall. She looked in the mirror, at the blonde bouffant hair, and she remembered seeing a butterfly, orange and auburn, beside the Palace pool, and she saw in the same instant, the orange light of the fire resting on her father's shoulders—uncertainly, like a pair of wings ready to take off. Gazing, she wondered how long it had been since she had taken her medicine. Are these my eyes? she wondered. Will Samuel know when he comes in and watches me? Yes, the eyes seemed to have lost their course, and she knew that within her the rising spring was only just beginning to gather its strength.

Without any warning, she hurled a cup across the room. With the smash, she saw the crack in the window and, too, the orange water lily. In her mind's eye, she was taken back to her grandmother's farm in Texas; she saw the small plants rising from the large garden plot—her grandmother was bending over, tending. In the crack in the window, she saw her profile. (Why is it that I can remember, Joanne thought, something so very much like that?)

"What month is it?" she asked Samuel.

"It's April, Gloria. That's why you must stop thinking about those opera sketches. You can't do those when you don't even know what month it is. You must," he said, holding her by the shoulders. How tired he looked! "You must rest. We haven't been able to get you to rest but we will."

But Gloria was thinking of the month—of the way it had been the year before. April. They had been at the coast and they were travelling southward. The rain fell in quarter notes, followed by equally fast descents of sun, which flew across the car, answered by more drops. "I'm about to tell him," she said to herself. Yet there was something about the way he took the road, reminding her of his restless, incessant movements back in the room—ellipses—which checked her to silence. The unlit moon had a dogged, flighty arc to it across the heavens. It was frightening. "Let's sunbathe," he would say and for a moment they would take off their clothes and go out on the sundeck. But then a squint would be coming into his eyes; he would hold up his hand as a shade and he would say, "Just look at the candles on those pines" (and it was true; they were as beautifully tiered on the shore pine as candles in a cathedral or the violins in the Mozart *Requiem*; hallowedness was everywhere; they were stretched across the island, all the way to the backwater from the breakers). "It's time to go for a hike." And to the island they would go. They hit a refuge of canaries, which exploded into an upward yellow flight. They were like a rain of arrows—myriads. And she decided, "yes—that's just like him, to make the discovery. The one that's instantaneous."

"Yes, I am so afraid, Samuel," she said. "I'm afraid something will creep up on me when I'm about to go to sleep. Or I'll simply rejoice too much in getting up in the morning and seeing all the flowers. The sight of those flag irises alone can make me wild."

"It's all worked out," he said. "We'll be checking you every day."

"But the clock-face," she said. "What if I have that dream again?"

"Your body will take care of it. And we're going to see to it that you get to a hospital."

For by now, he had discovered she was ill.

In the hospital, taken away from her painting, she opened a letter from her grandmother.

"Dearest loving Gloria," Lucinda wrote, "I have had a stroke. I asked your mother and father not to tell you until I was well. I was over at their house when it happened. I could see my mother coming back from the fields. She had such lovely auburn hair. I'm safe now. Quite safe. I have a cottage of my own. Some people wanted to put me away, but now I have a place of my own. Remember, dearest, if we have God in our hearts, we need never be afraid. I must go now, as the postman will make his pick up very soon. I sleep contented knowing your photograph is beside my bed, your painting of me on the wall with all my horses, and the irises such as you might have done them are not far from the window. I used to fancy, when I was a young and girlish art student—privately, of course, before I married your grandfather—that the horses were all shod on Neptune, who was the god of horses, and that they all galloped down here, wrapped in a billow of sea foam such as you might have done it. For you will always be a free spirit."

Gloria had a vision of her grandmother once again, but this time in a back room, ready to be wheeled to the mental ward. But there was Olivia, her mother, and Eleanor, her aunt, about to intervene.

Immediately she felt the cold steel of the wheelchair again, the one Samuel had put her in, when they had come into this place. She felt, again, Samuel's gaze wandering down from behind, as he gripped the cold bars. A greenhouse cracked open. Horses were inside, on fire. She pictured before her a scene—an actual photograph—of her grandmother standing before a bright stucco wall. There were red budding roses on a lattice. Then she remembered, Yes, the photograph had been a double exposure and there had been another picture in the corner—her grandmother standing with her aunt against a second trellis—yellow roses. The green was as fiery green as new leaves jutting out of a laurel. The parrot screamed, became a tulip in her mind's eye. She saw the turning zodiac around the sun; she saw a mountain on a screen—she and her grandmother had gone to a theater after visiting the Palace of Fine Arts. The mountain had seemed to be covered by an infinite lawn and then crowned by an auroral ring. In the valley below, there was the light yellow checker of flowered meadows.

"I must leave here," Gloria said to the nurse.

"It's not allowed right now."

"Yes, I must."

She packed. She flew out of the hospital unobserved, flew back West, where days later, she rejoined the Aqua Cavalcade. On the diving tower, she saw Samuel, who had finally caught up with her in the audience, saw three tiers against the sky, walked to the end of the high board suspended above the pool from the tower, turned, jumped.

In the air, she felt the energy of this husband who had held the cold steel behind her. Who had wanted to protect her.

In the air, she saw a vale of dogwood, as pink as a sunlit cloud in the refraction of rain. The rain descended hard upon the opening petals.

Raging dogwood?

Raging dogwood. Laurel leaves pushed through a screen of lilac. The crowded rhododendron trees formed a square. On the beautifully mown grass, she lay down in the widely dropping rain and took her ease at last.

◇

But I did not die, Joanne thought now, as she put the final things into the car for Hamilton. I was left behind to mourn Gloria and take up the campaign. Why was it that I was saved?

It's a spring afternoon. And so if there are moments of danger—of springtime panic—in these great squares of health, so there must be at least one instant of strength per day at a time when everything else in the world has receded from you.

I mean that at this moment and that moment, I felt strong. I put my arm around Sonya—she answered. And for this one instant I can recall the trust of Sonya.

Someone ought to compare (maybe they have) the flickerings and dimmings of a child's sympathy to a spring landscape, subjected to snows and shadows. Sometimes the sunlight and forsythia are there, twining out of the corner closest to the juniper. There is flowering quince and lilac in the warm air, and then suddenly it's gone, as if a cloud has passed, signaling that the season is going backwards—her voice is hollow suddenly, independent, and cut off, even while it's dependent on others, not you.

The light shut me out when I told Sonya about myself. At that moment way back—she was so happy to see me when I came into her bedroom. To talk. When I said I had something to talk about, she—lazy on a noon Saturday—drew the covers over her knees, and put a pillow in between. Already readying, protecting herself.

"Are you gay, Mom?"

"No, I'm bisexual, Sonya."

Is there any sense in trying to explain what this

is? One time, skipping rope, I overheard a boy say—
"Oh that guy—he's AC/DC."

"What does that mean?" Sonya asked.

"It means that I love your father very much, that
I'm very happy with him, but that there's another
need that I have—"

"I don't understand."

"For a woman."

"I don't understand but I'll always love you,"
Sonya answered.

"I had to tell you, Sonya, because your father
wants a separation. And you're going to have to
decide who you want to live with. He won't live here
anymore. He won't commute anymore."

I shut the door. In ten minutes, she called Samuel
in. I waited and looked out into the yard. Darts of
blue jays shaking the arborvitae. The zinnias beginning to heat up again. I wondered what the two of
them were saying. What the OPA was saying. About
me. This different person. I wondered if I was dying.
If others I loved were dying.

I went out for a walk. I came back in. "Sonya has
a question for you," Samuel said. He had the grace
of a long-distance swimmer who's powerful enough—
miles of conquered waves behind him—to stroll along
the shore.

"Have you ever had an affair?" Sonya asked. "I
need to know now because I don't think I can take
anymore."

"Yes, for ten weeks I was with Clare, the woman
you met."

"The one you said you were having the woman's group with?"

"Yes—but the tenderness I felt for her was like—"

But it was no use. I realized that long before—after all the scenes I'd been through with Samuel. The bisexual lives and breathes in a medium of living analogies and beguiles herself/himself into believing they exist in the minds of everybody else.

"I would have understood if you had been seeing another man," I had told Samuel, once we were alone again.

"But I'm not bisexual," he had answered. "So I don't understand."

"You don't need to be bisexual to understand—that Clare wasn't replacing you," I told him.

For I had stopped seeing her by then.

"But she was—is," he insisted. "You fantasize on her every time we make love. And all the other women who have been in your life. Ten weeks—that's what you told Sonya. But you've been in love with women ever since we got married."

"How do you know?" I asked.

"Because the women I imagine myself being with are your women, too. We both need those same people, not each other. I feel it when we're making love."

"No, no. I could still imagine myself being with a woman and have her *be* you."

"That's ridiculous," he answered. And yet he was chairperson of androgyny workshops, Men's Consciousness Raising Groups, and the Marathon Walk for the ERA. He had even been the one to see that Women's Issues had been established on his campus in Arden.

"I'm very needy for a woman," he went on. "One who's straight, monogamous, and fantasizes on me. It's a supreme dysfunction in our family to have me overaccommodating you."

"And what do you call what I've done?" I asked. "I've taken care of Sonya for years, held back my career because of her, and now you want to discard me."

"No, I've been the one who has been taking care of her for years while you've been off with your women friends. Besides, there's no use in our going on and hurting each other," he said. "I realize now that I've been pulling out of the relationship for a long time. You're just not there for me." Who is this talking? This isn't Samuel. This is some psychological formula. Ruthless, rigid, tallying. However, he'll never be able to bring off raising Sonya, I thought.

But after this talk—the first and the last—the door was shut, and the two of them were there, together. Sonya had made her choice. And he did bring off raising Sonya.

The sound of Samuel's car, taking Sonya away. I had to sit with her fear in the dark. Night could not pass, now, with the two of us alone, under the same roof. Why? Why? I knew it had been coming all along, and yet my flesh ached to nurture her— and yet spinning in between was her father—who seemed like somebody else—spinning when always before he had been the one to create the bridges. This humiliation—this all-motherly-systems-on-hold—was what was cutting into me. So that now, as I looked out the window and saw the trees, the flowers, the lawn, all analogies were over. There was not even the subject to write about in my poetry. Every step I had taken toward my daughter was seen as an act of smothering. Don't touch. Let go. While her father lived and flourished in her breathing medium. And so, as I looked out the window, they passed by, those various people, two by two, or three by three, mothers and fathers and daughters, sons and sons and fathers, grandfathers and granddaughters and mothers, and mothers and daughters and daughters and daughters and Since My Lady's Going into France, the Mother's Day billboard, fresh up from Sears presented me with most unbearable scorching, while I looked at this parade and the terrifying normalcy of their all-dominant lives. And I wondered why, back on that day, pulling the arborvitae from the car and scattering the soil everywhere, all over the car, on ourselves—we were mowing within the growth of the yard—while now all was disbarred and in the neighborhoods now all flowers—even, especially, the begonias—appeared from behind smoked glass.

April. I am in Woodland House. Eleanor and Appleton are shown in by Vy Coberg, the presiding nurse and Olivia's double, although younger. She has the same voice inflections.

"Joanne had a good rest," she says to them. "I've chalked that up—way high."

"What about the nightmares?" Eleanor asks.

"Less. Slept better."

It is as if I'm not there. I have not retreated into my pink bedroom of the 1950s—I have gone back even further. I have a kindergarten calendar on the wall—1 x 2 inch numbers, with a colored illustration residing in the position of the holidays.

"Have you heard from Sonya?" I ask Eleanor.

"No, dear, nothing. I called down yesterday. Samuel just said the same thing."

"That everything would have to be handled through the counselor?"

"Even the counselor won't mediate. It has to be the attorney. And Family Services."

"I've had my lesbian friends visit," I tell her, "and they even bring their children with them. Their children love them. Why won't Sonya see me?"

"That wasn't such a good idea," Vy says. "Next time, we're going to have to say absolutely no to any children. You know that it just upsets you."

"I know why," I say, not listening. "It's because I felt such terrible anger and she senses it and hates me for it."

"Do you have anything for me to read?" Eleanor asks, trying to cut me off.

"I already let you see my journal," I say.

"But I mean finished poems."

"No, nothing finished. But I would like to have something from you. That memoir about Gloria and Grandma. Because I had the most wonderful dream about them last night. We were out here in Woodland Park, and I ran through. And there were dandelions everywhere—I could smell them. You couldn't tell what was the sun and what was them."

I'm thinking of my old copy of *Alice in Wonderland* (A Children's Classic Book, from Modern Promotions). All the hard words explained in the margin so that the child's vocabulary is increased. I fall asleep and the whole book breaks down into its linguistic parts—just a bunch of random floating words explaining themselves—"globe, a glass fishbowl," 'Latin—the language spoken in Ancient Rome in the 2nd and 1st centuries, B.C.," "fire-irons—tools used to tend a fireplace, such as a poker, tongs, brush and small shovel," "gryphon—a mix of lion and bird, a fabulous creation," (this is my own) and figureposts, dahlias, chimneypieces, sundials, bellhandles, mountain rills, chrysalises, work boxes—all floating with a picture like those in grandfather's unabridged dictionary.

"I've had a hard sleep like that, honey," Appleton said. "That means you're going to recover."

It's later in the month of April. I am still in Woodland House. Still convalescing.

"This is quite a surprise," I tell Samuel as he comes in, sits down.

"Well"—his head nods in an odd way—"I'm here to give you hope that you can see Sonya."

"What sort of hope?"

"She's asking for you now," he tells me. "We had a family over the other night for dinner, you know, and the little girl sat on her mother's lap for a while and Sonya had to leave the table, she thought of you so much. She's also talked about all the times she enjoys being with you—especially the day you went out to the Crystal Palace."

Oh, yes, the one time Eleanor was allowed to leave us alone for a few moments. Sonya had told me then how she might change her first name since it belonged to my side of the family. To cover her roots.

He stops—he seems dressed for tennis in his athletic knits. "Of course," he says. "This isn't something I really want to discuss here. In fact, I find this place kind of depressing. Perhaps we could get your nurse to pack us a lunch, and we go talk in the park? Will they let you out?"

I put my arms at my sides. "What sort of picnic were you planning, Samuel?"

The thin sinews turn, restless. He's not sure I've revived enough to get my sense of irony back. "Oh I thought just a couple sandwiches, except of course if you're on some sort of special diet—we could stop off, too, at the grocery for some other things. I want to fill you in on how this Quincentenary is coming along—"

"Samuel," I tell him, "Vy Coburg my nurse will not be packing us lunch. Not now or ever. She saved my life—I don't give her menial tasks."

He puts his fingers together. "I apologize if I said something wrong."

"No harm done. Just tell me what you want."

He moves closer, or seems to. His whole thin skeleton is straining to get out. "I want you back. We threw everything away. Let's try to mend what we've done."

"That's too late," I say. "But if you really feel

these things, please encourage Sonya to let me see her. If you believe she loves me, you owe her at least that much. And me."

"You haven't been perfect either," he says.

"I know, but that doesn't change what I need now."

He gets up rapid-fire, moves about the room in a seeming figure eight. "It's because you still love Clare."

"Maybe—even that I don't know for sure. I have to find out."

"How can you find out," he asks, furious, pounding his palm, "when you are content with just this room and doting old ladies?"

"Because they are my recovery. And I'm going to have to ask you to leave, because you are disturbing it."

The end of April, Woodland, still again. The irises are out, looking like flagships in the wind. Above, the clouds are like islands in the stream, briefly gold at the right moment, and then iceberg white again. Today I try my hand at a couple of poems, the first since October. I say, one word, one sentence is a triumph. Now try two. Three. I hear the galloping of Lucinda's horses, all the way from Neptune.

Sonya comes up after her program in junior high. I was not allowed to attend. She has her friend with her.

"Is there a camera in the house?" I ask. "Maybe Vy could take a shot of Sonya and me together."

I am allowed outside, in front of the irises. Sonya and I stand slightly apart. Nevertheless, I put my arm around her, and she does the same, tentatively—the first time she's touched me in eight months. I feel myself shake a little.

And now there is something wrong with the camera. "Let's try it again." And as we pose ourselves once more, I feel terrified Sonya will let go her hand this time.

But the photo is taken. I will have twenty-five enlargements, please, and put them all around my living room—for I am going home. Or will go home.

But there is something else—a quick step here in Woodland House, now that Sonya is gone and I am beginning to think of packing. Of leaving here at last.

"I can't get over how improved you look," Caroline says, coming in. "May I have a hug?"

I concede. But I sense her.

She sits down. "Fine, then. I won't be a minute. I just thought you might be interested in knowing that our women's group voted unanimously to investigate putting out a newsletter with room for poetry. I always insisted that your work was of the first water, and I thought it would be a shame if you weren't included."

She has a pale grace. I say to her stiffly—"Thank you. I appreciate your coming, but I really must get on with putting things in order."

"You are leaving soon?" She smiles toward the corner, knowing one of the unopened Hallmark cards there is from her. "Congratulations. I really must send you another note. It really is much more than 'Get Well Soon,' then, isn't it?"

I let the silence fall.

"Seeing that you are so well," she says, at last, "I wondered if I might have Mr. Benton contact you."

"For what reason?"

"Just a simple affirmation, yes or no, if you think both you and Harold come from what they are now calling a 'gay configuration family.'"

"What do you mean?"

"That you come from the type of family which would be considered gay-inducing."

"You mean what—?" I ask.

"There's just an interest in having it studied. We thought we might have a look at Derek, too, if there's time," Caroline says.

I am Gloria in the wheelchair, with the feel of the cold steel in her husband's—my husband's—hands. "For reasons of pathology?" I ask.

"Well"—now with Samuel's same surprise and distrust at hearing irony but smiling through, of course—"I don't think we'd have to say it was quite that dramatic." Laughter.

"Why do you want to know? Why does he want to know?" I ask.

"We thought we might try collaborating again on an article. We are only trying to relieve a little of the pain in the world. Give people a chance. Like Samuel and I did back at Cornell."

Immediately I stand up. I give her a shove. "If you don't leave this minute," I say softly (don't they always say "softly" in the murder mysteries?), "I'll kill you."

And, horrified by what I discover is my shout,

I watch her flee—right smack into nurse Vy, who's heard me and now stands rigid in the doorway.

"This may set us back a another whole month," Vy says, sitting me down as though I were in kindergarten.

Humiliated, I drop back on the bed, safe again. Never, never, will I look that way again. Never.

⬦

On the day of the rally against Measure Nine, Sonya told her she wanted to move out of Samuel's apartment, and join her at the Castle. For Joanne had moved there temporarily, too.

So they had gone to get her belongings—later to join the Columbus Day renegade parade.

Samuel let her in without a protest. His living room appeared to be in order, but something still seemed amiss. There was a potted rhododendron there on the hearth, obviously a gift from his family, but it was dried out and neglected. So unlike Samuel. Outside, in the clearing sun, the eaves dripped strangely.

Sonya disappeared with her suitcase, into her room.

"If you're going to take her to that parade this morning, I'd advise you against it," Samuel said, looking after her.

Joanne stood there in her sneakers. "O.K."

But he wasn't satisfied with that reply. "It doesn't seem right that she join the very thing that's trying to put me down."

Joanne looked into the den, to the papers lying beneath the drafter's lamp. Shadows of hanging plants curved across the wall like a design in wrought

292

iron. He was an excellent writer. He revised so well, especially. And he had designed and realized the whole Arden Dome. Like a soap bubble out of his pipe. Many, many other things besides.

"Samuel," she said, "why don't you just join us?"

"Join you?" he asked.

"In the parade. Let go of the master plan."

"Joanne, you always were naive about politics. What makes you think I could give up what I believe in?"

"There's still time, Samuel," she went on, ignoring him.

"No, there isn't."

He waited.

"By the way," he went on at last, "I was going past some tables at the Renaissance Fair. Collectibles. I was expecting to see Eleanor, as a matter of fact. Anyway, when I saw all the antiques, I remembered that day when we went to the private auction and found that gold-rimmed china for almost nothing. Remember that we climbed the stairs of that hotel where everything was being auctioned off—all those dressers with dozens and dozens of mirrors?"

And in avoiding his glance, she saw the family china, hers and his, locked away behind the windows of his walnut cabinet—also a gift from his father. He had her favorite cup and saucer with the cardinal on it.

"Yes," she answered, holding the memory. An obvious attempt to spook her. "But I think it best if Sonya and I go now," she told him. "Let me know when you want to see her."

"Wish me luck," he said.

"Good luck, Samuel."

But he wasn't satisfied with that, either. He was restless. "Tell me what you can do for me. I miss you so much."

"No more than I've done for you already," she answered quickly.

"And what's that?" he asked.

"Ask you to the rally—and, wish you well."

"What? I don't think I heard you right. What did you say?" And he looked as if the hotel he had mentioned had taken fire with him in it.

"I've been wishing you well," Joanne said. "And the rest of us, too. I pray for the best things for you."

"No." He stopped as if to ward off a blow. But it kept coming out at him, again and again, even though she had said nothing more. "Wish me well? Praying for me? I'm supposed to speak at Balboa. Stop that! Say anything but that." His eyes were actually wild. He was nearly in a corner. He wiped his face and sat down. "You keep coming here. The OPA and I always said we were united in our causes, and I was glad to hear it at first and then later I started thinking, 'Causes! Causes!' and then later No on Nine started making everyone's nerves go funny. And now you're saying such terrible things to me. 'Pray for me'!"

"Samuel, I should leave—"

"I feel like this place has become a greenhouse with people at all the windows," he said.

"Samuel, I should leave—"

But I am here, she told herself, because I put myself here. I am here in the last ugly stages of a break-up, because years ago, way before Samuel, I allowed other people to make certain choices for me.

But he came up to her and squeezed her shoulder. "Please."

She pushed him off. "Don't ever try that again."

Suddenly he hugged her from behind. She turned and tore off his hands, and he insisted again. But then the cadence of the parade brushed past just outside, and he bolted from the room. Sonya, hearing the sound, appeared with her luggage.

"Anything wrong?" she asked.

"Not at all," Joanne answered. "Are you ready now?"

◇

The board meeting at Hamilton was a success. The *Review* would be out on schedule. Appleton's memoir would be the showpiece. No one in the world thought someone still wrote like that. It had been Appleton who had helped her get the editorship.

She took him to the meeting—he and Eleanor had driven up separately—in case anyone had any more suggestions. She'd rather have people say them to him directly, he could be so sensitive sometimes.

For example, they said that perhaps "the dark porphyry arc of the sea flowering like a camellia bell" was laying it on a bit thick.

"What do you mean?" he answered, pointing to the window. "Just look out there. Nature is wordy."

He and Eleanor were staying at the Sputnik Motel again. She had an adjoining room. On afternoons when she was working on the layout, she would look out at them on the boardwalk and wish that Sonya were here as well—but she was staying with Harold for a couple of days while she worked on a school project. Since the election, and the failure of Measure Nine, Samuel had not called Sonya. On this last day of her stay, when she was packing up and going back home alone—for Eleanor and Appleton planned to remain a few more days—she was reflecting on how she would be leaving Capitol City soon, away from the pull of Eleanor's Castle, and into a town of her own, Arden, with Sonya, and with Harold not far, a town where she could look for work as a teacher as well. And as she reflected on this, she was very much aware, once more, of Gloria.

But now it was time to see Clare. Visiting hours at Star of the Sea, at last. Joanne had been postponing seeing her, because she was afraid of what Clare might say. From the window of the recovery center, the shoreline made her think of two postcards she had seen of the Our Lady, one 1920, one 1975. They were of exactly the same water, the same sky, the same pebbles, but the shadings, the ink, made them look planets apart. In the 1920s, you would have named the color as aquamarine, and in speaking it in your mind, you would have enriched her dress. Now this sense followed her as she approached Clare's room. Everything reminded her of how directive she, Joanne, had been when she had seen Derek at Easter. And here Clare was, stooped on her bed, looking disoriented.

"We're supposed to talk in the presence of some other people," Clare said. "Some people who are in treatment, too. To show that I'm not isolating with friends from the outside and that I have no secrets. So don't move until I yank a couple of people from out of the hall." In a moment, she came back with an old woman and a male biker. "Talk in that corner," she said to them. They started in talking up a storm.

"This was more than I ever bargained for," Clare said. "I was just going to get detoxed while I read *Mariam* and made a few notes for a poem, and then I was going to walk out sober into a beautiful spring with the detox finished. It turns out this is just the start."

Clare looked very fatigued. She wasn't wearing eye shadow, but she had enough to last a lifetime. Meanwhile, the window became a lovely blue glass, wherein two Labradors, one yellow and one black, chased explosions of seagulls along the beach. The reflections dotted the room. In the background, from the biker and the crocheting woman, Joanne could hear "DWI" and "Jails, Institutions, and Death" and "out of the shadows."

"I'm so tired," Clare said, "you can imagine the ordeal they put you through. Every fifty minutes, day or night, is taken. And homework," she smiled. "I could sure dish it out but I sure can't take it."

Joanne had never seen her smile like that before.

"Do you miss Capitol City?"

"What I miss is Arden. It's what I pray for—no, lust for, if I've got any of that left in me. Know why? Arden is for people who live inside their own skins; they don't go beyond their fingertips. But Capitol City—that's for the people who live in their heads; it's always punishing people for not meeting its expectations. No accident the prison is there. Miss Arden? Yes, I miss it." She smiled. "You're my 'Miss Arden,' bringing it with you."

"But I live in Capitol City," Joanne said.

"But not for long, I understand."

There was silence in the room. Their visitors had stopped talking, too. Through the window, Joanne could also see Eleanor and Appleton moving along the promenade, his arm through hers and a parasol of light just above them. Waves, frilled like seashells, moved toward them. How she envied them! And the watery sketch of the rainbow was gone, and some artists were packing up their canvases and heading back home. The clouds, as they say in the eighteenth century, were starting to "mizzle."

"Clare, I can't get over how much you've changed."

Immediately, as if on cue, the venerable great-aunt and the biker came to attention in the corner and said to Clare—"You're supposed to ask her to say why."

Clare raised satirical brows. "Why?"

"You don't seem as arrogant as before."

"Excellent," the great-aunt said. "That's what everyone says about her."

"Well, that's for sure," Clare said, as if she hadn't heard. "I feel like I have about as much ego as a piece of wet tissue paper." Now she seemed aware of everybody looking at her. "Do you suppose, Jenny and Frederick, I've proven my communalness? Do you think I could have five minutes with her alone?" They obliged by sliding off the bed.

When the door was shut, she took Joanne's hand. "I know what you want. It's what I want, too. But if there's to be any hope for me, they say I'm not to have anyone in my life for an entire year, and they're absolutely right—I know they are, much as I complain. Every time I start hooking up with someone, I get drunk or loaded, and this time I know I won't get another chance."

Joanne still waited, remembering her back when they had first known each other, entering, ever so gently, a hot spring on a snow retreat—then it had been as if the Arctic air had swept the earth clean, with no division or dissensions between man and woman—in fact, men did not exist. It was only that bright pool with the bright configuration of snow beyond, with mountain peaks blooming like candles in the waning afternoon light, with only Clare and herself left on earth, two primal female spirits, interlaced as one, in the deepening blue, with the blue of her eyes, and her body as brilliant as ice, yet living.

But she was also reminded, seeing her now, that in the ghost of herself the change was wonderful, too. The red pencil had gone out of Clare's voice. This was something not to interfere with.

"I understand," Joanne said—and took both her hands. "I need to get my own life in order. I need to make my own amends to Sonya for having been absent or at least absent-minded for so long."

Jenny and Frederick came back and said it was time for meditation.

She got up, kissed goodbye.

But did she understand? She must wait a year? And there were no guarantees even then.

"Yes," she answered.

So she returned to Arden, went back to walking Isabella Court, to rooms Gloria had once occupied. Perhaps she could take them for herself and Sonya. Perhaps that would be the new life she had been waiting for, if Clare was to be unreachable, at least for the time being.

She climbed the stairs of the Court Apartments and as she reached the top of the landing, she felt she had been spared. Gotten off. And just by a hair's breadth. She had the newspaper listing with her.

An old woman showed her the rooms and smiled.

"These once belonged to my cousin," Joanne said. "Gloria Roget."

"You don't say?" the woman answered. "I remember her very well."

"Quite beautiful, right?" Joanne said smiling, sizing up the place, wondering if her own poetry would fit.

"There is a wonderful story about her," the woman said. "She threw a painting on a couple of thugs, three full flights down. Hit them on the head while they were trying to beat someone up."

"Gloria?" Joanne laughed.

"Yes, it was back when all those gay bashings were happening. But she stopped that one, *tout de suite*. You look like her, except for that dark hair."

"My God," Joanne said.

The woman told her how much the rent was.

"Thank you," she heard herself saying. "I'll think about it."

◇

She was driving at last into Harold's neighborhood, and in the yards, the bulbs, the autumnal crocuses, had emerged again from the soil and had shaken themselves out like wet toads, crawling toward the sun. There was another sudden rainbow, too, following her and waiting as she stopped at a stoplight, a bow with a stripe so popsicle green it brightened the mountain behind it, and you thought the distant livestock at either end must feel so softly its brush. The radio was alive again with the news that the state Supreme Court had thrown out Measure Eight.

But as she drove into Harold's driveway, she could tell, suddenly, just by the sight of the place that something was wrong again.

Inside, Sonya was sitting, blanched and silent, on the couch, and she could hear Harold on the phone in the bedroom. "No, dear," he was saying, "I'm not jacking you around, it really is important. It's just that I have to be there in ten minutes—"

"What's happened?" Joanne asked, thinking, in a horrified moment, Harold must be going back to Caroline. He had called someone "dear."

"Dad got shot in Capitol City," Sonya said. "The hospital called and they think he tried to commit suicide and missed! Missed! It really is funny." And with "funny," her face crumpled into a shaking, crying mask. To Joanne's surprise and shock, Sonya was laughing as the tears ran. She had never used the word "funny" like this in her life. "It's just a flesh wound but I thought he was going to die, and then they called back and said there was nothing to worry about."

"Who's Harold on the phone with?"

"Billings. He's trying to get someone to drive me to the hospital. Uncle Harold can't because he's already late to do a wedding."

Sonya took out a handkerchief and dried her eyes, but still the puppet-like face was there. "I know you won't let me go but I'm going anyway. What you say about him is true, but still he raised me when you weren't there. I love him and I want to see him. I'm not asking for more than just a few minutes." She started crying again. "It's never changed. I have to see him."

"All right, then," she said, "I'll drive you"—and in two minutes, after telling Harold, they were out the door.

But when they reached the hospital, he was gone. He had left, patched up, for parts unknown—perhaps, they thought, California.

That night she fell asleep thinking about the election in its last days. There had been a skirmish at a polling place—and at a junior high! The lines had been heavy, and standing there, an old woman had started talking to a transvestite about the outrage of Measure Nine. No one was sure whether she knew who she was talking to or not, but, still, someone from the back had come between and told them to shut up, and they had said they would not, and the man had drawn out a cap gun and started shooting imaginary holes in the ceiling.

As the polls neared closing, she had stood at the end of the avenue, holding one corner of a "No on Nine" banner, getting both the thumbs up and the finger, depending on whoever happened past.

And as she faded off into sleep, seeing herself on that corner, she remembered that on that afternoon when she had come out to Sonya, the one which had divided her life straight down the middle, she had left her still talking in that room with Samuel and had stumbled out on that walk, through the newly strange neighborhood of Capitol City, where she and Samuel and her child had lived undisturbed for years, but now where everything suddenly was going dark, punctuated by the sometimes lit garages, filled with bric-a-brac, hung tires, and scattered items from True Value—as alien to her as though they had been stolen from another planet, when just hours before they had been a part of the unwinking, unchanging world of their lives.

And remembering the granite mountain they had viewed just that afternoon when they had been looking for Samuel, recalling a mountain crowned with evergreens and even some initial snow, in the way a memory recovers itself after an emergency, she faded off to sleep, also seeing herself returning from her walk alone, with Samuel and Sonya standing frightened now at the window, and suddenly taking her in, as though she were someone entirely new.

LaVergne, TN USA
02 April 2010
177856LV00006B/1/P